THE
KILLER'S
GIRL

BOOKS BY HELEN PHIFER

DETECTIVE LUCY HARWIN SERIES
Dark House
Dying Breath

PREQUEL TO THE DETECTIVE LUCY HARWIN SERIES
Last Light

BETH ADAMS SERIES
The Girl in the Grave
The Girls in the Lake

DETECTIVE MORGAN BROOKES SERIES:
One Left Alive

THE KILLER'S GIRL

HELEN PHIFER

bookouture

Published by Bookouture in 2020

An imprint of Storyfire Ltd.
Carmelite House
50 Victoria Embankment
London EC4Y 0DZ

www.bookouture.com

ISBN: 978-1-83888-851-0
eBook ISBN: 978-1-83888-850-3

This book is dedicated with much love to my adorable Bonnie and Sonny, when you're old enough to read it of course xx

PROLOGUE

September 1999

Janet Marks read the front page of the *Cumbrian News* for the third time, staring at the headlines so hard, for so long, they were now blurry and had merged into one word.

RIVERSIDE RAPIST STRIKES AGAIN

Despite the warmth from the late afternoon sun as it blazed through the kitchen window, a chill settled over her shoulders. She glanced at the clock: Gary would be home soon. A lump formed in her throat and cold beads of perspiration formed on her forehead. She knew without a doubt that he was cheating on her and this was a good enough reason to tell him to leave. The babies were asleep upstairs; she clasped her hands together and prayed. Prayed that her children would stay asleep, that he would leave without a fight, or even better that she was clutching at straws. Putting two and two together to come up with five. She couldn't be right about this. She didn't want to be right about any of it, but that cold fear snaked along her spine whenever she thought about it and she knew with a bone-deep feeling of certainty it was him: he was the Riverside Rapist. The date of this latest attack was two nights ago. When Gary had gone fishing. He said he liked fishing at night because it was peaceful. The river was too busy through the day with families, tourists and other fishermen. He'd been out fishing the night of the other two attacks as well; she'd checked the calendar on the kitchen wall where she wrote down all her appointments. He didn't know it, but she also kept a track of the days he went fishing, working and running: a tiny asterisk next to the time he left the house. She didn't trust him, not since she'd caught him with her friend the day she went into labour with their second baby. He said it was a misunderstanding, that Claire had come onto him and it was only a kiss. Bent over double in agonising labour pains, she'd been too shocked to say or do anything about it. Hard to believe that was three years ago.

She heard a murmur from upstairs and jumped up, scrabbling to grab the bottle of milk she had ready. Her little boy, Taylor, was almost five now and too old to be still having afternoon naps, but Janet needed the rest, so when she put Skye down she told him to nap as well. Upstairs she crept into the small room both her kids shared. Taylor was fast asleep but Skye was stirring. Shushing her, Janet bent over and placed the rubber teat in her mouth. She started suckling and closed her eyes once more. The front door slammed, and she stood up straight. Kissing two of her fingers, she held them against Skye's forehead and whispered: 'Stay asleep, baby girl. Mummy loves you more than anything.'

She left the room, pushing the door to but not shutting it tight. Acid was burning the back of her throat, and any moment now he would see the battered, brown suitcase by the front door that he'd brought with him the day he'd moved himself into her home without asking.

'Janet.'

She stood still at the top of the stairs and wondered if she should have been the one to leave him, but she had nowhere to go. This was her house; the council had made her wait a long time for a three bedroom. She'd be homeless if she was the one to leave.

'Janet.' His voice bellowed up the stairs and she forced herself to run down them before he woke the babies.

He was glaring at her. Two perfect circles of red on his cheeks, the size of ten pence pieces. He pointed to the case.

'Going somewhere, are we?'

She shook her head.

'Why is that there then? Because you felt like it? Did you finally decide to get rid of those clothes that are too small since you gained all that baby weight?'

She wouldn't let him see how scared she was: it was time to make a stand. She had to do this for herself and her children.

'It's full of your clothes. I want you to leave.'

He laughed, bent over double and slapped his hands on his thighs.

'You're a funny one. Are you telling me to get out of my house? The house I pay for with my hard-earned wages.'

He was standing straight again now. He took a step nearer. He was taller than she was, but she stood firm, despite the fact that her knees were trembling so much she thought they might buckle underneath her at any moment.

'Yes, Gary, that's right. I want you to leave, now.'

He folded his arms, and he was standing so close, she could feel the heat radiating from him.

'Can I ask you why you want me to leave? What the hell is wrong with you?'

She could see by his posture and the way his eyes had narrowed into two slits that he was furious, but there was no going back.

'You and Claire, you're still screwing her. She told me, but that's not all.'

'She's a lying slut, don't listen to a word she says. She won't leave me alone. What do you mean that's not all?'

'I know what you did, what you've been doing.'

She began to back towards the kitchen, trying to put some space between them. He followed her, his entire face now a burning mask of hatred. She knew that look and she knew what would come next.

The hard punches that would leave huge bruises where no one could see because he was that sneaky. She ran into the kitchen, grabbing a large knife out of the sink. Its handle was slippery in her grasp, but she felt better knowing she had some protection. He followed her in, never taking his eyes off the knife, and she knew he would be even more furious that she'd picked it up and was now pointing it in his direction.

'What have I been doing, Janet?'

Her head was spinning; she didn't want to say it out loud, was petrified of speaking it. But she'd found his clothes in the washing machine when she'd got up in the middle of the night to make a bottle for Skye: his jeans had grass stains on the knees. Never, in the years they'd been together, had he ever come home with grass stains on his knees when he'd been fishing, because he always wore waterproof trousers. She could see the newspaper headlines inside her head: big, bold, black printed headlines telling of the horrors he'd put his victims through. He stepped towards her and she held up the knife.

'Get out, Gary, take your things and leave me alone. I'm through with this and I don't want you anywhere near the children.'

She screamed the words at him, but when he shook his head in disbelief she was no longer scared and gave him a look of defiance.

'No, I don't know what crazy shit you're talking about and I'm not leaving, so what are you going to do about it?'

'It was you, those women. You weren't fishing; you're a monster. Get out before I phone the police and tell them where to come find you.'

He lunged for the knife, punching her on the wrist so hard a burning pain shot along her arm up to her elbow and she thought he'd broken it. The knife fell from her grasp; he was fast, much faster than her. He scooped down and picked it up. This time he pointed it at her.

'You could get me in a lot of trouble talking crap like that. What's the matter with you, Janet?'

He took a step closer, so close she could feel the sharp tip of the blade poking into the soft flesh at the base of her throat. She opened her mouth to scream for help. The walls were thin. Surely someone would hear her and come to see what was going on or at least phone the police. Without warning, Gary swung his arm back and thrust the knife into her stomach. The scream died on her lips. He pulled the knife out, and she looked at the redness of the blood dripping from the blade. A maroon mess was spreading over the white dress she was wearing.

'You should have kept your mouth shut and your nose out of my business. Now look what you made me do.'

He thrust the knife at her again. As she fell forwards into his arms, she looked up and saw her beautiful baby girl standing on the bottom step, watching it all. She tried to tell her how much she loved her, but the only thing that came from her lips was a blood-filled air bubble. As she fell to her knees, dying, the only sound she could hear was Skye screaming for her mummy.

CHAPTER ONE

Present Day

Gabrielle Stevens decided to walk home from The Golden Ball where she had spent the last three hours laughing and chatting with her friends after her shift behind the bar had ended. It was a short walk; one she had made countless times. She wasn't drunk exactly, but she was struggling to walk in a straight line. The light from the last supermoon of the year illuminated the whole of the Lakeland fells and mountains that surrounded Rydal Falls; she stopped for a second to take in the view. It was magical; pulling out her iPhone she tried to snap a photo of it. When she looked at the screen she sighed: it always took a rubbish photo. A loud snap came from somewhere not too far behind and she let out a screech. She spun around, surveying the area to see if she was being followed. The narrow road behind her was deserted. She couldn't see any movement in the play park opposite. Her heart was racing and she let out a small laugh, probably some animal. All the same though, she crossed the road to the row of houses where she felt a little safer and not as exposed.

Forgetting about the moon, she hurried towards her parents' house where she lived at the end of the street. She didn't realise how shaken she was until she tried to get the key in the lock. After a couple of attempts she managed it, breathing a sigh of relief when it twisted and the door pushed inwards. Stepping inside she slammed it shut behind her, locking it and turning the hall light on. She was being stupid, *for God's sake, Gabby, stop it. You live in Rydal Falls, not The Bronx.* Still, she turned all the downstairs lights on just to make her feel better. Her phone began to vibrate in her pocket. She didn't recognise the number and opened the message.

Are you home?

No, who is this?

There was no reply; she waited, watching the screen for an answer. None came and she pushed it back in her pocket, *must be a wrong number.* Kicking off her shoes, she double-checked the front door was locked and went upstairs. The house was quiet without her parents; they were currently living it up in Madrid. It was saying something when your fifty-year-old parents lived a more exciting life than you did. She had to do something about it, get out of Rydal Falls for a start. As much as she loved living here there wasn't anything to do. If she wanted a life of excitement, she was going to have to move to a city and get a proper job. It was why she'd gone back to college despite how much she'd hated her school years.

She spat toothpaste into the sink and rinsed her mouth. Scraping her long hair into a topknot, she put her pyjamas on and went into her bedroom. She stared at the neatly made bed and felt the tiny hairs on the back of her neck prickle. She hadn't made it: she never did. One of the perks of living with her parents was her mum made her bed and took all the dirty pots downstairs. Gabby looked around to see if her breakfast bowl had been moved: it hadn't. It was still there, a few crusty Cornflakes stuck to the sides. Had she made the bed this morning? Her mind was a bit blurry after consuming a bottle of house rosé and a couple of vodkas. Had her parents come back early? They weren't due home for a couple of days. She looked out of the window down onto the drive. Their car wasn't outside. Had she made the bed herself and forgotten about it? An overwhelming feeling of tiredness filled her mind. She was losing it, another reason to move out of here into the big, wide world.

Pulling back the duvet she screamed. There was a folded piece of paper on the sheet. Her hands shaking, she plucked it between two fingers, opening it.

You look much better naked

A floorboard by the door creaked and she knew without a doubt that someone was standing in her room, right behind her. She felt the soft whisper of breath against the back of her neck and her body tensed, afraid to turn around. There was no escape; she could jump out of the window but would probably break her neck in the fall. It was a long way down. Her phone was in the bathroom. She'd left it on the corner of the bath when she'd undressed. Her feet were frozen to the ground and she prayed she was already in bed asleep and having some terrible vodka-induced nightmare. Whoever it was standing behind her wasn't in a hurry. She could hear his shallow breathing; he was waiting for her to make a move.

'Who are you?'

He didn't answer. The only noises in the room were the ticking clock on the wall and the heavy breathing behind her. Gabby forced herself to turn around and wished she hadn't. The man standing there was dressed all in black, wearing a ski mask. She could see his eyes and nothing else. He was leaning casually against the door frame with his arms crossed. Her legs were quivering and her breath was coming out in short bursts.

'My parents are on their way home. You'd better get out.'

Her voice cracked and despite trying her best to sound calm, the almost high-pitched scream at the end betrayed her.

He pointed to the bed. She shook her head and he uncrossed his arms. One hand gripped the handle of a large kitchen knife:

the one from the butcher's block on the granite kitchen counter she never used because it was so sharp, every single time she picked it up she ended up slicing her fingers. Her mind was screaming at her to fight, but her body was doing exactly what he was telling her to do, and she was disgusted with herself. She sat on the bed, numb. What did he want with her? Realising she had little choice, she opened her mouth to scream. But he was there in front of her, wrapping one arm around her and pressing a gloved hand against her mouth. He drew back his fist and punched her hard in the side of her temple, stunning her. Then he pulled a length of material from his pocket and gagged her so tight she felt as if she was going to suffocate. He hit her again and she fell back onto the bed, the light in the bedroom dimming. Despite the dizziness she reached out and pulled the ski mask from his head. Horror engulfed her, taking her to a new level of fear. She knew this man. Then her arms were being stretched towards the bed posts and she felt the sting as rope bit into her flesh.

CHAPTER TWO

Detective Constable Morgan Brookes had taken up running. At least that's what she called it if anyone asked. What she was actually doing with the 'Couch to 5K Programme' was a mixture of walking, then walking slightly faster, because she couldn't run to save her life. She had woken up at 04.25 again, the same time she did every morning without fail, and decided to put the extra time in her day to good use by trying to get fit. The weather was getting cooler as they headed towards the end of September. She liked Rydal Falls this early in the morning. The streets were deserted and the tourists weren't wandering around en masse. When she was almost back to tree-lined Singleton Park Road, where her ground-floor apartment was, she heard the ear-splitting peal of sirens. She paused, pulling an earbud out to judge how close they were. Another set of sirens joined the first and she felt her heart sink. Hopefully, it wasn't too serious, a drunken scuffle or a shed burglary in progress. She'd had her fill of murders to last a lifetime. She carried on home, checking her watch. She still had time to shower, grab some breakfast and get to the station before everyone else even thought about waking up.

Bent over double, Morgan was blasting her hair with the hairdryer when she caught the ringing of her phone. Picking it up, she saw she had two missed calls. The deep, gravelly voice of her sergeant, Ben Matthews, on the other end sounded rough, as if he'd been roused from a deep sleep.

'Morning.'

'Thought you'd have been awake. Were you asleep?' There was a hint of surprise in his voice; he knew about her insomnia.

'No, I was drying my hair. Why?'

'We're needed; there's been a sudden death on Park Avenue. Do you need picking up or can you meet me there?'

'I'll meet you there.'

He hung up, and she realised the sirens must have been going to Park Avenue. Despite being relatively new in her role as a detective, Morgan knew that this must be more serious than a run-of-the-mill sudden death. Ben had been called out to drug overdoses and suicides without the need to call her and request she joined him. She couldn't stop feeling overwhelmed. *You can do this; you know you can*, she whispered to her reflection in the mirror as she tied her shoulder-length, copper-coloured hair up and straightened the edges of her ponytail. With steady hands she applied two tiny black wings of eyeliner to her eyelids; her green eyes stared back at her. Already feeling better now she looked like a conservative version of her off-duty self – her freckles disguised under the Lock-It foundation she favoured; her tattoos covered – she dressed quickly in black trousers and a black shirt and felt ready to face whatever the day threw at her.

Turning into Park Avenue, Morgan was stopped by a response officer in the process of stringing blue-and-white tape across the width of the street. Ben's car was at the opposite end, behind the cordon. Parking, she got out and showed her ID card to the officer, with a greeting, before ducking under the tape. The officer smiled back. She walked briskly down the middle of the road towards where Ben was talking to one of the dog handlers. He waved at her and they watched as the officer unlatched the cage at the back of the police van and let out a gorgeous Fox Red Labrador. It jumped down, tail wagging, waiting for its instructions.

Ben turned to Morgan.

'The victim is twenty-three-year-old Gabriella Stevens. Her parents arrived home approx sixty minutes ago from holiday. They found the front door locked and all the lights off. When they went inside, the whole house was in disarray. Upstairs they found their daughter dead. Then phoned the police and here we are. As soon as the dog has searched the area, we'll go in and take a look at the scene.'

'I thought this was a sudden death?'

'It's a suspected murder. The first officer on the scene said it was pretty hard to get the full story from the victim's parents. He went upstairs and saw her tied to the bed with a rope around her neck. They are understandably hysterical at finding their daughter like this.'

Morgan let out a gasp, the horror bringing back her own situation: only a few short weeks ago, a killer broke into her apartment and attacked her. Ben's gaze softened and he reached out his hand to pat her arm.

'Is this okay, are you okay? I didn't think.'

'I'm fine, sorry. The poor woman.'

'Whoever the sick bastard was spent some time in the room with her whilst they rifled through her drawers and personal belongings.'

'That's awful. Were they looking for something?'

'The parents were focused on their daughter, so we won't know until they are able to come back home and go through her things after we've finished processing the scene.'

Morgan and Ben watched in silence as the dog and its handler came back out of the garden. It was straining at its long leash as it ran towards the parkland on the opposite side of the road. Whilst they waited for the all clear, they began to dress in the protective clothing that Ben kept in supply in the boot of his car. By the time they were suited and booted, the dog handler came back into view and gave them the thumbs up. The house was on the corner of a dead-end street; it had a front garden which was overlooked by the parkland opposite.

She knew Ben was concentrating so she didn't speak again, letting him lead the way through the garden gate and along the path towards the open front door. The heady smell of late-blooming roses filled the air. Morgan paused for a moment to admire the array of brightly coloured flowers which filled the front garden. It was compact, but every space was filled with containers of overflowing flowers and it was beautiful. There was even a trellis framework around the front door with a climbing rose growing around it. She paused, gently taking hold of a pale pink bud and whispered: 'It's like a cottage out of a fairy tale, it's so pretty.'

Ben nodded. 'Not much of a fairy tale once you step inside though.'

She followed him inside the house which was cooler than outside. The air was tinged with invisible particles of decomposition, and Morgan looked around in dismay at the mess. The house was homely and decorated with lots of flowery Cath Kidston wallpapers and fabrics. This made the overturned coffee table and ransacked drawers look even more out of place.

'What was he looking for, Ben? What makes someone break into a house, tie the occupant up, terrify the life out of them and then kill them? It doesn't look as if anything of value has been taken.'

She was pointing to the iPad on the floor, next to the sixty-inch television with a cinema surround sound system. There was a MacBook on the sofa, a set of car keys on the mantle and a stack of twenty pound notes tucked under an ornament next to the keys. She followed him upstairs, where the same mess greeted them. Bedroom doors were thrown wide open, and the master bedroom was an explosion of clothes; bedding was strewn all over the floor. It was chaotic; there didn't seem to be any reason for it. If Morgan had to describe this room, she would say it looked as if a teenager had thrown a hissy fit and trashed the place because they'd been grounded.

Ben carried on walking towards another door further along with a wooden name plaque which read 'Gabrielle's Penthouse'.

She followed and they stood staring at the carnage inside. Morgan's stomach muscles were clenched tight and she hoped she wasn't about to throw up the bowl of porridge she'd eaten for breakfast. From where Morgan was standing, the young woman looked as if she could be sleeping. Her head was turned away from her. It faced the window, and Morgan wondered if she had known she was going to die when she'd realised there was a stranger in her house. What had gone through her mind in those moments when she realised what was about to happen? The cold chill which had settled over her as she'd entered the house, had intensified so much she felt as if she was frozen to the floor. The only sound was that of Ben's slightly wheezing breath as he struggled with the face mask he was wearing. The woman's slender, partially naked body was bound at the hands and feet. Her once tanned skin was now pale and tinged greenish; a bloated jigsaw of blue and purple lines ran across her abdomen and chest. She was still wearing pyjama shorts which didn't look as if they had been disturbed. Morgan had never seen anything like it; she could feel her own breathing begin to labour. The putrid smell of decomposing flesh filled her nostrils, and she struggled to keep calm. She'd seen enough; she didn't want to look at the woman's face, but Ben gently pushed her into the room and she had no choice but to enter. A firm voice inside her head told her to pull herself together; she needed to see this woman. She owed it to her to look at her, study the horrible way she'd died and etch her face into her mind so she could recall her whenever she needed a reminder of why she was doing this job. When she was exhausted and working late into the night, she wanted to be able to see the image in front of her in full technicolour to keep her motivated. She needed to keep herself together. Whoever had done this hadn't cared about the victim's life one little bit. Morgan wanted justice for her and made it her priority to care. She would find the bastard who had done this and see him in court.

Keeping to one side, she slowly walked around the bed until she was staring at the woman's face. It had lost all of its colour and her skin looked waxy, reminding Morgan of those exhibits in Madame Tussauds she'd once been fascinated with on a school trip, convinced they were real people who had been covered in wax. Her glazed eyes had a milky film covering the irises; thick black lashes framed them and Morgan realised she had lash extensions. She felt her knees beginning to wobble. If she had to guess, she'd say she was in her early twenties. A large picture frame lay on the floor on a bed of broken glass. Without thinking she bent down and picked it up. Turning it over she saw a beautiful blonde woman, her arms around a much older woman, and felt her already broken heart tear in two. She assumed the other woman was her mum, because she had the same beautiful eyes and lashes with a few deep laughter lines around them.

Ben's voice broke her trance.

'Leave that, Morgan, there could be prints on it.'

She placed it back where she'd found it and stood up. 'Sorry.'

'It's okay, it's difficult. Don't touch anything else though, until CSI have been in, okay?'

Morgan spied a folded-up piece of paper sticking out from underneath the bed and pointed to it. 'Can I grab that?'

'Quick and don't touch anything else.'

She bent down, took hold of it and tugged it out then stepped back over the threshold. Unfolding it between her gloved fingers, she read it and held it towards Ben.

You look much better naked

'He's been watching her, waiting for this moment.'

Ben looked at Morgan. 'Why this, why all the mess, wasn't killing her enough?'

Morgan realised that this was where her years of being fascinated with serial killers and deviant criminals was about to pay off, and despite the fact that she didn't talk about it much she thought it was time to mention it. She felt more relaxed and confident around her colleagues. Amy, who was supposed to be her mentor, had told her last week she didn't need to be watching her every move and only to bother her if she really didn't have a clue. She didn't mind proving to Ben that she was more than capable of dealing with the serious stuff without anyone holding her hand.

'It could be a sexually motivated assault, but he's clever. I bet he didn't want to leave any forensics behind which could be used against him. He probably got off on the psychological terror of the attack without having to actually rape her; the note is a power thing he would have used to scare her.'

Ben's face was a mask of confusion. 'Who would want to do something like that?'

She shrugged. 'I'm not that good, at least not yet. I guess that's where we come in.'

Ben nodded. 'Come on, we need to speak to the parents and let CSI take over here. I'll get some PCSOs to canvas the street and knock on doors to speak to neighbours. See if they noticed anyone hanging around watching the place.' He turned and headed back towards the stairs.

She nodded and hoped the police community support officers would turn up some good information. Looking out the window, she noticed she could see the trees and bushes that bordered the park opposite the house.

'How did the killer know she was alone? She lives with her parents. Unless he knew about them being on holiday?' She pointed towards the park. 'I bet there are plenty of places to hide over there and watch the house. It's the perfect cover.'

Ben nodded. 'Yes, that's a possibility. Or he might know her. Stranger murders are very rare, especially here. As a rule, the killer is generally someone the victim knows. There is no obvious point of entry at the moment, so she may have let him in. It could be a boyfriend or friend.'

She didn't disagree with him because that was true, stranger killings were rare, but her instinct told her she was on the right track. Ben looked around the room, taking it all in then gave her the thumbs up. He turned and began to retrace his footsteps. Relieved to be leaving this scene of total devastation, she followed him. As she reached the door, Morgan took one last look at the crime scene and Gabby's body. Why did he choose you, Gabrielle? What made him want to do this to you? She didn't know the answers to any of it yet but knew that she would find them. She would work tirelessly to find out what had happened here and who had changed an innocent woman's life for ever.

They went outside, into the sunlight and the fresh air. The smell of decomposition clung to the pair of them. Despite the face masks she could still smell the putrid gas that had adhered itself to the white paper protective suit she was wearing. She couldn't wait to rip it off and have a hot shower, but she counted to ten. Ben beat her to it, ripping the face mask off and taking in huge gulps of fresh air. She removed hers a little more slowly, without the drama, and inhaled the scent of freshly cut grass. She looked around. Who was cutting their grass? She spied one of the council contract gardeners navigating a ride-on mower in the park opposite and began running as best as she could in the cumbersome paper suit. She ran out of the garden across the road, waving her hands at him and yelling 'stop'. Ben stared after her, a look of confusion on his face and then he followed suit. She had already caught the guy's attention before he even made it out of the gate.

'What's up?'

Morgan wondered if he was purposely ignoring the police activity opposite the park or was simply dim.

'I need you to stop right now. There's a major crime scene over there. You could be tampering with evidence.'

'What, how? I'm cutting the grass in the park; I'm nowhere near your crime scene.'

She opened her mouth to speak but heard Ben's voice.

'Detective Brookes is right. We need to search the park and playground. I need you to leave everything as it is and go wait in your van.'

'The boss isn't going to be happy.'

Morgan grimaced. 'Well the boss hasn't got a choice. I'm sure he has other jobs you can be getting on with. What time did you get here?'

'Just now, my van's parked by the other entrance. I unloaded the mower and drove it over here. Why?'

'Okay, well I need you to wait by your van, please. You can leave the mower.'

He rolled his eyes but climbed off and began walking away.

Ben grinned at her. 'Good shout, the entire park needs sealing off. I want a full search conducted.'

Morgan didn't say anything. She knew it did and was glad she'd realised before any potential evidence had been chopped into tiny pieces by the blades on the mower.

CHAPTER THREE

Morgan walked along the well-worn grassy path that had been trampled along the perimeter of the park over the years. She stood directly opposite the house where the body had been found and stared up at the window. She could see the bright flash from Wendy's camera as the Crime Scene Investigator snapped photos of the shocking scene inside the house. She caught a glimpse of Wendy as she passed the window and looked around, and realised it was a pretty exposed place to stand and watch the house. There must be somewhere the killer was able to hide discreetly yet in plain sight of the house. The note said she looked much better naked. Until they had a suspect, she was working off the basis that the killer had been watching, possibly stalking her, and here was as good a place as any.

There was a cluster of bushes a bit further back, and Morgan crossed the long grass towards them. A narrow opening was just wide enough for her to squeeze through. Waving her hands in front of her face to brush away any spider webs, she pushed herself through the gap, not quite believing what she was seeing. It was obviously used as a den by kids; there was a lingering odour of cannabis. Someone had dragged an old leather wingback chair in there at some point. The leather was almost worn out on some parts, and a couple of springs were protruding through the seat. She perched on the arm of the chair and could just about see the house opposite; but Morgan wasn't very tall. She was only five feet five on a good day: that was why she favoured platform Dr Martens boots on the rare occasion she went on a night out. They afforded her a bit of extra height. If someone taller than her sat or stood on the chair, though, they would have a perfect view of Gabrielle's bedroom, especially if they used binoculars or zoomed in on their phone. She looked around; the ground was littered with empty bottles and crisp packets. It would all need bagging up. Who wasn't to say the killer had left them behind? Even though she doubted he was so stupid, it would have to be ruled out.

'Morgan,' Ben yelled.

She pushed herself back out of the gap and saw him standing where she'd been moments ago, rubbing his head. She waved and walked towards him.

'How do you do that?'

'What?'

'Disappear. You have a habit of vanishing.'

She smiled. 'I found something interesting; you should come take a look.'

She led him to the bushes and pointed to the narrow opening.

'There's a den in there; if you are tall enough you can see the bedroom window from there. I think we need to send CSI in to do a search. There're lots of empty cans and crisp packets.'

He groaned. 'I won't fit through that.'

'Yes, you will. Breathe in.'

He took a step closer and she pushed him forwards. He lost his footing and almost crashed through the bushes, making a much wider opening.

'Sorry.'

He was muttering under his breath, but she couldn't make out what he was saying. A few moments later he squeezed back out.

'Good find, definitely needs a forensic search. However, I'm not too sure Wendy will be thrilled when she sees the amount of rubbish strewn over the floor. It's going to take her hours to process the scene, then this.' He paused. 'Actually, she can't touch this. I need another set of hands.'

He pulled his phone out of his pocket and headed back towards the house. Morgan spotted a PCSO getting out of a car and waved him over.

'Can you stand here and make sure no one goes inside until we get another CSI here to process it? Please.'

He nodded.

'Thank you, I appreciate it.'

She followed Ben, leaving the possible scene in safe hands. A cold feeling settled over her: this was a whole new level of scary. They needed to find this killer, and fast, because something told her he wasn't going to stop after this. If he thought he'd got away with this killing, what was to stop him from striking again? Just how safe were the residents of Rydal Falls if there were some crazed killer stalking people before breaking into their homes?

A white Mercedes GLS turned into the street. Its tinted windows and private registration, Dec 40, made quite an impression on Morgan. She kept telling herself one day she'd drive a car like that. She watched, wondering who was getting out. If it was the DCI then she was definitely sticking it out in CID until she made her way up the ranks. A tall, sandy-haired man got out and waved at her. Realising it was Declan, the pathologist, she grinned and waved back. He was really cute and down to earth for someone who spent most of his days with the dead. Not to mention he drove a very nice car.

Declan busied himself getting suited up while Morgan walked up to the cordon to sign him in. He had a heavy metal case in one double-gloved hand. Morgan held the tape up for him to duck under.

'Good morning, Doctor.' She realised she didn't know his surname. Ben referred to him as Dr Death. She couldn't call him that. She didn't know if he was aware of it and didn't want to upset him.

'Good morning, Morgan, what a fine one it is. Well it was fine, until your control room called me out here. I was supposed to be taking a few days' leave. Do you want to talk me through it?'

They carried on walking towards the house, and she realised that she liked him even more. He didn't act like she was still green under the collar. He was treating her as if she was a seasoned detective.

'I think I'll let my boss do that. I don't want to step on anyone's toes. Not this early in the day.'

Declan smiled. 'Wise answer, but I think you're more than capable of explaining a crime scene to me and don't let anyone tell you different. Some of these coppers are a bit old school, like to go by the book and all that. Not that there's anything wrong with that. I get it, I really do. But I like to listen to the people who know what they're talking about. I see from your current style of dress you've been in to the scene, which more than qualifies you to talk to me about it.' He lowered his voice as he turned and stared in the direction of the DCI, who was signing himself into the scene. 'Now take Tom, lovely guy. Knows his stuff, but watch: he'll come and try to tell me what's going on. Only I'm not going to be interested in what he has to say at the moment, and do you know why?'

She whispered. 'Because he's only just arrived and hasn't seen the body.'

Declan reached out and clapped her on the back. 'Exactly that, your insight is invaluable. So, Morgan, can you please talk me through it?'

She glanced back at Tom who was in the process of walking towards them. Declan carried on walking towards the garden gate.

'Don't worry, he's not coming in here. He's not got a shred of protective clothing on. Any moment now he's going to be intercepted by Ben. And there he goes; he's like a dancer with those moves.'

They both watched as Ben realised where Tom was heading and began striding towards him to stop him.

'How did you know?'

'I've been doing this far too long. So, Morgan, lead the way and tell me what's happened.'

She began to relay exactly what had happened since her arrival. They made their way upstairs to the room where Gabrielle's body was and where Wendy had just finished photographing the scene. She stuck her thumb up at Declan.

'Excellent timing, you can come in.'

Morgan didn't; she stood at the threshold to the room watching as Declan stepped inside and paused at the foot of the bed taking in the scene. He placed the case on the floor next to him and walked around to the side of the bed where Gabrielle's face was turned. He let out a loud tut; his head shook from side to side.

'I'm sorry we have to meet under these terrible circumstances. I'm going to have to take some samples, Gabrielle. It's not very nice, but I'm sure you won't mind because we need to find whoever has done this to you.'

Declan spoke quietly to the woman on the bed, the soft lilt of his barely there Irish accent giving his voice an almost poetic quality. Morgan felt her eyes begin to tear up. Declan opened his case and began to remove everything he needed. She watched as he took the victim's temperature and the ambient temperature of the room. He worked swiftly and methodically, first taking tapings for trace evidence from her skin, then combings of her hair, facial hair and pubic hair. Footsteps came up the stairs and Morgan turned around to see Ben. He stood behind her, watching Declan work. Declan had a pair of tweezers and was plucking hairs from the same areas and slipping them into evidence bags, writing on each one before moving on to the next. He took swabs from her mouth, teeth, genitals and the deep wound around her neck caused by the rope. Finally, he took scrapings from underneath her fingernails, which were short and painted white. When all these were safely stowed in his case to be sent off for analysis, he began to do a cursory examination of the body. Rolling her gently a little to look underneath her, Morgan let out a gasp at the angry red-blue bruising all over her back.

Ben asked him. 'What can you tell us, Doc? How long has she been dead?'

'Well, she died in bed. I know it looks obvious, but the hypostasis on her back confirms it.' He turned to look at Morgan and she shrugged.

'What is that?' She didn't know what that meant and wasn't afraid to ask him; she'd prefer he explained it than not have a clue what he was talking about.

'Hypostasis or more commonly called lividity is what makes her back look as if it's badly bruised. It's not; it's where the blood pools once the heart has stopped beating. Can you see the areas of white on her shoulders and buttocks? That's because she's been pressed against the mattress. In those areas the blood vessels have been squashed flat and couldn't fill with blood. If she had died elsewhere and her body moved, it would be in a different area. As for time of death, rigor has passed: putrefaction begins three to four days after death. That green discolouration on her abdomen is where it usually appears first, just next to the appendix.'

Morgan was still intrigued. 'Why?'

'Our gut is full of bacteria and it's usually contained quite nicely inside of it, whilst we're breathing that is. Once we die the little critters make a break for it, using the blood vessels as a kind of internal tube train system to run riot around the body. This is when the body is slowly turning to liquid and gas, which is what causes this delightful smell.'

A bluebottle flew in through the open bedroom door and tried to settle on Gabrielle's face. Declan shooed it away. 'This room must have been pretty airtight. I'm surprised there's no insect infestation already, considering she's been dead a minimum of three to four days. This little beggar must have smelt her. We need to shut the door until she's moved; otherwise, she's going to be crawling with them in no time.'

Morgan shuddered at the thought.

Ben shouted down the stairs to the officer outside. 'Shut the front door.' There was a loud slam as the front door was closed.

Declan continued. 'Cause of death looks like strangulation; there's a clearly defined deep, sharp groove around her neck caused by a ligature. Have you got that?'

'No, it wasn't there.'

'Well judging by the markings, I'd say you're looking for a piece of rope similar to the ones binding her hands and feet.' He gently lifted one of her eyelids open. 'Yep, that's confirmed. Can you see the tiny pinpoints of blood on the inner lining of the eyelids? Those are petechial haemorrhages, caused by strangulation.'

Ben stepped closer to take a look; Morgan didn't.

'I'm not sure why your man took the rope away from the neck yet left the ones tying her to the bed, but I imagine you have your ideas. I'm happy for the body to be moved to the mortuary if you are. It's going to need a bit of extra care. I don't think the skin is ready to explode yet, but it could when you try to move her. Much better to be safe and take precautions. I'd prefer her to arrive at the mortuary as intact as possible.'

Morgan grimaced. How did he do this day in, day out and with such a lovely manner? He must be a saint.

CHAPTER FOUR

Morgan and Ben supervised as the undertakers arrived to remove Gabrielle's body to the mortuary. She was wrapped in a cotton sheet and then placed into a black body bag, which was sealed with a yellow tag. Much to Morgan's relief, Gabrielle hadn't exploded or lost any of her skin. She hadn't been able to say whether she'd pass out or not if that had happened. The two men from the undertakers had been so gentle with Gabrielle that she found it touching watching them work. Both of them were middle-aged, possibly had daughters the same age. What a difficult job to do, she thought, they must see some tragic sights. Working with the dead every day, you would think they'd be hardened to it. Yet there they were, talking in hushed tones and telling Gabrielle what was happening and where they were taking her whilst blinking back tears. She wondered where her parents were; no doubt they would need to speak to them as soon as they could. She couldn't imagine coming back off a nice relaxing holiday abroad to discover your daughter had been murdered in her own bedroom. It didn't bear thinking about. Who would do such a thing? It was evil, cold and in her opinion very calculating. The killer had taken his time and planned this so he was undisturbed. Now it was up to them to follow up on every lead and clue as to why they had chosen Gabrielle as their victim.

They went outside and, along with the officers and PCSOs still at the scene, bowed their heads as the undertakers wheeled the trolley holding the body bag to the waiting private ambulance. Gabrielle

Stevens looked tiny inside the black bag. Morgan wondered if it was claustrophobic being wrapped in a sheet then zipped into a heavy-duty bag; even if you were dead, would you know what was happening?

'Give you a penny for your thoughts?'

She turned to Ben and shook her head. 'You don't want to know what I was thinking.'

He smiled. 'No, but I bet it's pretty similar to what's going on in my head. Come on, we need to remove these sauna suits, tidy ourselves up and go speak to her parents.'

'I was afraid you were going to say that. I don't know if I can. I feel so sad and angry at the same time.'

'Good, so you should. I'd be worried if you weren't fazed by it.'

She hoped he didn't think she was being soft, but she couldn't help it. This was how she felt; if in ten years' time she was still doing this job, she knew she would still feel this way about tragic, senseless losses of life. If she didn't, then it would be time to call it a day.

They walked to Ben's car. Wendy passed them brown paper evidence sacks for the protective clothing they were wearing. At the boot of the car they undressed. Morgan's shirt was clinging to her back and her hair was stuck to her head. The quick make-up job she'd done before leaving the house hours ago was non-existent: only red marks across her cheeks and the bridge of her nose were visible where the mask she'd been wearing had dug into her skin. Ben didn't look much better: there were dark circles under his armpit. Luckily, his head was shaved so he didn't need to worry about his hair.

'I feel like a sweaty, yucky mess. I can't go and speak to Gabrielle's parents looking and smelling like this.'

'Yes, you can. There're some tissues in the back of the car, blot yourself down. They aren't going to care what you look like. All they care about is what we can tell them and do for them.' He leant across and sniffed her. She pushed him away in horror.

'Besides, you don't smell. Well maybe there's a hint of decomposition lingering in your hair. But her parents have seen the worst thing they could possibly see; they can probably still smell it as well. That image is never going to be pushed from their memories.'

Morgan nodded. 'Where are they?'

He pointed to a house at the opposite end of the street. 'A family friend.'

He began to walk towards the house and she had no choice but to follow.

As they got nearer to the front door, where a PCSO was standing by the gate, Morgan felt her pulse begin to race. She didn't want to face them but she knew she'd have to. She owed it to them and to Gabrielle to do her best, and she knew she would.

Ben knocked and walked inside, until a voice shouted: 'In the kitchen.'

They walked towards the room where the voice had come from. Sitting inside it were a couple whose faces were so ashen they looked grey, in stark contrast to their tanned arms. The woman who had called them in was standing at the kitchen counter dropping tea bags into a teapot. She spoke first.

'I'm Sue; this is Charlotte and Harry, Gabby's mum and dad.' She stopped speaking, her hand flying to her mouth and she turned away from them. The couple looked to be in shock; both of them had a look of disbelief etched across their faces. Their eyes were wide open and they both stared at Morgan, who realised she was probably a very similar age to their daughter. It was Ben who broke the silence as he pointed to a chair.

'Do you mind if we sit down?'

They shook their heads. Morgan slipped onto the chair and tried to smile at them without it being too much. Sue placed the teapot on the table and some mugs; there was already a jug of milk and a sugar bowl. Along with a plate of untouched chocolate digestives.

No one spoke until Sue said: 'Tea is really good for shock. I'll be mother.'

She poured out four mugs of tea, passing them around. Gabby's mum shook her head. They waited until she'd finished and Ben began to speak.

'I'm so sorry for your loss. I can't even begin to imagine how you must be feeling. Do you need a doctor, someone to come and check you're okay, maybe give you something to help you settle?'

They didn't say a word, but Harry shook his head.

'We need to ask some questions, find out a bit about Gabrielle's background so we can start speaking to her friends and find out what her last movements were.'

'Gabby, not Gabrielle. She didn't like being called by her full name,' Charlotte whispered. 'She turned twenty-three last week; how old are you?'

Charlotte was staring at Morgan.

'I'm twenty-three.'

'Did you know Gabby?'

She shook her head. 'No. I'm sorry.'

Harry reached out for his wife's hand and gently clasped it in his.

She continued to speak. 'I thought maybe you would have gone to the same school or college. Gabby couldn't decide what she wanted to be when she was growing up. First it was a police officer, then a nurse; she ended up working in The Golden Ball. I hated her working there; she should never have gone there.'

Ben nudged Morgan. She realised that Charlotte had struck up a conversation with her and not him and he was happy for Morgan to take the lead. She felt as if there was a tennis ball lodged in the back of her throat, it was so hard to speak.

'Did Gabby have trouble whilst she worked there? Why didn't you like it?'

'Do you know that pub? You must do. I bet the police get called there all the time. It's rough, full of kids who drink far too much for their age and with no ambition to get a real job. Not to mention the alcoholics and drug dealers. That's what happens when you're open all day and sell cheap beer.'

Harry shook his head. 'You can't say that. Gabby liked working there. You don't know those people.'

'I can and I will, you know it too. She spent far too much time hanging around with the losers in there. It would be a good place to start asking questions. Who would do this to my beautiful girl? She didn't deserve this; we don't deserve this.' Her voice began to quiver as the tears began to roll down her cheeks.

Harry nodded. 'Did they, was she? Oh God.' He buried his head into his hands and began to sob.

Ben gave him some time before he reached out his hands and took hold of both of theirs.

'We don't know. We won't know anything until the post-mortem. I'm sorry I can't tell you much at the moment because I don't know myself, but I can tell you that my team will not stop until we find out who did this to Gabby. We will find them and bring them to justice.'

Charlotte never took her gaze off Morgan. 'I want you to find him and when you do make sure he has to look you in the eyes because of what he's done. As soon as you find this monster, I want to know who he is. I don't want you to keep anything from me. Do you promise? You come straight here and tell me his name.'

Morgan felt as if it was hard to catch her breath. The room was spinning and it was far too hot in this small kitchen. The smell of the tea in the mug in front of her was making her feel queasy and she wanted to run out of this house, out into the front street and get away from here as fast as she could. Instead, she gulped, nodded and answered.

'Charlotte, I will do everything I possibly can. When we find him, I'll be the one to arrest him and read him his rights before we lock him up and throw away the key.'

'Good.'

Morgan couldn't look at Ben. She didn't know if she'd just overstepped her mark but she knew that she was speaking the truth. She would hunt down whoever did this, slap handcuffs on him and enjoy every single minute of it.

'Can you give us a list of Gabby's closest friends? We need to speak to them. Do you know the passwords for her phone, laptop, and iPad? It would be a big help,' Morgan asked.

Sue got a pen and notepad out of a drawer and placed them on the table in front of Harry, who pushed them towards Charlotte. He looked at Ben.

'I don't really know. I didn't take much notice. Charlotte knew Gabby's friends, her personal stuff. You write them down, love.'

Ben added: 'Do you have somewhere to stay? I'm really sorry, but we can't let you back into the house until we've finished searching and processing the scene, and that might take some time.'

Sue spoke. 'They can stay here as long as it takes. You both have your suitcases. I'll wash whatever you need.'

Ben smiled. 'Thank you, that's great. We'll try and be as quick as we possibly can, but we need to be thorough. I know you will want us to make sure we've got every shred of evidence we possibly can. There's a family liaison officer who will be here soon; they will be your point of contact and keep you up to date with everything that's happening. If you have any questions, they will help, and if you need to speak to either of us then they will let us know.'

Charlotte nodded. 'We never should have gone away. It was a cheap holiday. It's my fault, I kept moaning at Harry about needing a break. If we hadn't gone, this wouldn't have happened.'

Morgan noticed that Harry didn't reach out for his wife's hand; instead, he stared down at the floor, and she felt awful for them both. She wondered if their marriage would survive this, if he would for ever blame her for insisting they went away. If he didn't, would she be able to live with the guilt that had no doubt lodged itself inside her heart? Humans seemed to be good at blaming themselves whenever things went wrong, even if it had nothing to do with them.

'You can't blame yourselves. This isn't your fault and it's not Gabby's fault. The only person to blame is whoever decided they had the right to break into your home and kill your daughter.'

Charlotte smiled at Morgan, but it never reached her eyes as she whispered: 'Thank you.' Then she bent her head and began writing some names for them. The pen was shaking in her fingers but she continued then ripped the page from the book, passing it across the table to Morgan.

'I've put them in order of who she was closest to; the password is at the bottom. I don't think she's changed it recently. I think she used the same one for all her accounts: Facebook, emails, et cetera. I only know it because we both share a couple of accounts for online shopping.'

Morgan looked at it then folded it, tucking it inside her notebook. 'Thank you, this will be a huge help. Can you talk us through what happened when you arrived home?'

Harry sipped his tea. 'There isn't much to tell. We got dropped off by the airport taxi at almost six this morning. When we went inside we knew immediately something was wrong. It was such a mess and then there was the smell; oh God it was my girl that awful smell.' His breath caught in the back of his throat.

'What was the house like? Was it secure? Did you have to unlock the door to get inside? Can you remember if the lights were on or off?'

Charlotte shook her head. 'No, the lights were off. It was in darkness and we had to use a key to open the door. When we turned the light on, we thought we'd been burgled then I saw the money still there and the iPad. Gabby's key ring was on the floor. I just knew something was terribly wrong. I shouted Gabby; I thought maybe she'd had a party and the house had got trashed, but Harry was already running up the stairs to check on her. He knew, knew what that awful smell was and I followed him. Her bedroom door was shut but the others were all open. He knocked then pushed it open and—'

The tears began to flow; this time Harry did reach out for his wife, holding her close as she sobbed into his chest. Ben stood up and Morgan followed, desperate to get out of the confined kitchen, which seemed to be getting smaller by the minute.

'Where's Gabby's key ring now?'

Harry pushed his hand into his pocket. Tugging it out, he held it in the air. Morgan stared at the picture of Gabby and two friends, mouths open, mid-scream, as it dangled in front of her. It had been snapped by an automated camera on a ride at a theme park, the sort of photo you normally cringed at when you saw what you looked like. Gabby had a sense of humour and she liked her even more for it. Her heart ached even more at the loss of her life. Ben pulled out a glove, slipped his hand inside and took it from Harry.

'I need to get this checked for prints.'

'I didn't think. I just shoved it in my pocket when I saw it on the floor. I'm sorry.'

'It's okay, anyone would do the same. Thank you. Once again I'm very sorry about Gabby.'

Sue led them to the front door, giving the grieving couple some space. She didn't speak and watched Ben and Morgan as they headed back to the car.

It was time to go to the station for a briefing.

CHAPTER FIVE

In the large office which housed the CID department, Detective Constable Amy Smith tucked her long fringe behind her ear. She was regretting having her blonde hair cut into a bob. It was too short to tie up and got in the way when it was down. Glancing at her reflection in Ben's office window, she wished she'd worn trousers instead of a dress. She looked as if she was ready to go out for afternoon tea not work a murder investigation. Thank God Ben had called Morgan out and not her. She was quite happy to be in the office gathering the information she needed to give to the PCSOs, so they could start the house-to-house enquiries regarding Gabrielle Stevens's murder. Amy had been shocked to come into work and be notified by the duty sergeant of the morning's events. Straight away she'd rung Ben, who was her supervisor, to see if she was needed at the scene. He'd told her to get the questionnaires ready, so she had. She was in the process of hunting down clipboards to attach the still-warm sheets of paper to, when the door opened and in walked response officer Dan Hunt, carrying a small gift bag with a large pink bow stuck to the front of it. She took one look at him and the bag. Despite him being in love with himself, there was no denying his black hair, tanned skin and brown eyes were easy on the eye. It was no wonder women swooned over him, not that she'd ever tell him that; his head was big enough.

'Aww, how kind of you, Dan, you didn't have to. It's not my birthday so what have I done to deserve this?'

'It's not for you.'

She gasped and placed her hand over her mouth. 'What, why would you say that? Who's it for then?'

His cheeks flushed a deep shade of red. 'Which one is Morgan's desk?'

She pointed to the desk at the back of the room nearest the window with a large chunk of pink rose quartz on it. 'That's Morgan's. It's not her birthday, is it? Because I didn't know and I'd feel bad if I missed it.'

He shook his head. 'Not that I know of.'

'What's that for then? Last I heard you were being a dick to her because she got to come work up here and you never.'

'It's because I wasn't very nice about that; it's an apology.'

'What's in it?'

'A pair of earrings.'

'Expensive?'

'What's it got to do with you?'

She shrugged. 'I'll tell you whether it's a good enough apology or whether you need to try harder.'

'Pandora.'

'Suppose they'll do. I wouldn't expect her to come crawling back and be your best friend just because you bought her earrings though, not unless she's a pushover. Do you fancy her then?'

He shook his head. 'No, I don't. I was an arsehole to her when she got transferred up here and I feel bad. It's been worrying me for weeks. What is this, Amy, an interrogation?'

She laughed. 'No, I'm just making sure you're not making things worse with a crappy present. You must like her a little bit if you're buying her Pandora.'

He crossed the room to Morgan's desk and put the small gift bag on it. 'Get lost, Amy; don't go stirring things when there's no need. It's an apology, not a marriage proposal.'

He strode out of the room to the sound of her laughter. She was still grinning when Ben and Morgan walked in.

Ben took one look at her and asked: 'What's so funny?'

'Nothing really. Morgan you have a present on your desk off an admirer.'

It was Morgan's turn to blush. 'Who's it from?'

'You'll have to open it and see. I'm not spoiling all your fun.'

Ben had no idea what was going on. 'Amy, have you sorted the questionnaires out or have you been pissing around all morning?'

That wiped the smile off her face. 'They're all done, boss. I even hunted down clipboards.'

'Good because I want the house-to-house started immediately. You can go see the community sergeant and gather every available PCSO, then get down to the crime scene and oversee the enquiries.'

Gathering the pile of clipboards in her arms, she didn't answer him back like she usually would, realising whatever had happened must be terrible to put Ben in this sort of mood. He went into his office and shut the door.

Amy turned to look at Morgan, who was staring at the gift bag.

'Your best mate, Dan, brought it about thirty seconds before you walked in.'

'Why? He's not my best mate. He's not even my mate at the moment.'

'Open it. I want to see it. He said it's because he was a dick to you. It's an apology.'

Morgan pushed the bag to one side. 'Yeah, well I don't need an apology or a present. I don't want anything off him.'

'Aren't you going to open it?'

She shook her head.

'You're a tough cookie, Morgan Brookes. I like that. You're not easily bought, but maybe you could open it and take a look just for my sake. He must feel bad if he's buying you presents.'

'You just want to know what's inside.'

'I know what's inside. He told me.'

'Then you can have it; there's no need to open it. I don't want it.'

Amy shrugged. 'I don't think that's the way an apology works. You don't give the present away; you're supposed to keep it.'

'What's wrong with a simple "I'm sorry"? I don't need presents.'

'Don't shoot the messenger; maybe he likes you more than he realises.'

'Dear God, I hope not. He's not exactly boyfriend material if he can be mean to someone when they haven't done anything wrong.'

'Not for me to say. It's a bit like the boys at school. You remember, the ones who were horrible to you because they liked you really and wouldn't admit it. Don't you think you're being a bit too harsh on him? He's—'

She never got to finish her sentence because Ben shouted: 'Amy, what are you waiting for?'

She rolled her eyes at Morgan. 'He's in a right mood.'

Morgan whispered: 'It's awful, Amy, that poor girl was tied to her own bed and strangled. He left her for days, her body decomposing for her parents to discover her. The smell... she was going green; they thought she might explode when the undertakers came to move her.'

'No, that's terrible. See you later, open your gift. See, that's exactly why you should forgive Dan. Life's too short to hold a grudge.'

She left Morgan staring at the small bag with the oversized pink bow and took her clipboards to go find as many PCSOs as she could.

As she went downstairs to the community office, she could see Dan hovering around by the brew station. She looked the other way, not wanting to be the one to tell him his peace offering was still unopened and Morgan had been less than impressed.

CHAPTER SIX

Morgan wished she'd gone back out with Amy to help with the house to house. Anything was better than sitting here waiting for the briefing. Ben came out of his office, carrying his laptop and a paper file tucked under one arm. 'Please can you go get the printouts I sent to the printer?'

She jumped up, nodding. Pleased to have something to do. She knew what was coming after the briefing. As soon as the Crime Scene Manager and Claire, the DCI from the Murder Investigation Team, had been spoken to about the scene, the body had been taken to the Royal Lancaster Infirmary for a post-mortem. Ben would no doubt attend and take her with him, not that she didn't want to. It's just she couldn't get it out of her head the way Gabby had been brutally murdered and left like that with not a shred of decency. He hadn't even had the heart to pull the duvet over her nakedness. He left her on show like some prized possession. Had he thought of her that way, as if she belonged to him? Gathering the sheets of paper, she made her way down to the blue room, which was still painted a weird pink colour. The oval table was almost full, so she squeezed into a gap between DCI Tom Fell and Wendy, who was nursing a huge mug of coffee which smelt really good.

Ben shuffled the papers she passed to him. Then brought up the crime scene photos Wendy had already emailed to him. The outside of the Stevens' end-terrace house looked like any normal house on the street: the pots full of scented roses that Morgan could still smell and white walls luring everyone to a false sense of security.

The atmosphere in the room was one of fraught anticipation; it almost felt static and she was tempted to reach out a finger to poke Tom and see if she gave him a shock. She glanced around: everyone was sitting up straight; some were gripping pens in their fingers so hard the ends of their fingertips were white. They wanted to see the scene, look at the body, yet at the same time would rather not. Realising it looked as if she wasn't paying attention, she focused on the whiteboard. She didn't need to see these photographs because the horror from inside Gabby Stevens's bedroom would be etched into her mind for ever. Then the photographs from the inside of the house flicked across the whiteboard: the mess, the expensive electronics and cash which had been left behind.

Tom spoke.

'It's obviously not a burglary, too many valuables were left untouched, yet he wanted the occupiers to think so. Why the mess? Was it a control thing, or was he looking for something?'

Ben shrugged. 'At this point in time, I can't say. The bedrooms are in a similar state, particularly Gabby's. Her mother insisted we call her Gabby when we talk about her, not Gabrielle.'

Morgan spoke without even thinking about it. 'I think he was looking for something specific. I think when her parents are allowed in they'll discover something personal is missing from Gabby's room. It won't be obvious though; I think he's made the mess to hide the fact that he's taken something, a trophy. He wanted something to remember what he did to Gabby whenever he looks at it, a reminder of the good time he had.'

She stopped, realising the whole room was staring at her. 'I mean, it's what they do, isn't it?'

Tom turned to her. 'It's what who does?'

'Killers, especially the sexually motivated ones, which I think this is. They like to relive the fantasy, the killing and take something personal that belonged to the victim, to look at in their own time whenever they want. Ted Bundy liked to keep his victims' heads;

he'd display them in his apartment and sometimes apply make-up to the faces or wash and brush their hair. Jerry Brudos liked to collect shoes, especially black high heels. He would then dress up in them to masturbate. Joseph DeAngelo, the Golden State Killer, took jewellery from his victims...' The look of disbelief on Tom's face told her to stop talking, so she did.

'Are you saying we have some crazed serial killer along those lines on the loose, Detective Brookes? You do realise this is Rydal Falls and not New York City? Those are all American killers you have just named. It could have been some disgruntled boyfriend, a lover's tiff gone horribly wrong and he's trying to make it look like a burglary. It may even have been some sordid sex game that didn't pan out how it was supposed to.'

'Yes, sir, it could, it was just a thought worth mentioning.'

Ben quickly flicked to the next photo, catching everyone's attention as they turned away from Morgan back to the whiteboard, and she let out a sigh.

Wendy leant over and whispered: 'This lot wouldn't know a sexually motivated killer if he invited them to an orgy and brought a severed head out on a silver platter. I think you have a valid point.'

Morgan smiled at her, and then turned her attention back to the board. She would keep her mouth shut in future even if it killed her.

Ben scrolled through the photographs, each one building the anticipation in the room until he came to one taken from the bedroom door, looking at Gabby Stevens's naked, decomposing body, lying on a double bed, the pastel pink cotton sheets and pillows a stark contrast to her white, marbled green torso and vivid, red-blue back. A collective gasp echoed around the room.

'It's bad, in fact it's bloody awful. Sir, you have a point: it could be a disgruntled boyfriend; we can't rule that out. But in my opinion, a boyfriend would have killed her without the need for the peep show. I definitely think there is some sexual motive to it. Wendy, did you find any evidence on the body of a sexual assault?'

She shook her head. 'There were no obvious signs of semen, but it doesn't mean she wasn't sexually assaulted. The pathologist will be able to tell us a lot more when he takes a closer look.'

'The property was secure when her parents arrived home. They opened the door with a key. They found Gabby's key on the front doormat, so whoever left locked the door behind them and posted the key through. Wendy, can you get the key sent off to be fingerprinted? It's on your desk.'

'I will as soon as we leave this room.'

'Excellent, thanks. Did you find any prints around the window frames, any signs of a forced entry?'

'No. Whoever it was had either been let in to the property by the victim or had a key.'

Morgan, who firmly believed it wasn't someone Gabby knew, held up her hand.

'Yes, Morgan?'

'What if they'd been stalking her and knew how to get inside? Maybe she left a window open and he cleaned around it before he left, or she hadn't locked up properly. If they knew her routine, it would make it easier to get into the house without being seen or leaving evidence behind.'

Ben didn't disagree with her, but he didn't agree either. She knew it might sound far-fetched and, yes, this was Rydal Falls, a quiet Lake District town nestled between Keswick and Ambleside, but it wasn't that long ago an entire family had been murdered in cold blood in their home. Crazy stuff happened everywhere, not just in big cities.

'At the moment, I have Amy and PCSOs conducting house-to-house enquiries. I want a full search team to go in now the body has been removed. Her mum gave us a limited list of friends to speak to; she worked at The Golden Ball, so myself and Morgan will go and speak to staff there until Declan is ready to start the post-mortem, which we will also attend.'

'What about the area in the bushes where someone could have hidden and been watching the house?'

'Yes, thank you, Morgan. There is an area which the local kids have turned into a bit of a den, but Gabby Stevens's bedroom window is visible from inside of there, just. I want that searching as well, just in case the killer has been stalking her and that is his hiding place. I don't want to rule anything out.'

Ben shut his laptop, gathered his papers and stood up. The officers, search team and Wendy all filed out of the room. Morgan followed, leaving Ben and Tom behind. She didn't want to know what they said about her. It was their decision whether they took her input on board, but she wouldn't be silenced when she might be right, regardless of what they thought. Gabby Stevens didn't deserve to die this way, no one did, and if he did take a trophy then he was more than likely going to do it again. If this was a sexually motivated killing, he would want to repeat it; he wouldn't stop after Gabby. Who was going to be his next victim? They had to find him and stop him before he had the chance to strike again. There was no telling what chain of events this murder could have set in place.

CHAPTER SEVEN

Morgan waited back in the office for Ben. She opened the bottom drawer and dropped the gift bag inside. She'd give it back to Dan when she had the time; she was far too busy today. Her stomach let out a loud groan. Despite feeling queasy earlier, she was hungry now and desperate for coffee. It was lunchtime and she always felt tired by this time of day: waking up at 04.25 every morning meant she was ready to have an afternoon nap by lunchtime. The days she was on a late shift was fine, but today was going to be one long day. There was so much to do still and they hadn't even got to the mortuary.

Ben walked in.

'Come on, we need to go to The Golden Ball. I need food first though; otherwise I'll flake out at the post-mortem later.'

She smiled at him, relieved they were both thinking the same thing. Walking out to the car, he didn't speak until they were outside of the station. The sun was peeking through the clouds, a cool breeze was blowing and Morgan felt refreshed as it blew away the suffocating stuffiness of the last thirty minutes.

'That was a pretty impressive speech about serial killers.'

'Yeah, you think so? I don't think the DCI was too impressed with it.'

Ben laughed. 'No, he did look a bit shocked at your suggestions. He's okay, Tom, you just have to remember he's been doing this job longer than you've been alive and probably never come across a sexually motivated killer. The Potters were the closest thing to something so serious in a very long time. It's almost unheard of around here for someone to be murdered by a complete stranger; you know what it's like, almost everybody knows everyone else. There isn't much you can get away with without someone seeing you or gossiping about your business.'

'I get that, but it doesn't mean that it couldn't happen. People have access to much more information through social media, television, Netflix shows about all kinds of killers. It only takes someone who is a borderline psychopath with too much information overload to make them think they can live out their wildest fantasies, regardless of whether they live in London or here. It happens, Ben, and we can't decide it's not possible just because it's never happened before.'

'I don't; I'm not small-minded. I'm trying to explain why Tom and probably most of the officers in this station would think like that. I'm willing to explore every available avenue to catch whoever did this to Gabby Stevens.'

He threw the car keys in her direction and she caught them in one hand.

'You never fail to impress me, Brookes. Drive me somewhere to get coffee and cake before I pass out.'

She laughed. 'Thanks, Sarge. I'm glad you're so easily pleased.'

She drove them to her favourite café, The Coffee Co., and waited outside, letting Ben go in and buy his lunch. When he returned with an assortment of paper bags and two large lattes, she nodded with approval.

She drove the short distance to a small lay-by with a view of Lake Thirlmere.

'Tuna or cheese savoury? You can have first pick because I'm that impressed with you.'

'Cheese, please.' She didn't tell him she didn't think she'd be able to stomach tuna, which might repeat on her whilst watching the post-mortem. As fast as the thought entered her mind she blocked it off. She needed to eat; they both did if they wanted to keep going for as long as this would take. They ate in silence. Morgan was trying to recall as much information about the kind of offender she had read so much about as she could.

There was a group of kids messing about in canoes on the lake and Ben asked: 'Didn't you used to work at an outdoor education centre? Or did I imagine that?'

She laughed. 'You have a good memory. Yes, I did.'

'Did you like it? I mean I don't mind a bit of exercise, but spending all day with noisy kids whilst canoeing, ghyll scrambling and whatever else, is not exactly a pleasurable job to have.'

'I liked it. I'm not particularly sporty. I love being outdoors though, and I worked with primary school kids who were pretty cool. They're just the right age to not care about life and enjoy everything you throw at them.'

'That's a big change to what you're doing now, why this?'

She looked at him. He was far more relaxed around her now than when she'd first started working for him and she realised he was asking a general question because he was interested in her life. He had lost weight in the last few months. Not lots, but enough to be noticeable, and he looked better in himself. At one point, she'd been worried he was going to have a heart attack or kill himself, but he seemed different now. She'd have to congratulate him: it wasn't easy dieting with the stress of this job. She knew how easy it was to put on a few pounds with all the takeaways and coffees, which was part of the reason she was trying to do the stupid running a few times a week.

'You already know.'

'Do I?'

'I thought you did. I've always been fascinated with serial killers ever since I read *The Silence of the Lambs* when I was fifteen and realised that these kind of people existed. I then began to read every true crime book I could get my hands on. How their minds work. I realised that I'd like to be a detective one day. Actually, I wanted to move to the US and work homicide there, but I realised you need to be American to do that. I was pretty devastated about that. I quite fancied walking around in a bomber jacket with FBI on the back.'

'So here you are.'

'Yes, here I am.'

'In rural Cumbria with possibly the lowest murder rate in the country. But you do get to work with me, so that's kind of a bonus.'

Morgan laughed. 'Hmm, I suppose it is. I don't know, maybe I'll get some experience and transfer to a city.'

'Maybe, why not a definite plan because you're young and keen enough?'

'I like living here. I love the beauty of the lakes. I also kind of like working for you. Are you trying to get rid of me after giving the DCI a heart attack at the briefing?'

He grinned. 'Not yet and I'm glad to hear it. I think you'll end up running rings around us all one day; maybe you'll end up being my DCI. Don't let anyone hold you back, Morgan. If you get the chance of promotion, take it. I spent too long being a DC before deciding to become a DS.'

'Why don't you go for your inspector's board? It's not as if you're ancient, Ben.'

'I might, but I like being here. Working the cases hands on, not from behind the desk. I'd hate to be stuck in the station all day attending meetings. It would drive me insane.'

'Yeah, I understand that. It's much nicer being able to eat your lunch staring at this than the flaking walls in the canteen.' She winked at him, brushed the crumbs from her trousers and pressed the engine start button.

The Golden Ball was in walking distance from the station, they could have walked there, but then they'd have had nowhere to catch a bite to eat and it was nice chatting to Ben about stuff other than the cases they worked on. Despite the tragedy and horror surrounding Gabby Stevens's murder, they were only human.

CHAPTER EIGHT

Morgan knew The Golden Ball had been one of Stan's drinking spots, and she looked around with interest at the place her dad had spent so many hours of his life. It looked as if it had been involved in a floral explosion, there were so many hanging baskets and planters outside the front. Morgan parked the car. The tired picnic benches which shared the car park could do with a lick of paint and tidying up, she thought.

'I bet those plants are a nightmare for the customers. They'll attract every bee and wasp in a ten-mile radius. Imagine sitting there spending your whole time wafting them away.'

Ben laughed. 'I wonder what it's like inside. I haven't been in here for years. It used to serve a half decent pint.'

He pushed open the door and she followed him in. It was very green inside. Almost everything was painted a different shade of green. The bar area was empty, and a large man appeared. He had the build of a rugby player, with a fading black eye, which Morgan thought he'd either got fighting with drunken customers or playing sport.

'We're not open yet.'

Ben answered. 'Police, can we have a word?'

He looked up from the glass he was polishing, stared at them both and nodded. They crossed towards the bar, perching on stools.

'What's wrong now? I did what the licensing officer advised me to do; I can't do anymore.'

Morgan glanced at Ben. She didn't have a clue what he was talking about and judging by the expression on his face neither did he.

'We're not from licensing. I'm Detective Sergeant Ben Matthews and this is Detective Constable Morgan Brookes. Are you the licensee?'

'I am, John Walden.'

'John, we're here about your employee, Gabby Stevens.'

'Oh, that's okay then. What's Gabby done? I can't see her getting into much trouble. She's one of my best workers, lovely girl.'

Morgan let Ben talk and wondered how many lives were about to be changed because of Gabby's murder.

'I have some bad news. I'm afraid Gabby was found dead by her parents this morning.'

The barman, who moments earlier had ruddy cheeks and seemed larger than life, deflated in front of them both. He put the glass on the bar and leant forward, closing his eyes. Opening them seconds later, blinking away tears that were threatening to fall.

'Had she been in an accident?'

'No, she was murdered at home.'

The man gasped. 'What are you saying?'

Morgan knew he was in shock, but it was pretty obvious what Ben had just said.

'Her parents came home from holiday and found her dead. Can you tell us the last time you saw or spoke to Gabby?'

He turned to Morgan, nodding. 'I can't... it's just hard to imagine.'

She gave him a few moments to process the devastating news and tried again.

'I'm very sorry, I know this must be really difficult and a terrible shock, but can you tell us when Gabby was last at work?'

'What day is it, Monday?' He began counting backwards on his nicotine-stained fingers. 'Thursday evening. She finished her shift around eight but stayed on for a few drinks with her friends.'

'How was she? Did she leave with anyone?'

'In good spirits, although that might have been the bottle of wine and vodka shots. Those girls can drink me under the table and I drink a lot, especially after a match on a Sunday. I didn't see her leave, to be honest, it was fairly busy. I remember her shouting "see you next week, John"; I don't think I even looked her way. I just waved. Oh God. I didn't even say goodbye to her. But you don't expect that to be the last time you see someone, do you? I mean you don't think about stuff like that. How did she die?'

Ben took over. 'I'm afraid we can't say at the moment but it was under suspicious circumstances.'

'No, no, no. Was she was murdered? By who? Have you got the bastard? I'll kill them.' He placed his elbows on the bar and rested his face in the palm of his hands. He was rocking, and Morgan wanted to reach out to comfort him but stopped herself.

Ben's voice softened as he spoke. 'No, we haven't got anyone in custody yet. It's very early days but it's only a matter of time before we do. Gabby was only discovered this morning when her parents returned from holiday in the early hours. Did she have any trouble with anyone, a boyfriend, an ex?'

Morgan asked. 'Did you see anyone hanging around her? Did any of the customers like her a lot more than they should have?'

John shrugged. 'Not that I know of. She had a boyfriend but he went off to uni a couple of years ago and they drifted apart. I don't think he even comes back to visit his parents; you know what lads are like when they get the chance to escape from here. We didn't really talk about that kind of stuff, you know. Her friends would be able to tell you a lot more about her personal life.' He reached behind him, ripping some paper towels off a roll and blew his nose.

'Do you know which friends she was with on Thursday night?'

He nodded. 'Becky and Kate. I don't know where they live though.'

'That's fine, thank you. Could we have the CCTV footage from Thursday? From when Gabby started her shift until she leaves. And can you confirm your whereabouts Thursday evening through to early hours Friday morning?'

'Yes, I can. I was here all night, and then after I locked up I went upstairs to eat supper with my girlfriend. After that we watched a couple of episodes of *Mindhunter* on Netflix and went to bed. What are you saying?'

'That's great; we just have to rule everyone out. It's not personal, like you say. If you didn't leave there's nothing to worry about. These are routine enquiries in a murder investigation; we have to eliminate everyone. Is your girlfriend here?'

He shook his head. 'No, she's gone to meet a friend for coffee, and I suppose so. As to the CCTV, I'll get it downloaded for you. The system is a bit slow or you could have taken it with you. Would you like to take a quick look at it now?'

'Yes, please.' Ben glanced at Morgan, who opened her notebook. She'd written down 'Mindhunter' and underlined it. Above it were the names on the list Gabby's mum had given her. Becky and Kate were cousins who went to school with Gabby. They both worked at the nail bar in town.

John lifted a part of the bar up so they could come behind. He led them to a small room.

'Excuse the mess, but I like it this way. I know where everything is.'

Morgan couldn't stop herself. 'I loved *Mindhunter*; I binge-watched them all one weekend when it was first released. I wish they'd do another series. Those guys were unbelievable. Where are you up to?'

He shrugged. 'Not really my thing. I only watch it because Saffie likes that sort of stuff. I think we're on the one where they accuse the school principal of doing inappropriate stuff.'

She smiled at him.

There was a monitor on what she assumed was a desk. She couldn't tell because it was littered with pieces of paper, beer mats, pens and empty mugs. John began to type Thursday's date onto the hard drive and then waited for the footage to load. After a few minutes of cursing and trying different date formats, images finally filled the screen.

'Do you know what time she left? Could we look at that to see whether she was alone?'

He shrugged. 'I'll go to ten and see if she's still here, then work my way back.'

Finally, he pressed play and the screen was filled with black and white images from the bar area nearest the front doors. John pointed a stubby finger on the screen to a table in the corner with three women sitting around it.

'There she is: that's Gabby. She's the one with the bun on the top of her head, her back to the camera. I think she always chose to sit that way. She told me she hated knowing there were cameras watching her. I told her there was nothing I could do about it: they're part of my licence condition.'

A heavy ball lodged itself in Morgan's stomach. Knowing what had happened to her, she couldn't bear to see Gabby alive, having fun with her friends. Ben was looking at the other customers in the pub. If he recognised anyone, he never said. Morgan forced herself to watch as Gabby and her friends stood up and they both took it in turn to hug her. When she turned so she was facing the camera, Morgan sucked in a breath. She looked so happy, so pretty, and now it was hard to associate the body from earlier with the girl on the screen. She threw her small bag over her shoulder, waved at her friends and walked towards the exit. Pausing, she turned and shouted something, which must have been to John because he lifted an arm and waved at her, all the time continuing to serve two men at the bar.

Ben pointed to a man on his own, sitting nursing a drink. He was facing the table of girls.

'Stop, who's that?'

John rewound it a little. He shook his head. 'I wish I could tell you, but I don't know everyone that comes in for a pint. I don't exactly ask them to sign in. There's been a lot of contractors lately with the Armadale Hotel being refurbished.'

They watched, the man was turned away from the camera but he kept glancing over his shoulder to look over at Gabby and her friends. As Gabby left, he watched. A minute later, he downed his pint and stood up to leave, following her outside.

'Do you have external cameras?'

'Well yes and no. They're rubbish; I'm waiting on new ones to be installed.' He switched camera view and Ben swore. The images were too grainy; you couldn't see anything on them.

Ben stood up. 'Thank you, John. I'm sorry we had to be the bearers of such bad news. I'll ask a PCSO to pop in and collect the CCTV in an hour if that's okay.'

He stared at them both. 'What do I do now? I don't know what to do. Should I go and see her parents?'

'I wouldn't, not yet. Give them some space.'

'Okay, if they need anything at all I'm willing to help. Can you tell them that?'

Morgan smiled. 'Yes, of course. Thank you, the camera footage is more than enough at the moment. If you do think of any incidents with customers, or anyone who may have been hanging around Gabby, you can ring me anytime.' She passed him a small blue and white business card with 'Cumbria Constabulary' stamped across it. He tucked it into his pocket.

They walked back into the bar area and he turned, pouring himself a large whisky. Morgan didn't blame him. His hands had been shaking when he took the card from her.

Outside in the car park, Ben asked: 'What did you think of him?'

'He seemed genuine, but he admitted to watching a programme about serial killers the night she was murdered. Why?'

'Just wondering if he might have a bit of a crush on Gabby. But I don't think we can lock him up because of his viewing taste. You've already watched it though. Is there anything on it similar to Gabby's murder?'

She shook her head. 'He also has a girlfriend, and an alibi. I didn't get the impression he was the kind of bloke to be able to sneak into a house and murder a woman in cold blood. For one thing, I think he's too big to be discreet. She would have heard him coming in and maybe had time to phone the cops.'

'Why, what's his size got to do with it? If anything, it would give him an advantage. He would be able to overpower her easily.'

'Just a hunch. I didn't get any bad vibes from him at all.'

'We can't arrest people on whether they give off bad vibes or not. It wouldn't hold up in court, would it? We need concrete evidence, and until we've spoken to his girlfriend and confirmed he didn't leave, then I'm not ruling him out. It's up to us to find the evidence to eliminate him. Once that's ticked off we'll move on. What about the guy who was watching Gabby and her friends?'

Morgan realised Ben was right: she shouldn't be so easily swayed. Point taken. She would ensure John's girlfriend was spoken to and his alibi corroborated. It should be easy enough to prove his innocence, and if the pub CCTV didn't show him leaving the premises, he was off the hook.

'I think we need to locate him as soon as possible. He was taking a keen interest in them and then he left a minute after she did. It could be a coincidence, but it's strange.'

Ben nodded. 'You're right, he is definitely someone we need to be speaking to. Hopefully, Gabby's friends might know who he was or be able to give us a description. I don't like the way he never once faced the camera, not even when he was leaving.'

'How did he get his drink at the bar?'

Ben shrugged. 'There's another room to the pub, maybe he came in that way, bought his drink and then went to sit down by the girls.' His phone began to ring.

'Hello, yeah right, that's great. Thank you, Declan, we're on our way. We should be with you in the next hour depending on traffic.'

He ended the call, and Morgan felt tiny butterflies in her stomach at the thought of seeing Gabby Stevens's dead body again so soon, and under the harsh mortuary spotlights. It was even worse now she'd watched her on the television screen so full of laughter and life, with only a few hours left before someone would come into her home and kill her so cruelly. A cold shiver ran the full length of her spine as a chill settled over her shoulders, which was only going to get worse under the air conditioning at the mortuary.

CHAPTER NINE

Stan Brookes waited until the others had left the building, before he began a final check of the toilets and kitchen in the community centre where the local AA meeting had just been held. He was six weeks into the programme this time, but it was six weeks longer than he'd ever lasted before. This time he had a reason: he'd almost lost his daughter to a killer and had never felt so helpless in his life. Thankfully, he'd managed to stop him and almost severed an artery in his leg in the process, but he was here to tell the story, and so was Morgan. He'd spent the last five years since his wife, Sylvia, had died on a downward spiral and he knew he'd been a lousy father. He had been so focused on his own feelings of guilt and remorse that he'd stopped seeing and talking to the one person who meant the most to him. She had hated him so much, but she couldn't blame him anymore than he blamed himself for Sylvia's death and the spectacular way he'd ruined all of their lives.

He stared at his reflection in the cracked mirror above the sink. Deep lines and grooves filled his forehead. What was left of his grey hair was thinning; the one thing that had improved was his skin tone. It had been a dirty, jaundiced colour due to the damage to his liver. Six weeks without a drop of alcohol, though, and he looked a little less yellow; his blue eyes were much clearer too. He missed Sylvia. He'd been a terrible husband then he'd turned into an even worse father. He leant his too-hot forehead against the cold glass. Tonight's session had brought up a lot of raw memories; most of them he'd rather forget. He'd usually find the answer and relief to his sadness in a bottle of cheap cider, or Jack Daniel's on the day his benefits got paid into his bank account.

He heard a loud crash from inside the hall and jumped; it startled him and his heart was racing. He threw open the bathroom door.

'Who's there? What you doing?'

The lights were still on. His voice echoed around the empty hall. He walked out to the front door.

'Oh, shit.' Shattered glass covered the floor and a broken piece of breeze block lay on top of it. He rushed outside, the glass crunching underneath his shoes. This time he was extra careful; he had no one's life to save. There was no one outside; in fact, he'd never seen the street so empty. He turned around and sighed. He was going to have to phone the cops, and he hated them. Not quite as much as he did before he realised Morgan meant more to him than her job, but still, he didn't like them.

He went back inside and took his phone out of his jacket pocket. This would be the third time he'd ever called them in sixty years: the first was when he found his wife's dead body; the second when he saw a madman trying to murder Morgan, and now this. He listened to the automated voice until he finally heard a man's voice. Stan gave him the address and told him someone had caused criminal damage. The call handler told him an officer would be with him in the next hour and hung up. He wondered if it would be Morgan, then realised that she was working in the offices now and not out on patrol. Already training to be a detective after such a short time, she'd probably be too busy to attend broken windows.

He phoned the number pinned to the wall in the kitchen for the centre manager and relayed to her what had happened. She sounded annoyed and he had to stop himself from telling her it had ruined his morning.

'How long will it take you to get here?'

'An hour; I'm in Kendal, shopping.'

'I guess I'll wait for the cops then, should I?'

'Thanks, Stan. I'll come as soon I've finished up here.'

He wasn't angry, he quite liked Joan. She was feisty and took no messing around. She reminded him of Sylvia.

'Hello, police.' A voice echoed around the entrance.

'I have to go; cops are here already.'

He hung up and walked towards the entrance, where a copper not much older than Morgan was standing. They all looked so young these days, or was it because he was getting old?

'Hi, I see someone kindly put the window through. Did they steal anything?'

Stan shook his head. 'I'm Stan, and not that I'm aware of. I was checking the toilets were empty when I heard the glass smash. I came out and found the mess; no one was here.'

'This is the second report of smashed windows this week in this area. We think it's the group of teenagers who seem to be running riot at the moment, but I'm sure the cameras will help us to identify them. Are you the caretaker now? Has Joan left?'

'No, I just help out with the AA meetings. I offered to lock up; kind of wishing I hadn't now. I could have been home now making my lunch.'

The cop laughed. 'Sorry, being a Good Samaritan can really suck at times.'

'Hey, do you know my daughter? She's in the police?'

'I may do, but there are quite a lot of us. What's she called?'

'Morgan Brookes.'

The cop smiled. 'I do know her very well; in fact, I was her tutor. I trained her.'

Stan felt his guard slip a little. If he knew Morgan he must be okay. 'What's your name then, fella? I'll tell her you came to my rescue next time I see her.'

'Dan. Do you know how much the door is worth?'

He shrugged. 'No idea. Joan is shopping in Kendal and will be here soon. She might be able to tell you. I'd just be guessing.'

'I guess she'll be able to sort out a joiner then. It's expensive if we call one out. They charge a call-out fee before fixing the problem. I'll give you my number. Can you ask her to call me? I can take the details for the damage over the phone from her, then I can go start an area search and see if I can find this group of pain-in-the-arse teenagers.'

Stan took the card from him. 'Cheers, I'll give her this. If you see Morgan, tell her I said hi. Can you let her know where I was? I'd like her to know I'm still sober, even though it's early days.'

'If I see her, I will. She's tied up with a murder investigation so I might not.'

'Another murder; dear God what is the town coming to.'

'We're certainly having a run of bad luck at the moment, Stan. You can clean that up. CSI won't be able to get here today and they wouldn't be able to get prints off the block anyway. Best hope of catching the little sods is from CCTV footage.'

Stan nodded. 'Thanks, I'll do that.'

Dan smiled at him then turned and walked back to the patrol car. As Stan began to sweep up the broken glass, he wondered who had been murdered and if Morgan was okay. For someone so early in her career with the police, she seemed to be in the middle of some of the worst cases the county had had in the last ten years. He would phone her later and see how she was holding up. Things weren't perfect between them, but they were much better than they had been in a long time, and he'd take that any day over never seeing her.

CHAPTER TEN

The mortuary was always a pleasant surprise to Morgan. She'd been here several times in the last couple of months and the thought of it was always much worse than actually being here. It didn't smell of anything bad at the moment, just the clinical disinfectant smell that hospitals smelt of, but they weren't inside the actual room where the post-mortems were carried out yet. They were about to get gowned up. She could hear Declan's voice from inside, giving orders to Susie, his assistant. She walked into the small changing room and took a gown from the basket, along with a pair of gloves. Not that she was going to be touching anything. The door opened and Wendy rushed in.

'Phew, that was a panic to get here. Traffic is terrible this time of day.'

Morgan smiled at her. Wendy dressed in protective clothing because she was going to be in close proximity to the body, photographing and possibly taking wet and dry samples to send off to the forensic lab.

'How do you do it?'

Wendy turned to her. 'What, this?'

She nodded.

'I guess I want to catch the bad guys as much as you do.'

'Then why didn't you become an officer?'

'Ah, I don't mean I actually want to catch them like go after them and arrest them. God, no, I don't think I could do it. In fact, I'd be really crap at that part. I like being a part of the team that catches them; I've always loved forensic science. I grew up watching shows like *Silent Witness* and *CSI Vegas*; they do make it look far more glamorous than it actually is though, don't they? I think they should come with a warning label which says, not at all like real life. I can't tell you what a shock to the system it was at the first sudden death I attended when I couldn't see the corpse for flies and maggots. I still feel like vomiting in my mask when there's insects. I flipping hate them. But it's like anything. You get used to it, even the bad stuff, and if what I do helps you to go and find the person responsible then that makes me happy.'

Morgan laughed. 'I grew up watching every serial killer documentary and reading all the books; anything ever written by an FBI profiler, I have on my bookshelves. *The Silence of the Lambs* was the catalyst though.'

'Social media and television have a lot to answer to, don't they? Rydal Falls wasn't really the murder capital of the world until this year though – do you think it's something to with the fact that you wanted to work murders so bad that they're dropping in your lap like some gift from the Universe, or is it just an unlucky coincidence?'

'Gosh, I don't know. I've never thought about it like that. I hope they're not happening because I'm subconsciously wishing for them. What a terrible thought that is.'

'Are you two ready? Declan is having a shit fit; said he can hear you gossiping and he wants to crack on.' Susie, whose hair was jade green today, smiled at them both, then lowered her voice. 'He's been a miserable sod all day. I'm sick of listening to him.'

'Susie.' Declan's voice bellowed from inside the mortuary and she shrugged. 'See.'

Morgan and Wendy laughed, but followed her into the mortuary where Declan and Ben were waiting for them.

'Glad you could join us. Can I begin?'

Susie did the smallest eye roll Morgan had ever seen then turned to Declan.

'Yes, sorry.'

He smiled at her and his face softened. 'That's okay. Is everyone ready to rock and roll?' Every head in the room nodded at the same time.

'Good. Susie why did you turn the radio on to this bloody awful station? If I have to listen to one more song by a spotty boy strumming a guitar who can't sing, I'm going to lose my shit.'

She crossed to the shelf where the radio was balanced, its antenna extended all the way out because the walls were so thick, and turned the dial until Smooth FM began to play.

'That's better. This is what you call music. Real music you can actually dance to, by singers who can actually sing.'

Morgan loved Declan but wondered why he was so mean to Susie. She seemed to always try her best and he still told her off; but it was nothing to do with her. Susie must not mind because if Ben was like that with her she'd tell him to bugger off. With the soft sounds of the Four Tops in the background, Declan began to unwrap the sheet from Gabby Stevens's body. Without needing to be asked, Susie was by his side and they worked in perfect harmony.

Once Gabby was on show for them all to see, they stepped back to let Wendy take some photographs. Under the harsh lighting, the discolouration on her skin looked even worse and the smell was too. Morgan wished she wasn't here, wished that Gabby had stayed in the pub longer or gone home with her friends. Wished that her parents hadn't left her and gone on holiday. But all the wishing in the world couldn't change what had happened to the once-beautiful young woman lying on the steel table in front of them. And she owed it to Gabby to be here for her until the very end. She was going to see this through and then she was going to hunt down the sick bastard who had brought them all here to witness this final intrusion into an innocent woman's life.

CHAPTER ELEVEN

By the time they arrived back at the police station it was late. Morgan looked at her watch: up to now, she'd worked a fourteen-hour shift. They went up to the office, where Amy was going through the pile of clipboards returned by the PCSOs, looking for any relevant information the neighbours may have seen.

'Anything decent, like a positive ID of the killer and a lovely piece of camera footage showing him leaving the house?' Ben asked.

She shook her head. 'Not really. The woman next door but one was on her way home from work when she saw Gabby going through her front gate around twenty-two hundred hours. She was alone; she didn't see anyone following her. Said by the time she'd got her bag from the back seat of her car, Gabby's front door had slammed shut. She didn't see her after that.'

'We still need to speak to her friends, but Declan thinks time of death was sometime around the early hours of Friday morning, so that fits. Amy, do you want to come visit her friends with me? Morgan you can go home. You've been working this since the early hours.'

Morgan didn't want to go home despite being exhausted. 'What about you? You were there before I arrived at the scene.'

'I get paid more than you. Amy can make herself useful. You can come in early tomorrow to continue with the enquiries.'

She wasn't going to argue. She'd seen enough sadness for one day. Watching Gabby's friends' lives fall apart in front of her eyes was a good reason to call it a day and let Amy deal with it. She nodded, too tired to argue any further. Grabbing her bag, she headed out of the door, ready for a long, hot shower and a glass of something strong to help her sleep.

At home, she took a bottle of wine from the rack in the fridge. Filling the glass, she sat down in her one oversized armchair, looking out into the blackness of the communal gardens. Standing up again, she drew the curtains shut. She couldn't bear the thought that someone had spent time watching her. How naïve she had been, living her life without ever thinking the nightmare stuff she loved to watch and read would ever come to haunt her in reality. Her phone began to vibrate and she wondered if Ben had changed his mind. Picking it up from the small, circular coffee table she saw Stan's name flashing across the screen.

'It's late, is everything okay, Stan?'

He laughed. 'I was about to ask you the same thing. Yes, I'm good. Apart from some little bastards who smashed the glass in the front door at the community centre earlier. But that's nothing compared to what you've been dealing with.'

'Did you phone the police, Stan?' She still couldn't bring herself to call him dad; they weren't quite at that stage of building their relationship yet. She also knew he hated phoning the cops and was interested to know if he did, because drunken Stan would never ring them, but sober Stan seemed a much nicer guy.

'I did and he seemed like a decent lad, the copper who turned up. Said he knows you. Was the one to train you up. Dan his name is.'

She blew out her cheeks. 'He did, and yes I suppose he is a decent copper.' She didn't add he was just a rubbish friend.

'Is there a bit of friction there? Not that it's anything to do with me, love, but you know at my age you can sense when something's a bit off.'

'I suppose we had a bit of a falling out, but it's in the past.'

'Good, life's too short as we both know. Look what it's taken for us two to get our act together.'

She couldn't argue with that; he was right.

'Anyway, I'm only checking you're okay after everything and you're not working yourself too hard.'

'I'm good, tired, but good.'

'Right, I'll leave you to it. Night then, love.'

'Night, Stan. Oh, and Stan?'

'Yes.'

'Thank you for phoning. I'm glad you did.'

There was a bit of a cough, a sniff and a sob-like sound then the line went dead. The more she talked to him, the more she liked him and was glad they were repairing their fractured relationship. It was a shame it had taken a near tragedy for them both to realise that.

She finished her wine, checked her windows and door were locked for the second time and went to bed to read a book she hadn't looked at in a very long time, written by John Douglas, an FBI profiler. Reading made her eyes tired and after an hour, knowing that it wouldn't be long before she was awake again, she put it down and closed her eyes. She needed some rest so she was ready to start a new day to find Gabby Stevens's killer.

CHAPTER TWELVE

Ben and Amy knocked at the side door to the flat above Pretty Fingers nail salon on the main street of Rydal Falls. They listened to the sounds of heavy footsteps running down the stairs and then the noise of the key being turned in the lock, followed by a high-pitched voice that shouted: 'Hang on, the bloody key is stuck. Becky, can you get the door open?'

More footsteps. Ben looked at Amy: he didn't want to do this. He was tired of being the bearer of terrible news, but it had to be done. Finally, the key turned after some high-pitched giggling and swearing. The door opened inwards and there were two women, both wearing pyjamas, with bright blue gunge smeared across their faces. Despite the majority of their skin being covered, they still looked shocked to see Ben and Amy: they clearly had no idea who they were.

'Oh, it's a bit late. Sorry, we're not into religion and don't need to buy anything.'

Ben frowned, wondering what they meant. Amy smiled at them both.

'We're not Jehovah's Witnesses or door-to-door sales people, we're from the police.'

'Oh, sorry about that. What do you want?'

It was Ben who took over. 'We have some bad news. Is it possible we can come inside for a chat?'

The blonde girl nodded and stepped back; the brunette held up her hand to stop them.

'Sorry, this is rude but do you have any ID? It's late and, well, you have to be sure, don't you?'

Amy nodded and tugged the lanyard from around her neck, holding it out for them to study. Ben pushed his hands in his pocket and pulled his out, passing it to them. Both girls looked at them and then their pictures on the small, plastic cards.

'Thanks, come in.'

The girls led the way upstairs to the flat above the shop. It was compact and untidy: there were half-eaten cartons of Chinese takeaway on the coffee table and an almost empty wine bottle. Ben's stomach groaned; he was hungry. The blonde girl held out her hand.

'I'm Becky; this is Kate. What sort of bad news? Is the shop okay?'

'Why don't you sit down?'

Both girls did, squeezing next to each other on the armchair to give him and Amy the two-seater sofa. They sat so close together their knees were touching.

'I'm Detective Sergeant Ben Matthews and this is my colleague, Detective Constable Amy Smith. We're here about Gabby Stevens. Her parents said you were her best friends. Have you spoken to them today?'

They shook their heads.

Kate spoke. 'No, we've been to Manchester on a Primark run. We only got back an hour ago. Gabby was supposed to come, but we couldn't get hold of her, so we went without her. Is she okay?'

'I'm afraid not. I have some sad news for you both.'

He had never passed a death message to women who looked like Smurfs before and found it really disconcerting.

They waited, eyes wide open, staring at him, their mouths slightly parted. Kate was visibly shaking and Becky's head was turning from side to side. He inhaled deeply.

'Gabby was found dead this morning by her parents.'

There was a loud screech. He jumped. He didn't know who had done it as both of them were trembling. Becky was sucking in air as if she couldn't breathe properly.

'It's not possible. How can she be dead? I don't believe it. You must have the wrong person.'

Amy reached out for Becky's hand. 'I'm sorry, but it is Gabby. Her parents found her and positively identified her.'

Tears were flowing freely from Kate's eyes, making track marks through the blue sludge that was smeared over her face. She whispered: 'When? How?'

'That's why we're here. We don't know everything yet.' Ben knew he wasn't strictly telling the truth: they knew how she'd died and where, but he was trying to spare them the awful details. 'We need to know when was the last time you spoke to Gabby and to get a little background information on her.'

Becky answered. 'At the pub, on Thursday night. We always go and see her on Thursdays because she's at college on a Wednesday night and we like to get the gossip.'

'Was she drinking on Thursday? Did she leave to go and meet someone?'

'She was a little tipsy, but not hammered like we get sometimes. She left on her own; she doesn't have a boyfriend at the moment. Her mum and dad were on holiday for a few days.'

'They came back in the early hours today. When you were in the pub, did you notice anyone watching you? Had Gabby fallen out with anyone or mentioned having bother with anyone? Did she use dating sites?'

They both shook their heads. 'No, she's so lovely. She doesn't do falling out; even when we were at school and would be a bit bitchy like teenagers are, saying things like "spotty Trevor smelt sweaty again", she never joined in. She always stuck up for everyone; she was so kind. She didn't have a bad word to say about anyone. Not even about her ex after he left her to go to university and didn't even tell her in person they were through. She wasn't on Tinder because she said she wanted to focus on her college work.'

'Does she ever see her ex?'

'God, no. Mark Shepherd never comes back here. He couldn't wait to get away when he left a couple of years ago. She really loved him though; he broke her heart and I think that's why she hasn't had a serious boyfriend since.'

'Do you have an address for him?'

'Only his mum's. No idea where he lives. She lives at 52 Wood Grove.'

'Thank you. What about her employer, John? How did she get on with him?'

'John's all right. She liked him as her boss. We've all known him since school. He was a couple of years above us. He still thinks he's fifteen, though, and plays rugby, even though he's not the best at it. Saffie keeps telling him to pack it in before he does some serious damage to himself.'

'What about college? Which one did she attend and what was she studying?'

'The sixth form, in Kendal. She was trying to resit a couple of GCSEs. She was studying psychology and sociology. Gabby said her psychology teacher was a bit of all right – I think she only signed up to his class because she fancied him. She was always the brainy one out of us all.'

'Thank you. I'm sorry we had to tell you such bad news. If you think of anything that might be important, can you let us know?'

Amy scribbled her phone number on a Post-it note and passed it to Becky who seemed to be coping far better with the awful news than Kate, who had now managed to smear the blue stuff everywhere, up her arms and onto the backs of her hands. Ben stood up. He would normally shake hands, but he couldn't touch the snot-smeared gloop.

'I'm sorry for your loss.'

He led the way, Amy following behind until they got into the car and shut the doors. He looked at Amy, who smiled.

'What the hell was that?'

'Face masks; it's what us girls do. We go to Primark, stock up on pyjamas and cheap knickers, get a Nando's, have a few cocktails, then go to Lush to stock up on bath bombs and tubs of face masks for a pamper session.'

He stared at her. 'And you call us blokes weird for liking watching rugby in the pub with a pint? Is it some kind of cult thing? Do you have to do that every time you step foot in a Primark?'

She shrugged. 'Not really, but it's popular. Then you go home, have a takeaway, drink wine and snap photos to put all over Instagram.'

'Christ, thank God I'm not a woman. That sounds like a lot of hard work just to buy some knickers.'

Amy snorted with laughter. 'It's just fun.'

'Do you do that?'

'Sometimes.'

'I thought I knew you, just shows you never really know anyone. My mind is blown.'

'You're just a grumpy git. You're behind the times. You need a girlfriend so you can keep up better.'

Ben sighed and started the car engine.

Amy lifted her hand to her mouth. 'Ben, I'm sorry. That's awful. I didn't mean that how it sounded. It's just Cindy would probably do it too, if she was still here.'

He looked at Amy. 'It's okay, but you know, I don't think she would. And I'm not ready for a girlfriend yet anyway. It's only been just over three years since she died. And if women have changed that much in three years, I'd rather not; it's terrifying. Come on, let's call it a day. Tomorrow we can speak to Mark Shepherd's mum and see if he's been in town lately.'

They drove back to the station in silence, Ben wondering if Morgan partook in the shopping, face mask thing as well. She was bound to; she was even younger than Amy. He would ask her next time he got a moment. He felt as if his perception of the opposite sex was so far off the radar he might as well become a priest.

CHAPTER THIRTEEN

He looked at the phone in his hand and wondered if he dared risk it. The outdated iPhone 8 had so many cracks on the screen it was hard to see the picture; he could just make out three girls, all pouting. He'd made her tell him her password before killing her. It hadn't been hard. She'd sobbed the letters out before he'd gagged her again. The phone had no value to it whatsoever, but for him it was priceless. He was currently weighing up if he should use it to send a text message to whoever was dealing with the murder investigation. It wasn't difficult; he'd done his background research and knew Rydal Falls had a very small criminal investigations department.

It was risky, he knew that, but that was part of the fun. Part of the chase. If he used it sparingly when they weren't expecting it, and turned it straight off, he might just get away with it. They would only be able to trace it to the nearest phone mast to where he had turned it on. Google had told him that even using cell site analysis to trace it, would roughly give police a three-kilometre radius from the phone mast it connected to when it was powered on. So, if he used it as far away as he could from his house, it wouldn't trace back to the area he lived. He could have so much fun with this. He was parked on the busy A590 watching the cars race past; no one was going to take any notice of him. The hardest part was deciding which detective to message. He'd seen the older guy at the scene and knew he was called Matthews; he'd also seen the woman, who was more his type. It had been relatively easy trying to get their phone numbers, easier than anything else he'd done up to now. He just had to decide who to send the message to: who would figure it out first? And how would they feel when they realised they were getting text messages from the grave?

He knew they'd found the girl: the street had been sealed off and the area flooded with officers this morning. Coppers were still there when he had passed again tonight. He didn't care. He was confident they wouldn't have a clue who he was or what he was doing. He liked playing games. He always had as a child. He picked up the piece of lined notepaper he'd written the phone numbers on and tore it in half, then folded each piece over. He passed them between his fingers as if dealing a deck of cards then stopped. Whoever's phone number was in his left hand was who he would message. Slowly he unfolded the piece of paper. An articulated lorry flew past his stationary car so fast it vibrated and shook. He stared down at the name and number, a huge smile on his face. He was glad it was this one; he would have chosen this one anyway. This was going to be fun. Dangerous, but exciting. Did they even realise the girl's phone was missing yet? Possibly not; the house was still sealed off. He didn't know where her parents were but he would bet it wasn't at home. Therefore, the house was out of bounds to everyone except the police. Would they be looking for her phone? He'd purposely left everything else of value just to throw them off the scent. It didn't matter. They soon would or was he giving them more credit than they deserved? Were the detectives running this as clever as he was thinking? He hoped so.

Pressing a gloved finger on the side button, he waited for the phone to come to life. Using the stylus, he typed in the password. The phone began beeping as a flurry of notifications began to come through. Going into the messages, he typed in the number from the piece of paper and saved it as 'Bait' then typed one word:

Hi.

He sent the text then turned it off again. Smiling, he put the phone back into a small lead-lined box and tucked it under his seat. It was time to move. He would be long gone before the recipient even figured out what that meant. *If* they even figured it out. It might take quite a few more messages before they realised. He smiled to himself; this was going to be a great game and he would be the winner because he didn't like to lose. Losing wasn't an option.

He hadn't had much in his life while he was growing up. His mother was a devout Catholic who didn't believe in luxuries, and her favourite proverb had been 'spare the rod and spoil the child'. In Winifred's case, that rod had been a wooden ruler that she would rap across his knuckles or spank his bottom with, and by Christ it had stung. She had not used it sparingly at all; in fact, she'd used it more than anything else. He'd never cried though. He wouldn't give her the pleasure. He wouldn't show her weakness, or anyone for that matter. He'd hold it in until he was alone and even then he would sob quietly into his pillow. Not for long, just enough to get his anger and frustration out. He hadn't cried when Winifred had been killed in a car accident the day after he got his driving licence. He had quietly rejoiced. The police had never found the car or driver. To be fair, he didn't think they'd looked too hard, which was just as well because he hadn't known as much about forensics as he did now. He'd bought a knackered car from the scrapyard, telling them he was looking for something for banger racing. It had been kept under cover in the back street. He often wondered if she'd realised what was going to happen when she'd heard the engine revving as she crossed the road by the church that was like her second home. Had she known it was her son who had his foot on the accelerator as he'd floored it and hit her at forty? He liked to think that she did, that she had prayed to her precious God to save her when she realised what was about to happen. But who knew? If he was honest, he didn't care. She was out of his life for good. When the police had come to tell him, he had acted suitably distressed. He'd recently read a book about the murders at White Hall Farm and realised Jeremy Bamber would have made a decent friend. It seemed they both despised their religious mothers with a murderous passion.

CHAPTER FOURTEEN

Morgan jolted awake; she had been thrashing around having a nightmare. As she lay there, cold beads of perspiration on her forehead, her heart racing, she picked up her phone off the bedside table: 04.25. 'Dammit.' She punched the pillow next to her. She was so tired and just wanted to sleep for an hour more. This had been going on far too long; it didn't matter how late she went to bed or how tired she was. As she lay there with a pillow over her face, she tried to remember what she'd been dreaming about and couldn't. The nightmare happened a couple of times a week and no matter how hard she tried she couldn't remember much about it.

Admitting defeat, she threw her duvet to one side and got out of bed. She had tried everything. Meditation was great for getting to sleep, but it didn't keep her asleep; hot baths; no television or screen time an hour before bed; yoga – you name it she'd tried it. The only thing that seemed to have kept the nightmares away was the herbal tea that she'd got off the strange but lovely woman who lived in the woods near to the Potters' house. Ettie, she was called. She didn't remember her surname, but she'd liked her. She was kind and funny, and the jar of loose tea she'd given her had worked, even though she'd been reluctant to try it at first. Maybe she could pay her a visit, buy some more from her. To be honest, she'd freaked her out a little, but she liked to think she was a good judge of character and she reminded her of her mum. Sylvia had liked to make her own teas and grown her own herbs.

As she brushed her teeth, she decided she would go and see her as long as she had a little bit of time to spare, and maybe it was time to get some real help with the bad dreams. Did she need to see a counsellor or a psychotherapist? Maybe they would be able to help her out.

An image of Gabby Stevens's dead, bloating body filled her mind and she squeezed her eyes shut, trying to force it out. Today there was a lot to do, lots of enquiries to follow up on, and she wished she didn't feel like crap. She glanced at her reflection in the mirror. Dark circles under her green eyes, and she was sure there were a few lines that had appeared around her eyelids that she didn't have a couple of months ago. Christ, at this rate she'd look like she was fifty before she reached twenty-five. Was this the price she had to pay for her career choice? They don't mention that on the application form when you apply to the police… may prematurely age you, but there are some great benefits.

She decided to make herself a hearty breakfast; today was going to be another long one. They had a killer to apprehend. First though, she would have another go at this walk-jogging thing. Picking up her phone, she noticed she had a notification of a text message. Opening it up, she didn't recognise the number and there was just one word.

Hi.

It must be a wrong number. She didn't think anything of it as she got dressed and laced up her trainers. The roads and streets of Rydal Falls were deserted and as she walked, walked faster, and then attempted to jog, a message came through the earbuds she was wearing in the robotic voice.

Message from unknown number; are you not speaking to me?

Morgan stopped in the middle of the road to take her phone out of the armband and look at it. It was the same number. Who was this? A horn blared and she jumped. Lifting a hand in apology, she crossed to the pavement and typed back.

Who is this?

G.

Sorry, I don't know you. I think you have the wrong number.

She tucked her phone back into the armband and carried on, red-faced, almost back at her apartment. It felt much better now she wasn't the only person living in the renovated Georgian house. A woman around her age had moved into the top-floor apartment a couple of weeks ago and it was nice knowing she finally had a neighbour. They were a bit like passing ships, but they both stopped for a chat whenever they did see each other in the communal hallway, and she had the cutest little sausage dog.

Going inside, Morgan stripped off and had a quick shower, then dressed for work. When she checked her phone again, the message had been read. Good, whoever it was obviously realised they were texting the wrong person. She began to grill the tomatoes and mushrooms she'd promised herself, popping two slices of bread in the toaster. She ate her breakfast whilst continuing reading the book from last night. She might drive Ben mad with her comments about killers and their motives, but she wasn't going to stop. If it helped this case, it was worth all the funny looks and stares in the world.

Driving to work her phone beeped again; if it was G, whoever that was, they could do one; she didn't know anyone called G. Once she'd parked her car, she took her phone out of her bag and stared at the screen.

That's not nice, we only just met and you've already forgot me.

Baffled wasn't the word. This time she ignored it. Whoever it was would get blocked if they messaged again; she didn't have time for this kind of crap. They must either work nights or not have to go to work at all if they were up texting random strangers at all hours. She was annoyed now, but it was nothing she couldn't handle.

She walked into the office, usually the first in on an early shift, so she was surprised to see Ben's office light on. Unless he'd forgotten to switch it off last night. She threw her bag onto her desk and crossed the room. Knocking on the door, not expecting an answer, she jumped when he threw open the door.

'Good morning.'

'You scared me, morning.'

'How, you knocked on my door?'

She shrugged. 'I didn't actually think you were in there. Why are you here?'

'I work here?'

'Very funny; why are you here so early?'

'I couldn't sleep. I kept thinking about Gabby Stevens. I want to know if anything is missing from her room. It's been bothering me since you mentioned it at the briefing yesterday.'

'The only way you'll know is if you let her parents go in and have a look.'

'I know.'

She nodded. 'Coffee?'

'Yes, please. As soon as it's a respectable hour, we'll pay them a visit and ask them to check. Why are you here this early?'

Morgan, who had turned to go and put the kettle on, looked over her shoulder. 'For the fun of it.'

He laughed. 'I can think of much better things to do for fun. Hey, talking of fun, do you ever subject yourself to smearing gloop all over your face to make yourself look beautiful?'

She squinted one eye at him. 'What? Like a face mask?'

He nodded.

'Occasionally, if my skin is looking a bit tired or spotty. Why the sudden interest in my beauty routines? Are you saying I need all the help I can get?'

He was shaking his head. 'Amazing, you just don't know, do you?'

'What are you talking about?'

'The friends last night; Gabby's friends answered the door looking like bright blue Smurfs and Amy reckons it's a common thing amongst women. I'm intrigued to know how common.'

'That's weird.'

'Yeah, Amy said something like that. Hurry up with my coffee, I need something to kick-start my brain. It feels as if it's died inside of my skull.'

'Then I'm suggesting you need much more than the tin of dried-up Nescafé in the brew cupboard that you have to scrape with a knife to get some out. Let's face it, it's seen better days.'

'Haven't we all?' He sighed, turned around and shut the door.

Charming, Morgan thought to herself and went to make the drinks.

After passing Ben his and sitting at her desk with her mug, she opened the drawer and saw the gift bag from Dan. Letting out a sigh, she picked it up: maybe Stan was right and she was being too hard on him. Untying the bow, she took out the cream box with 'Pandora' stamped on it. Carefully opening it, she saw a pair of small, silver angel wing earrings with a tiny diamanté stud. They were cute and the sort of thing she would wear; he'd chosen wisely.

Amy walked through the office door, and she slammed the box shut. Dropping it back into the drawer, she closed it, not wanting to spend the rest of the day being teased because Dan had bought her an apology gift. She felt herself warming to him a little more and decided to call a truce and thank him.

*

Amy was followed by the DCI and they had a team briefing. Ben had already scrubbed the extra-large whiteboard clean and Blu-tacked a picture of Gabby Stevens's laughing face on it, below one of her very dead face. Morgan knew he did this to ensure no one on the team forgot the horror of what they were dealing with. She stared at the picture of Gabby laughing. She was almost the same age as her and this was a small town, yet she didn't remember her from school. Although Morgan didn't really attend much school the last year because her mum had died and she'd gone off the rails a little.

She let out a loud yawn. Ben stopped talking; his gaze fell on her.

'Am I keeping you up?'

'No, definitely not. I'm sorry.'

Amy smiled at her and whispered: 'Busy night? Did you see Dan?'

Morgan couldn't stop the look of horror that spread across her face at the thought of her and Dan being more than friends. She glared at her, shaking her head then turned to look at Ben and asked: 'What did task force find when they searched her bedroom? Where was her phone? Did she not have chance to call for help? Do we know the last person she spoke to?'

Ben looked at the A4 sheet of handwritten notes.

'No phone. They seized an iPad, laptop and a Kindle which have all been sent up to the high-tech unit at headquarters.' He ran his finger along the itemised list again.

'Definitely no phone on here. I'm gutted to say that the finger-print results off the key were negative; the rubbish bagged up in the park is still being processed, but it's unlikely we're going to get a hit back off any of that either. It's a long shot.'

'Well, did they check in her handbags, coats, trouser pockets? I can't believe she didn't have a phone. Not many twenty-three-year-olds don't have phones, and that photo on the board is a selfie, so that would have been taken with one.'

'You're right, well spotted. Maybe it's broken and being fixed. We'll ask her parents. Morgan, you can come with me and we'll ask them to go through her personal belongings to see if anything is missing like you suggested.'

Ben began to talk and she found herself staring at the photo once more.

That's not nice, we only just met and you've already forgot me.
Who is this?
G

She jumped up; the colour had drained from her face.

'I think I know where her phone is.'

Ben was looking at her as if she'd gone mad but she didn't care, and Tom had a mild look of amusement on his face. Grabbing her phone off the desk, she opened the messages from the unknown number and thrust the screen in front of Ben's eyes.

He read them, then looked at her. 'Surely not; isn't this just a wrong number?'

Morgan showed the phone to Amy.

'Why would I suddenly get a text message off a wrong number in the middle of the night, from someone who signed off as G? I don't know anyone called G, and I definitely don't know that number. We need to find out Gabby's phone number.'

Ben nodded. 'How does whoever this is have your phone number? That's what worries me more.'

Morgan hadn't thought of the consequences of a killer sending her messages. Her knees gave way as she flopped down onto the nearest chair. The room was too hot and she felt as if she couldn't breathe. She heard Ben's concerned voice but it sounded really far away.

'Morgan, Morgan, are you okay?'

Amy began to speak. 'Christ, give her some space; she needs a couple of minutes, that's all. No wonder she can't breathe with you two suffocating her. Go on, you may be in charge but sometimes you have no common sense. Go grab a coffee and give us a few minutes, gentlemen.'

Morgan felt a hand on her back. 'Bend your head between your knees, it will pass. Take some slow, deep breaths.'

She bent down and began to slowly inhale through her nose and exhale through her mouth until the room stopped spinning. Feeling better, she slowly lifted her head and looked around. Amy smiled at her.

'That's one way to clear a room. What a pack of fannies. Honestly, you should have seen the panic on Ben's and Tom's faces. Are you okay?'

'Yes, I think so. Why did that just happen? I feel stupid.'

'Tiredness, shock. Have you eaten breakfast?'

'I'm beyond tired. I never sleep past four twenty-five. I haven't for years but this morning it was so hard to get up.'

'No wonder. Why do you wake up at that time?'

She shrugged. 'I have since my mum died. I have these bad dreams, only I can't remember what they are except for a few glimpses of the same woman.'

'You need to speak to someone. I know who can help actually.'

'I'm not going to see a psychiatrist. I'm not that bad and I don't know if counselling will help. I don't know what the dreams are about so I can't tell them what's bothering me.'

'My cousin's boyfriend is a psychotherapist and an excellent one. Highly recommended, he deals with stuff like trauma and childhood issues. I'll give you his number, it might help, and what have you got to lose?'

Amy rooted around in her desk drawers. Finally finding a crumpled business card, she passed it to Morgan. 'He's worth a shot. You could go and see him for a free consultation and if you don't think it's for you at least you tried.'

Morgan clutched the card in her hand, looking down at the name Isaac Cross. Tucking the card into her pocket she smiled.

'Thanks, I'll give him a ring.'

Amy nodded. 'You're welcome. Should I let the guys back in?'

Morgan felt her cheeks begin to burn. 'How embarrassing. Yes, I suppose you better had.'

Amy disappeared, and she stared at her phone on the desk. How had a killer got her phone number and why was he texting her?

Ben followed Tom back into the room. Neither of them said anything to her and she realised Amy had probably told them to leave it.

'Morgan, we may need to seize your phone. I've just got off the phone to Charlotte Stevens and I have Gabby's phone number, her mum said she had a cracked iPhone 8.'

She picked up her phone and opened the messages. He rhymed off the same number the messages had been sent from and she nodded.

'It's her number.'

'Sick bastard,' Amy murmured.

'Yes, very. But also not very clever; we can track the phone and hopefully it will lead us straight to his front door. With a bit of luck, we could have him in cuffs in the next few hours. This could be the break we need to catch whoever it is.' There was excitement in Tom's voice.

Morgan didn't say anything but she didn't think the killer was stupid; if anything, he was probably far cleverer than they were giving him credit for. He must know that phones can be traced and tracked. For a start, there's Find My iPhone then Snapchat and other apps have location trackers on them. Why would he risk it? He must have Gabby's password, and she wouldn't be surprised if he'd put the phone onto airplane mode and deleted all her social media apps.

'Sarge, I don't think this is some random act of stupidity by a killer with a huge ego. I think this is a cleverly thought out move. The crime scene looked disorganised because of the mess, but it wasn't. He wants us to think that, but in fact he is highly organised. He knew she was alone in the house; he'd been watching her; he got inside without arousing her suspicion. I wouldn't be surprised if he picked her because she fit some kind of profile. I think he has a type and specifically chose her because she met those requirements. The same way he has chosen to communicate with me. Maybe not because I'm his type – I'm a redhead and Gabby was blonde, but I'm the same age and he wants me to feel threatened without directly threatening me. If anything, this is showing us how clever he is. You won't be able to track the phone or if you can it will be a false lead.'

'For Christ's sake, Morgan, you don't know this – any of this.' Ben's cheeks were flushed red and he had almost hissed the words at her.

'No, I don't. I'm not an expert, but…'

'But what?'

Everyone was staring at her and her mouth had never felt so dry. She wished she could get up and walk out of this room that was too hot and stuffy.

'I think we need to keep a watch on the Stevens' house. Killers like this, they revisit the crime scenes; he may go back or try to involve himself in this one somehow.'

She stood up. 'Excuse me, I need some fresh air.'

She walked out of the office. She needed some breathing space because she had just been dragged into the middle of a murder investigation by a killer who liked to play games and she didn't know what that meant for her. She also knew she'd managed to make her superiors angry with her because of her outspoken opinions. But she had to tell them. This was a small town, but it didn't mean whoever was doing this didn't have a big-city mind and an even bigger agenda. Rural Cumbria might not seem like the ideal place for a serial killer, but if they didn't take any of this into account how many more women might die? No matter what the cost was to her, she couldn't sit there and watch that happen. Uncurling her clenched fingers, she realised she still had the card

Amy had given to her. Before she could change her mind, she went to the front office.

'Morning, Brenda, can I use the phone?'

'Morning, lovey, of course you can.'

The bell rang, signalling someone was at the front counter. Brenda got up and left her to it. Morgan spoke to Isaac Cross. When she told him she got his number off Amy and worked with her, he managed to squeeze her in for a chat at four o'clock that afternoon. She thanked him and hung up, not sure if she was doing the right thing but it had to be worth a try. She had never felt so physically exhausted or drained and now she had to worry about a killer who had her phone number. Did that also mean he knew where she lived? That thought slammed into her, knocking every last ounce of fight from her. She walked outside to sit on one of the benches for some fresh air.

CHAPTER FIFTEEN

Ben looked at Amy and Tom, who was shaking his head, and asked: 'Now what do we do? This is not what I was expecting to have to deal with today.'

Tom's phone rang and he excused himself, leaving them alone. Amy waited until the door closed behind him.

'You can be as annoyed with Morgan as you want, but what she's talking about makes sense. This is more than some drunken idiot who decided to have a good time at Gabby Stevens's expense. For a start, we have to keep an eye on Morgan as well. I don't like it. Why choose her to contact and not you? It's a power thing; he must get off on having power over women, especially women in their early twenties.'

'We need to get Morgan's phone sent off.'

'Yes, but if you do that he won't be able to contact her. Get someone to come here and get what evidence they can from it today, so she still has access to it. I'm worried about her, Ben. She's not sleeping and now this. After what happened last time, she can't be left alone. She either needs to stay with someone or have someone stay with her.'

'She only has Stan. I don't think she'll want to stop there. Her apartment is only a one bedroom and she doesn't even have a sofa for someone to sleep on.'

'Then she has to stop at yours; you have that massive house and live there on your own.'

'Hang on a minute, she won't come to my house. Especially now I've pissed her off so much.'

'Well she's going to have to. I'll tell her. You don't mind, do you? Unless you want to ask Tom to pay for her to stay at a hotel for a few days.'

'That's not going to happen, and she won't be any safer in a hotel than she is in her own home.'

'Well then someone is going to have to watch her twenty-four hours a day. Do we have a budget or the staff for that?'

He shook his head. 'I'll do what I can. I'll ask her if she wants to come to mine. Amy, please go find her and bring her back. What a mess. We can't have her wandering off on her own until we know what's happening.'

Amy saluted. 'Yes, boss. Does she have a magnet built inside of her that attracts trouble; I've never known anyone like it.'

She left him alone in the office staring at the whiteboard. Part of him excited that things were happening that could lead them to Gabby Stevens's killer and a part of him terrified about at what expense it might be. He really liked Morgan, and the thought of her being dragged into this investigation on a personal level made his stomach churn and the back of his throat burn with acid. Before she came along, things were so much simpler in this department and he wondered if he'd made a bad decision by asking her to join them so soon after her training. No, he told himself, she wasn't a bad decision at all. She was the best one; his life had turned around since she'd begun working with him and he enjoyed her company. It wasn't her fault she seemed to get involved with all the criminals in the county. They would sort this out.

He picked up the phone to ring the high-tech unit at Penrith, to get someone to come down here to retrieve any evidence from Morgan's phone, and to get some advice about what to do.

*

Amy came back with Morgan, who was carrying a paper cup carrier filled with steaming hot coffees that smelt amazing. She handed one to him. 'Peace offering.'

He smiled. 'Absolutely no need for that but thank you. I need this more than you could ever know.'

She laughed. 'Me too. Sorry if I spoke out of turn; I don't mean to, but I can't help what goes on inside my head.'

'No, you didn't. It's just, well, you know. We don't want to think that sort of thing goes on around here, but you are right, just because we don't expect it doesn't mean that it can't. The last thing I want is to be blinkered and let Gabby's parents down. So thank you for bringing it to our attention. Darcy from the high-tech unit is on her way to take a look at your phone, and did Amy tell you about her wonderful idea?'

'Not yet?'

'Amy, why don't you explain?'

Ben picked up his coffee and walked into his office, closing the door. He needed paracetamol to go with his caffeine fix, and he didn't want to witness Morgan's reply to Amy's crazy idea. If she did agree to come stay at his house, he was going to have to go shopping and clean up. Living alone meant a different takeaway every night and getting the polish out when the dust was too thick to see the image clearly on the TV screen. A bit of company might be nice though, and they could discuss the case whenever they wanted. And he'd know that she was safe. Not that he thought Morgan Brookes needed a man to keep her safe; no, he knew she was capable of looking after herself. But she'd been through so much the last few months and it might be nice for her to have some company, and the more he thought about it he would enjoy it even more. His house had been too quiet since Cindy's death.

His door opened and Morgan walked in.

'Amy said I had to stop with you. Is this a direct order?'

He shook his head. 'She has such a way with words. No, it isn't.'

She took him by surprise by smiling, and her green eyes crinkled at the corners. 'I'm joking, I honestly don't need to stop at your house. But it might be nice for a couple of days until we know what's going on, as long as you don't mind and she didn't blackmail you into it because I don't need sympathy from her or you.'

'No, she didn't blackmail me, not directly. And I know you don't need sympathy. It makes sense; we can work the case from there if we need to. I have plenty of spare rooms.'

'The spare room is fine and, yes, I suppose we could work even longer. Thank you, I have an appointment at four then I'll go grab some stuff.'

'No problem.'

She left him to it and he wondered if he was going to regret it, or would it be the opposite and would he enjoy her company so much that it would be difficult to let her go when the time came?

CHAPTER SIXTEEN

Rushing out of the office with her head down, she walked straight into Dan, who held out his arms and caught her.

'Oh, I'm sorry. I wasn't looking where I was going.' She lifted her head from the piece of paper she was reading and was mortified.

He smiled at her and she didn't sense any animosity from him. She smiled back.

'Thank you for the present, but you didn't have to.'

He shrugged. 'I'm glad you like it and, yes, I think I did. I was an arsehole to you for no reason other than jealousy. I'm sorry, Morgan, can we call a truce?'

She laughed. 'Of course we can. I hate falling out with people.' She didn't add, *especially when I've done nothing wrong.*

'Awful news about that girl yesterday. How are you getting on?'

'Not wonderful, lots of things to look into. No definite leads as of yet though. What are you on with? Much happening?'

'I've got to go see the DCI. That bloody idiot, the mayor Greg Barker, told them I passed information on to him.'

'Did you?'

'Nothing about the cases or the Potters' murders. He used to ring and ask me stuff occasionally, but I never told him anything that wasn't already in the public domain.'

'God, that's all you need. Just tell him that; he's probably grasping at straws and trying to cause trouble for you.'

'Hey, do you fancy grabbing some lunch later or a coffee if you get the chance? We could have a proper catch-up.'

Morgan nodded. 'That would be great. I don't know what time though. We're going to visit the victim's parents soon.'

'Just call me when you're free. I can come meet you or pick you up, if I haven't been suspended.'

He laughed at his joke, but Morgan just smiled because there was a good chance if there was any evidence against him for passing on information he would be.

'Yes, I will. Good luck.'

She walked off, feeling much better. At least she didn't have to worry about the uncomfortable feeling whenever she saw him now. Had he been passing on information? She really hoped he hadn't because he'd lose his job, and despite everything he was a good copper.

Going into the storeroom, she grabbed some boxes of evidence bags to stock up their cupboard. They needed to take plenty with them to visit Gabby Stevens's parents, in case anything had been missed in the initial search yesterday. Once she'd replenished the huge, black kitbag with bags, gloves, search forms and everything else they needed, she knocked on Ben's door.

'Coming.' He came out and looked at the bag. 'That was quick. Have you been home to get your stuff?'

'No, it's the search bag. I thought we might need it. Better to be prepared than waste time coming back for it.'

He smiled. 'You're good, Brookes, very good.'

'She's also a teacher's pet,' Amy muttered from her behind her computer.

'Come on, let's get this over with. I'm not looking forward to seeing the Stevens again. It's so hard knowing that nothing we say or do is going to make any of this any better.'

'What if we catch him, lock him up and throw away the key? Surely that might help.'

'It will, but they're still left without their daughter.'

Morgan couldn't argue with that.

*

The blue-and-white tape had been removed from the entrance to the street. There was now a piece across the front gate to the Stevens' house and a PCSO was sitting in an unmarked car outside. Ben parked in front of it and they got out. Morgan immediately felt a huge weight pressing down on her shoulders. The PCSO got out of the car with a scene guard booklet in one hand and a fluffy key ring with the front door key to the house in the other.

'Morning. Are the parents around, do you know?'

She nodded. 'Yep, they're still in the house up there with Susan.'

Ben thanked her. 'I'll go get them if you want to sign us in, Morgan.' He was already briskly walking up the street.

The PCSO lowered her voice. 'He's so lovely; he never snaps or gets moody. Not like our sergeant.'

Morgan finished signing their names and looked at her. 'Yeah, he's nice and isn't as moody as he was when I first started working for him.'

'He's lost weight as well, looks a bit of all right. God knows there are not many decent blokes to look at in this station.'

Morgan laughed. 'I didn't really notice.'

Ben came out of the gate with Charlotte Stevens and Morgan felt her heart tear a little for the woman who looked dazed. She quickly signed Charlotte Stevens's name into the logbook: they needed to keep a record of everyone who went in and out of the scene for continuity when it went to court. No one could go inside who didn't have a good reason to; the preservation of evidence took precedence over everything else.

Ben opened the gate for her.

'It's like something out of a television show, isn't it? I mean you don't expect this to happen, do you? It's not what your life should look like,' Charlotte said quietly.

Morgan felt as if her throat had closed up. It was hard to find the right words to say but Ben didn't falter.

'It's horrific. I'm sorry that you're having to do this, Charlotte. We really appreciate it, but we need to make sure nothing is missing from Gabby's room and we need to locate her phone.'

'Is it missing? It should be on her bedside table. She never went anywhere without it. Her dad would tease her, saying she'd have to have it surgically removed.'

'The search team didn't find it yesterday.'

'They can't have looked hard enough. Was it a team of men?' Charlotte gave a strained laugh at her joke, and Morgan smiled.

'Yes, it was.'

'Well if they're anything like Harry then God help you; he can't find his glasses when they're on his head.'

As they stepped into the house, Charlotte lowered her head and crossed herself. The smell of decomposition lingered in the air, although not as strong now Gabby's body had been removed.

'That smell. I'm scared after everything is over, all I'm going to remember about my baby is how bad she smelt. She always wore Chanel Chance; Gabby would be horrified to know she smelt this way.' A sob escaped her lips, and Morgan reached out her hand, gently clasping Charlotte's.

'You can give her perfume to the undertakers when they release her body, or you could spritz the clothes you want her to wear in it so she smells like she used to.'

'That's nice, thank you. I never thought of that; Gabby would like that. I will.'

Morgan glanced at Ben who looked almost as distraught as Charlotte, and she wondered if he was thinking about Cindy, his dead wife. Did this bring back memories for him?

He led the way upstairs to Gabby's bedroom, pushing open the door. Charlotte stepped in behind him.

'Can I touch anything now?'

He nodded. 'Yes, of course. If you could check through her personal belongings to make sure everything is there. Did she keep a diary at all?'

She shrugged. 'She was twenty-three; there are some things you don't tell your parents. Actually a lot of things, but she was a good girl. She never hurt anyone and she loved her family and friends.'

The words came out barely a whisper. Morgan tugged a pair of gloves from her pocket to offer to Charlotte, and Ben shook his head. He motioned to her to keep her hands in her pockets; if needed they would glove up when Charlotte gave them anything to take away. She realised he didn't want to put her through having to wear nitrile gloves to touch her daughter's things. Morgan expected her to fall apart, but she surprised them all by beginning to search through the open drawers and under the bed with a steely determination etched across her face. She pulled out a jewellery box and lifted the lid. Giving it a once-over, she shut it again. Finally, she turned to them and shrugged.

'Everything seems to be here. The only thing missing is her phone.'

'Thank you, we really appreciate you looking. I know how difficult this is.'

She shrugged. 'What else can I do? I feel helpless. I let her down. I was so selfish wanting to get away for a bit of sunshine and cocktails. She's dead because of that, and now I have to live with it. The least I can do is help you to find her killer. I want to look him in the eyes and ask him what fucking right he had to do this. Who told him he could play God with my daughter's life? And then do you know what I'd do? I'd stick a knife straight in his heart and watch him die.'

'You did nothing wrong, Charlotte, you're allowed to go on holiday. Gabby wasn't a child; she was an adult, more than capable of looking after herself for a few days. The only selfish person is the bastard who decided to come in here and take her life. Neither you nor Harry are to blame for any of this.'

She bent her head and whispered: 'Thank you.'

Morgan asked: 'We don't know how he got inside yet; everything is secure and we found no footprints around the windowsills. Did you keep a spare key anywhere?'

She nodded. 'Yes, under the pair of ceramic wellies by the front door.'

Ben turned to go and check. The search team hadn't found a spare key yesterday but they might have missed it. Morgan followed and watched as he tugged on a pair of gloves. Opening the front door, he bent down and lifted the planter to reveal a key. He didn't need to tell Morgan to get evidence bags because she was already running towards the car for them. She returned with a large sack and a small plastic bag. Ben apologised as he put the plant pot into the paper sack, then the key into the much smaller one. Both of them praying there were prints on either item that might give them a much-needed break: the killer must have known about it and used it to get into the house. It explained there being no signs of a forced entry if he had access to the key.

'I think it might be wise to get the locks changed, Charlotte.'

'Why, do you think he's going to come back?'

'I don't know, but it's possible.'

'I hope he does; I'll be bloody waiting for him.'

Morgan liked her. Despite everything, she was strong and feisty.

Ben answered: 'If anyone tries to get inside your house, Charlotte, you must ring 999. You can't take the risk.'

'Oh, I will. Don't worry.'

'Good, I'm going to release the house soon. So you can come home. Would you like us to arrange someone to come in and clean Gabby's room for you?'

She shook her head. 'No, thank you. There have been enough strangers in my home. I'll clean it.'

She walked back up the street to her friend's house, and Ben turned to Morgan.

'She's tough.'

'I know, I like her.'

'I thought you might. Come on, let's get these back to Wendy and see if she can work some magic. A set of prints would be amazing.'

'He must have taken Gabby's phone as his trophy. I suppose, to most people, our phones are our most prized, personal possession.'

She signed them all out of the scene and told the PCSO she wouldn't be here much longer, then climbed into the car. As she did, she caught a whiff of Ben's aftershave; it smelt nice, especially after the awful smell from inside the crime scene. She looked at her watch; she had thirty minutes to get to the station for her car and to get to her appointment.

CHAPTER SEVENTEEN

He watched from his car. So many girls, so little time. The sixth form college car park was a favourite place of his to spend time. Nobody ever gave the car a second glance, everyone was too busy scurrying from their cars into the main entrance or vice versa. The only problem was most of them were just a little too young. He didn't want an immature teenager. He preferred a woman in her early twenties; one who was just beginning to ripen nicely like a decent wine. He didn't want anyone too old either. He wasn't after a mother figure, despite what the psychologists would say. Yes, he hated his mother but he didn't want to relive killing her over and over. Christ, that would be like some kind of torture. He wanted someone who was his type. Someone he would enjoy thinking about for the rest of his life. If he was going to see their face in his dreams, why would he pick some ugly, wrinkled old cow? No, he wanted someone pretty, someone like that copper. Now she was his type. He'd spied her going into the station yesterday. The sunlight had glinted off her copper hair, tied into a high ponytail. Her skin had a warm glow to it with a smattering of freckles and her eyes, those green eyes. He wanted her but not in the way he wanted his girls. They were for a specific purpose; they were the players in his game. The policewoman had been an added bonus. If he was going to get caught, he'd like it to be her that straddled him, cuffed him and read him his rights.

He had to stop thinking about her because he was getting hot under the collar.

A car reversed into the space next to him and he glanced at the driver and smiled. She was older than most of the girls who had been in and out. She smiled back, grabbed a bag off the passenger seat and got out of the car. She was tall, athletic and had a high ponytail. She was blonde, but it didn't matter about hair colour. She reminded him of her and she looked around the same age.

Turning on the engine, he began to reverse out of the parking space, simultaneously watching which door she went through whilst trying not to run any of the teenage idiots over who walked around in a world of their own. She walked a little further along than the main entrance, and he smiled. She was heading for the art department. As he pulled out, he looked at her number plate, memorising the make and model. He was happy. He'd found the next one after only a couple of hours' hunting. Now the fun would begin. He enjoyed this part almost as much as the killing.

It was almost four, so that meant she might be attending an evening class or possibly getting ready to teach one. He knew there were several classes that started late. All he had to do was narrow it down to the art classes and he'd know exactly when she'd be in and out. Then he could park up on the street and wait for her to leave. He'd follow her home and find out where she lived. Easy pickings. He grinned, wondering if she had a boyfriend or a partner at home. Those kinds of things complicated stuff a little, but it wasn't impossible. It hadn't mattered with G; he would have still killed her if her parents hadn't gone away on holiday. That had been an added bonus. It had meant they had the house to themselves and he'd been able to take his time instead of having to rush.

CHAPTER EIGHTEEN

Morgan looked at the row of houses, picking out the one Isaac lived and worked from. Her stomach felt weird, a combination of nerves and hunger. She realised she hadn't eaten since breakfast. She would meet Dan for a late lunch after this if he was free. The thought of the pair of them calling a truce made her feel better. The only other person she had fallen out with for a long time had been Stan. But in her defence, he hadn't helped the situation. She was glad they were okay now. Forcing herself to get out, she crossed the quiet road. It was a modern new-build, three-storey house with a garage. Before she could knock on the door, a man a little older than her opened it. He had a shaved head and dark stubble on his chin. He was wearing a pair of jogging pants and a Captain America T-shirt. He smiled, holding out his hand.

'Isaac. You must be Morgan. Come in, excuse the casual dress, it's my day off and I only have a college lecture later, so I don't bother with formal clothes.'

'I'm sorry, I had no idea. You didn't need to see me today. I can come back another day.'

'No way, if Amy sent you then you're a priority. She doesn't really get the whole psychotherapy thing, but I don't hold it against her. She's very close to Sophie and spends a lot of time here.'

He led her to a door and she was sure it led into the garage. Opening it she followed him into a modern office.

'It was the garage; we converted it when we realised the spare room wasn't going to hold all my filing cabinets. Amy comes back and forth whenever she argues with Jack. Don't tell her I said that, though; she'll go mad.'

Morgan laughed. 'I can imagine. She's lovely but she speaks her mind a lot.'

'You noticed that, yep, she does. Some people have an automatic shut-off button but not Amy. But enough of her. Take a seat and tell me how I can help you.'

She sat down and felt herself sinking into the soft, leather chair.

'Comfy, eh? I think most of my clients come here to snooze in that chair, but who am I to judge?'

'I'm so tired I could definitely fall asleep.'

'Why are you so tired? On the phone, you mentioned not sleeping and bad dreams. So is this a regular thing?'

Nodding her head, she felt as if she wanted to tell him everything, even though there wasn't much to tell.

'I've woken up at the same time every morning for the last five years without fail and it's driving me mad. I'm exhausted. I can't think clearly some days. Plus, I know I have bad dreams, but I don't ever seem to be able to remember all of them. Sometimes I see a red-haired woman who looks a bit like me, but I don't know who she is. It's not someone I've ever seen in real life.'

'I can definitely help you with that. Not today, of course, because this is just an informal chat and it might take quite a few sessions to get to the bottom of it. But it's something we can work together on. This woman though: you say you don't know her, but you probably do on some deeper subconscious level. When we sleep, the filter we keep on top of everything gets weaker and all the suppressed memories begin to float up to the surface. Do you remember anything at all about your dreams?'

'I think I'm very young in them, a toddler maybe. That's about it.'

'It sounds to me like some kind of repressed memories that are resurfacing or trying to. Did you have a normal childhood? By normal, I mean absent of any kind of abuse.'

She closed her eyes and thought back to her earliest memories. They were of her and Sylvia in the garden, picking herbs and vegetables, but she wasn't a baby; she was about five or six.

'Nothing really before I was five or six and, no, no abuse; in fact, there's nothing out of the ordinary.'

'Hmm, I'm wondering if you suffered some kind of trauma at a very early age and you've managed to block it out up to now. Childhood memories are usually present before the age of five or six. Is there anyone you can ask, family perhaps, about your early years?'

'Stan, my dad. It's kind of a complicated relationship. My mum took an overdose when I was fifteen and we kind of fell out and drifted apart.'

'Do you not speak to each other?' He was sitting forward, his elbows on his knees and his chin resting on the palm of his hand. Morgan felt a little uncomfortable at the way he was staring at her.

'We do now; we've been working on it.'

'Good, that's very good. Why don't I book you a proper appointment? They usually last an hour. In the meantime, you could speak to Stan and ask him if anything happened when you were a baby that may be causing these problems. It may be that he doesn't know or can't tell you anything, of course. But don't worry, Morgan, we can fix this. Maybe not in a couple of sessions but we can work towards it.'

He smiled and stood up. Walking around to his desk drawer, he pulled out a large, black diary. 'Now let's see. I imagine you want to start as soon as possible. I have a gap next Tuesday at 3.15.' He passed her a clipboard.

'Please, can you put your details on there for me, just basics: address, doctor, medication, that kind of thing.'

Taking it from him, she began writing down the answers to the questions.

'I saw the news about the murder earlier. Gabby was such a lovely girl. What a terrible waste of life. Have you caught the killer yet?'

The tiny hairs on the back of Morgan's neck prickled.

'Not yet, but it's only a matter of time. You knew Gabby?' Signing her signature, she handed the clipboard back to him, then forced herself to get out of the ridiculously comfy armchair and stood up.

'Good, because no one should have to die so young. It's so unfair and she was so lovely. I saw her around the college. I didn't know her very well but she was always very friendly. I lecture there a couple of times a week.'

Morgan felt as if the breath had been pulled from her lungs and the room began to go black around the edges. She whispered, 'It's tragic.'

'Are you okay?'

His voice sounded far away.

Squeezing her eyes shut, she opened them and smiled.

'Sorry, I've been feeling a bit peaky today. I think it's the lack of sleep and stress. I'm working Gabby's case with Amy. We may need to speak to you and get a statement about Gabby.'

'Of course, anything I can do to help. Although I've probably just told you as much as I can. I only knew of her to recognise.'

He walked out of his office and she followed him. He opened the front door for her and she stepped into the deserted street.

'Nice to meet you, Morgan. I'll look forward to seeing you on Tuesday. Good luck speaking to Stan.'

She smiled and lifted her hand to wave at him. 'Thanks, Isaac.'

Inside her car, she felt a chill run through her body. She was being totally ridiculous. He worked at the college; he was bound to know some of the students. She was torn: did she mention this to Amy and Ben or did she tell Ben and let him deal with Amy? Or did she have the worst overactive imagination anyone was ever born with? That was more likely. She took her police phone out of the glove compartment and sent a message to Dan.

Starving, need to talk, are you free?

Immediately a message came back.

Yes, Coffee Co. in five?

She sent a thumbs up. Maybe food and caffeine would kick-start her brain again and clear the fog which seemed to have settled over it.

CHAPTER NINETEEN

The café was empty. Morgan took a table as far away from the counter as possible. She didn't want the poor staff overhearing the conversation she might have with Dan. Regular people didn't need to know the horrors of what they dealt with. If they did, they'd probably never sleep either. She didn't wait for him before she ordered, she couldn't. If she didn't eat something soon she was probably going to pass out. He arrived still in uniform but he'd removed his bright yellow body armour. She'd forgotten how good he looked in black. He had shaved and the stubble he normally favoured was gone. Sipping her coffee, Morgan stared out of the window as the first drops of rain began to fall, and people began to hurry along the high street just before the heavens opened.

The loud scrape as he pulled the chair out next to her made her jump.

'Sorry, didn't mean to scare you.'

'I'm tired and was daydreaming, it's okay. Have you been busy?'

'Not too bad, shoplifter followed by a minor road traffic accident. I bet you can't say the same.'

'No, it's been hectic and grim. I went with Ben to see Gabby Stevens's bedroom.'

'Again? What for?' He was ripping open packets of sugar and tipping them into his huge mug of coffee.

'To make sure nothing was missing. Task force didn't find her phone yesterday. We just wanted to double-check.'

'Did you find it?' He took a huge slurp of coffee. 'Bloody hell, burnt my tongue. It's boiling hot.'

She smiled. 'Hate it when that happens. It will be all furry now for a couple of days.'

He stuck his tongue out at her, and she laughed.

'No, but we didn't really expect to.'

He arched an eyebrow at her, and she wondered if she should be talking about the case with him like this, but she couldn't see why not. He was a copper, just like her; he worked for the same side. Just because they were in different departments, she wasn't telling him anything that anyone in the station couldn't find out. She'd missed this, the easy way they could chat about cases and help each other out. It felt good to be speaking to him, and she was relieved that they'd made it up.

'This isn't public knowledge.'

'Good, because I'm not a member of the public, Morgan. I work with you.'

'I got a message, several messages actually, from Gabby Stevens's phone.'

He stared at her, his eyes so wide she was afraid they would fall out of their sockets.

'No fucking way, you can't be serious.' His voice was loud, so loud the guy behind the counter had stopped what he was doing.

Morgan nudged Dan's arm.

'Sorry,' he whispered. 'What did they say? How did they get your number? I don't understand why they'd text you.'

'You tell me, I don't know either. They were a bit creepy to be honest.'

'Is that why you messaged off your work phone?'

'Yeah, someone from the high-tech unit was coming down to take a look at my phone.'

'Morgan this is serious. I know you don't like being told what to do but you can't have some nutter messaging you. If he knows your phone number, who's to say he doesn't know where you live?'

The guy brought their bowls of soup and toasted sandwiches over. Morgan thanked him.

'I need to eat before I pass out.'

Dan nodded and they both ate in silence. When she pushed her plate away, he asked: 'So, what are you going to do? Do you want to come and stay at my house for a bit, or I can come sleep on your armchair? Not that it's a great bed, but you know I will.'

'Thanks. Amy has already sorted something out.'

'Are you stopping at hers?'

For some reason, she felt awkward telling him she was going to Ben's and nodded.

'Hey, what happened with the DCI? I guess he didn't suspend you.'

'No, but he told me if he found out I'd passed any information to Barker that was confidential, he'd have my badge and my bollocks.'

'Ouch.'

'Yep, he was serious as well. But he has nothing except Barker's word for it, which kind of means jack shit seeing as how he's a liar.'

'We both seem to be up to our necks in it.'

'Speak for yourself, Brookes, you seem to find yourself in all sorts of messes without any help from me.'

She laughed. 'I need to get back; they'll be sending out a search party for me.'

Dan smiled. 'This was nice. I'm glad we're okay. If you need anything ring me, anytime. I have to take the van back, it's nearly home time.'

They both stood up, shouted thank you and walked out of the café back to her car. Dan's van was parked behind it.

'Bye, Dan.'

She got into the car. At least something had gone right today.

CHAPTER TWENTY

Ben looked up when Morgan walked into the office. He was sitting at her desk talking to a tall woman with the most amazing dreadlocks she'd ever seen. She didn't miss the glance he gave to the clock on the wall.

'Sorry, my appointment took longer than I anticipated and I stopped off to buy something to eat on the way back.'

He nodded, accepting her apology. 'This is Darcy from the high-tech unit. She came to look at your phone. It's a good job you left your password for her or it might have been a wasted journey.'

Morgan realised he was well and truly annoyed with her, but she was too tired to care about Ben's feelings. She felt as if she wanted to curl up in a ball on the floor and sleep for a year. Exhausted wasn't the word.

'So what did you find out?'

It was Darcy who answered. 'I've run a trace on it. I've also cloned your phone and have everything up to now that we might need as evidence. So you can carry on using it in case you get any further messages. I've requested a cell site analysis for Gabby's phone, so we'll know which mast it triangulated to when those messages were sent to you.'

Morgan liked to think she was pretty up to date with stuff, but this was way above her head.

'I'm sorry, you've done what?'

'When an analysis is carried out, it checks which phone masts the phone was nearest when it was turned on and sending the message.

It usually has a choice of three but will automatically choose the nearest mast with the strongest signal. We can then triangulate the three masts and come up with a three-kilometre radius of where the phone was used.'

'Can't you just track it to wherever it is?'

Darcy laughed. 'If we were the FBI or MI5 possibly, but we don't have that kind of technology available to us at the moment.'

Morgan stifled a yawn; her head was pounding and she was tired. She also needed to speak to Stan. Isaac had said that everything could be due to some kind of childhood trauma she was blocking out. Maybe something happened that she didn't remember; once she knew, it might put an end to the ridiculous early morning wake up calls and nightmares she never remembered. The only thing was: would he tell her if anything had happened or would he be too embarrassed in case it showed him in a bad light?

'So you can use your phone for now. I've shown Ben how to use the software to download everything from it. There would be little point taking a point of contact away from the killer. It's a bit scary for you though, isn't it?'

After what she'd been through the last couple of months it felt as if this was another level of scary that she never even knew existed. 'Well, you know where I am if you need me. I've put my number in your contacts list: my own number not my work one. I only work days because of the budget cuts or if there's a rush job on.'

'Can we not use Find My iPhone? Or some other kind of tracker? What about location services?'

Morgan had found her second wind.

'I tried, whoever it is has the phone switched off or on airplane mode. They've also turned off the location tracker. Our boy knows what he's doing, which is why you need to be very careful.'

'He'll only come out to play when he's ready.'

Darcy nodded. Morgan realised the magnitude of what she had been drawn into: a killer was messaging her for fun.

Her head began to spin and she felt as if she couldn't breathe. The room was too stuffy; she needed fresh air. Crossing to the window behind her desk, she pushed it open as far as it would go and stuck her head between the gap.

Ben's deep voice was full of concern. 'Morgan?'

'I'm good, I just need a bit of air.'

'I'll get going then. Same applies, Ben. If you need to speak to me about anything ring my mobile. Don't wait until the next time I'm in work.'

'Thanks, Darcy, I really appreciate this.'

She heard the office door open and close. There was only the two of them. Footsteps as Ben crossed towards her vibrated the floor.

'So what's going on with you? Darcy is right, this is some messed-up stuff.'

'Where's Amy?'

'Gone to take statements from the landlord and his girlfriend at The Golden Ball.'

Sucking in a couple of gulps of the damp, fresh air she turned around. 'I went to see her cousin's boyfriend. He also said he'd heard about the murder and was devastated at the senseless loss of life.'

'Why did you go see him?'

'He's a psychotherapist. I told Amy I wasn't sleeping and she recommended him.'

'Was that your appointment?'

She nodded.

'Did he say anything else?'

'Nothing confidential; he just said he was upset because he'd seen her around the college where he lectures a couple of times a week and she was such a lovely girl.'

'He knew her? That's interesting. Maybe we should speak to him officially about it. At this point, I'll take any leads we can get.'

'What about Amy?'

'Leave her to me. I'll discuss it with her. Hey, do you want to go get some stuff from your apartment so it's in the car for when we knock off?'

'Yes, I can do.' She also thought she could pay Stan a quick visit on her way there.

Her shoulders heavy and her brain aching, she left Ben to it.

CHAPTER TWENTY-ONE

Ben was about to call Amy when his desk phone began to ring.

'Good afternoon, is this Detective Sergeant Ben Matthews?'

He recognised the soft Irish lilt in the voice and smiled.

'It is, Doctor, why so formal?'

'I'm trying to show my assistant the proper way to address someone on the phone. I overheard her earlier answering my desk phone with a very distinct "Yeah". No good morning or anything, it was horrifying.'

Ben laughed.

'I bet you don't get that with your protégé, Morgan, do you?'

He rubbed a hand over his chin. Despite shaving this morning it felt rough already.

'No, her phone manners are impeccable. However her ability to attract disaster is on another level. But you didn't phone to discuss our colleagues.'

'You, my friend, are very perceptive: no, I did not. I phoned because I fast-tracked the swabs and hair samples for you. There were two possible matches: one of them is being retested because it's a mistake.'

Ben sucked in his breath; this was too good to be true. 'How is it a mistake?'

'Well one is a close match to Morgan's.'

'Christ, how has that happened? I told her to be careful. What about the other?'

'Well this is where it gets a little complicated because hers is also similar to the other. To be fair, I don't know what's going on with that one. I understand the basics, but I'm no DNA expert.'

'How?'

'Do you remember that terrible case from back in the nineties? The rapist who attacked women out alone walking or jogging.'

'Vaguely, the press called him the Riverside Rapist because all his attacks happened along the banks of the river.'

'Well the other is almost identical to his. There are a couple of slight differences, but it's good enough and things have improved a lot since his initial sample will have been taken when he was arrested.'

'What the hell? He's in prison, isn't he?'

'Yes, I googled him. Unless he gets out on day release for good behaviour. It happens. He would probably be nearly at the end of his sentence, wouldn't he?'

'Well, at least we have a starting point. Thanks, Declan, I appreciate it.'

'You're very welcome. Don't be too harsh on Morgan.' He hung up.

Ben logged on to his computer and began to research the Riverside Rapist. Photographs of a smiling man, dressed in a grey two-piece prison jogging suit, filled the screen. He was waving – his arms and legs in shackles – as he was put into the back of a van. He had raped three women along the bank of the River Rothay then murdered his wife. The arrogance radiated from him. Ben could tell by looking at him that Gary Marks thought he was God. He needed to speak to him and find out what was going on, and he would have to take Morgan with him because he didn't want to leave her alone at the moment. He paused, should he have let her go off on her own now to collect her things? Probably not. He searched for the phone number for HMP Manchester. He needed to pay a visit to Gary Marks as soon as he could.

CHAPTER TWENTY-TWO

Morgan didn't bother knocking or ringing the broken bell that was smashed to pieces; instead, she pushed the front door to the block of bedsits where Stan was living. It opened, and she tutted under her breath. This was the third time she'd visited, and each time the door was open for anyone to walk inside. As she stepped into the dark, gloomy narrow hall which smelt of cooking oil and sweat, she began to breathe through her mouth. It smelt awful. There was a stack of crumpled letters on the bottom stair. The filthy, threadbare carpet looked as if it hadn't seen a hoover in ten years. Stan lived on the top floor. Tucking her hands in her pockets so she didn't touch the banister or walls, she ran up the three flights of stairs to his door. It smelt much better up here, and he'd hoovered the stairs which led to his front door. She knocked on the plywood door and heard footsteps inside. It opened, and he smiled to see her.

'Morgan, how are you, love? Come in.'

He stepped to one side and she went inside. His flat smelt of bleach and lemon – a much better combination than further down. Bless him, he was really trying to impress her.

'I'm good. Busy, but you know how it is.'

'Sit down. I'll put the kettle on.'

'I can't stop long, sorry. I've just called for a quick visit. How are you?'

'I'm good.'

She looked around the compact bedsit. There were no telltale empty cans of alcohol or whisky bottles; it was clean, and he'd even scrubbed the grime off the windows.

'You've done a good job with the place.'

He laughed. 'I've done what I could with it. I know it's a shithole, love. But it's better than a park bench and it's warm. Thank God I'm up here so I can't hear what the idiots downstairs get up to. I think the woman in the bottom flat is dealing, but you never heard that from me. It doesn't bother me, except when people are shouting, banging and throwing things at the windows in the early hours.'

She nodded, acknowledging his comments, but not making a big fuss of them because he'd more than likely clam up and not tell her anything else. He still disliked the police, although with not quite as much passion as he used to.

'I'm tired, really tired. I wake up at the same time in the early hours every morning. It started after Mum died. I have bad dreams too, but I can never remember what they are. I know they're not about Mum; sometimes I get a tiny sliver of it come back to me and a few times I've seen a red-haired woman. She's tiny, with green eyes a bit like mine. But that's it. I never remember anything else, just her face. Things have got so bad I decided to see a psychotherapist and he thinks they might be repressed memories from some kind of childhood trauma.

'I don't remember anything like that happening apart from Mum dying. But I was fifteen, not a kid. I was wondering if you knew about something that had happened when I was little that, for some reason, I might have blocked from my mind?'

She looked at his face; the colour had drained from it and he looked stunned.

'I, I don't know, love. There's nothing that I know about. As far as I know, you had a great childhood. We protected you the best we could from everything. Well, I'm not saying you didn't fall over and scrape your knees or crash that little pink bike you had when you were trying to learn to ride it, because you did, quite a lot, but no matter how bad it hurt you always got back up and tried again.'

'Oh God. I didn't mean it like that. I'm not accusing you of anything, Stan. I know you and Mum did your very best. I was wondering if I'd been in some kind of accident or saw something terrible happen to someone else.'

He shook his head. 'No, we looked after you from day one the best that we could. I'm not saying we were perfect parents; I don't think anyone ever is and I know I made mistakes after Sylvia passed. All you can do is try your best and hope that you're doing it right.'

She sighed. 'Thanks. I wonder what the hell these bad dreams are then.'

'If you're seeing a shrink, they'll be able to work it out. You'll be paying them enough for the pleasure.'

Morgan didn't correct him that it wasn't a shrink, realising she was too tired for anything. 'I have to go, but thanks. Sorry if I upset you.'

She stood up, taking the few steps from the sofa to reach the door.

'Be careful, love, you work far too hard and after last time…' He didn't finish his sentence. He didn't need to: both of them had paid a price that had almost cost them their lives.

'I will, thank you. See you later, Stan.'

She shut the door behind her and trudged down the stairs, relieved to be back outside in the fresh air. She was proud of him; he was trying really hard. Next time she'd tell him this, maybe even ask him around for tea on her days off. This thought made her feel much better; they'd had some ups and downs but they were sorting it out and she owed him. Who was she to judge anyone's parenting? She'd never had kids and didn't think she'd ever want them. It was too hard bringing them into a world where evil stalked innocent people and killed them for pleasure.

CHAPTER TWENTY-THREE

He'd searched the college website for the class timetable, then he'd searched through the department pages until he'd found a picture of her. She was stunning, even more so on the headshot she'd used. Obviously a professional one, not a selfie from a drunken night out. He also had a name: Emily Wearing, and thanks to Facebook he knew that she was twenty-five in three weeks, single, lived alone and loved her pet sausage dog more than anything else. He'd studied her photographs closely. He knew she liked to drink rosé wine, enjoyed the cinema and Italian food. Thanks to Instagram, he knew her hobbies included running, fell walking and reading, especially thrillers. She baked lots of cakes; she also burnt a lot too as she posted pictures of the disasters as well as the edible ones. The only thing he didn't know was her bank account number, but given a little more time, he was sure he could find it out. All this had taken him less than thirty minutes. It was unbelievable, really, and stupid, so very stupid. How many people posted their most private information onto the Internet for the whole world to see? More did than didn't, except for him. He had a Facebook page, but it was set to private. The only people he had as friends were actual friends; he didn't accept every idiot who sent a friend request. He only posted generic pictures, nothing personal. Why would he? His life was very private. He didn't want anyone knowing anything about him that he wouldn't tell them in person.

It hadn't been hard to figure out where she was from either. Although the college was in Kendal, she spent a lot of time around the Rydal Falls area. He recognised the places her photographs were taken, and she always added the location on her Instagram posts. He knew all her personal information. If he got the chance, he'd follow her home tonight to see exactly where her house was. If he couldn't, there was tomorrow. Although it had been almost a week since he'd strangled G, he was itching to do it again. He'd fantasised for so long about it; he hadn't realised exactly how delicious it would be to be in such control of another person. He didn't think she would be as much fun as his first. He knew that the first was supposed to be the best, like the first of everything, first love, first kiss… first kill had been far too superior to either of those. He wanted to at least try and recreate it though. If anything he was a trier; his mother had always told him that. And didn't her precious God love a trier too? Yes, He did.

He waited in the car by the side of the road, a book propped against his steering wheel. He looked as if he was cramming for college or getting ready to teach. No one bothered with him, which was fine, he liked it that way. Invisibility was a great ability to possess when you needed to be discreet and when hunting for your next kill. Discretion was invaluable. There weren't as many cars parked out the front of the college as the last time he was here; he'd stand out if he was still parked there when she came out. He looked up; people were filtering out of the doors. It was almost seven; she was either going to leave soon or be here until the bitter end. The words on the page in front of him were a blur. Inside his mind, he was already getting to know E a little better than he already did. What was her bed like, was it big, did she make it every morning when she got up or did she leave it a mess? G had been messy; he'd had to make the bed for her and he doubted she'd even appreciated his efforts.

His patience was finally rewarded when he saw E's blue Mini appear at the junction of the exit; but she wasn't alone. He was a little disappointed with this. In the passenger seat was a much older male and he wondered who this could be. Friend, colleague? He would follow her. Hopefully, she would only be offering this man a lift somewhere and not taking him back to her address. He'd got himself worked up about the fun he was going to have with her and didn't want it to be spoilt before he'd begun.

Placing the book on the seat next to him, he indicated and pulled out behind her, slowly and keeping a safe distance. He didn't want her to see him just yet. He preferred the element of surprise. It made the whole thing so much sweeter, especially when the fear in their eyes turned to recognition and disbelief.

CHAPTER TWENTY-FOUR

Amy walked into the office with Detective Constable Des Black, who had thankfully come back to work after his recent hernia operation. They needed every hand they could get.

'Anything?' Ben asked.

'Nothing decent, lots of gossip about how Charlotte is a bit of a diva and gives Harry the runaround. Apart from that, they're a happy family, married for twenty-five years and like their city breaks.'

'Can I have a word, in my office?' He walked towards it; she put the clipboards down and followed him.

'What's up, Ben?'

'Morgan went to see your cousin, the psychotherapist. He mentioned knowing Gabby.'

'I know, I suggested it. And he's my cousin's boyfriend, but I don't hold that against him. He teaches at the sixth form, so yeah I would imagine he did.'

'Do you think he'd be able to help us with the investigation? Maybe come up with an idea of who we might be looking for? I know it's a long shot, but Morgan's ideas about serial killers have got me wondering.'

'I can ask. I think he'd be able to help, or at least advise us. Let me phone him.'

Amy rang and waited for him to answer, putting the call on speaker. 'Hello, it's me.'

'Hello you.'

'Isaac, my boss was wondering if you might be able to give us a hand with something?'

'Like what, are you short-staffed? I don't think I'd be any good at enquiries or scene guard.'

'Not that kind of hand. He wants some advice but isn't sure if this is anything you would be able to help with.'

'Go on. If I can, I will.'

'You know about the murder? We're trying to get an idea what this suspect could be like and wondered if you might have any insight into the kind of person we should be looking for?'

'What, like an offender profile, that kind of thing?'

'Yes.'

'Ah. You know I would love to be big-headed and say yes, but unfortunately I can't. It's not something I'd be comfortable doing really. You need a forensic psychologist for that.'

'Oh, right. Yeah, I suppose we do. We can ask for one maybe. God knows how long it would take though. Thanks, Isaac, it was worth a shot. We're looking for any kind of lead we can get right now. What he did to that poor girl was horrific. She didn't deserve that.'

'No, she didn't, and neither will the next girl.'

'What do you mean "the next girl"?'

'Are you not assuming he'll strike again? This kind of thing, if you're telling me it was horrific and you have no obvious leads or any suspects with connections to her, then he might be a stranger and he'll probably do it again.'

Ben buried his head into his hands. He was the second person who thought this was what was happening. Amy knocked the speaker off and finished her conversation. He didn't listen to the rest of it because he was trying to figure out what to do next, how likely this killer was to strike again and if he already had another victim in his sights, and then it hit him. Morgan. He'd contacted her. Somehow he'd got hold of her personal number and had been texting her. He was bold, he wanted attention, was looking for it. If this was a one-off he'd have tried to make himself invisible. He wouldn't be blatantly rubbing it in all of their faces.

He rang her number and breathed a sigh of relief when she answered.

'Hi.'

'Hi.'

'What?'

He realised he felt a bit awkward, then pushed that thought to one side.

'Where are you, what are you doing?'

'Do you also want to know what colour underwear I'm wearing?'

'Good God, no, I do not.'

He heard her laughter and felt better. 'Your sarcasm gives me heartburn. Don't be so mean to me.'

'Not on purpose, sorry. I'm just leaving my apartment. I've packed some things ready for my big adventure. Do I need to go shopping for some food? I don't want to take all of yours.'

'It's up to you. I think I have enough stuff in for tonight.'

'I'm bringing what fresh stuff there was in my fridge; no point letting it go off. What time are you finishing work?'

There was a slight pause as he tried to figure it out and then she whispered: 'Oh God, I didn't mean that how it sounded. I meant should I come back to work or go straight to yours?'

'I don't know, I'm tired. Maybe we could meet at mine, have something to eat and figure out whether to come back or not.'

'Sounds like a plan to me, boss.'

'Oh and, Morgan, I'll give you a spare key. No breaking any windows to get inside.'

He began to laugh and then hung up the phone. Grabbing his jacket, he told Amy he was nipping home. She waved a hand at him. Her head bent, she was reading her notes off a clipboard, and Des was concentrating as he typed what she was telling him onto the computer. They might only be a small team, but they were bloody good at their jobs and dedicated. He couldn't ask for anything more.

CHAPTER TWENTY-FIVE

Morgan felt better in herself. She was still shocked at Gabby's murder and the fact that her killer had chosen to communicate with her out of everyone, but she felt more at peace. She wasn't sure if it was the fact that she was finally getting professional help with her insomnia, that she and Stan were getting along much better and working hard to repair their broken relationship, or that she was going to be staying at Ben's for a few days. There was no denying she liked him; he was funny and being with him was enjoyable. He was good company and caring for a boss. She couldn't ask for anyone better to work with. She reached Ben's house moments before his car arrived and smiled to herself, thinking about the first time she came here; worried for Ben's welfare, she had thrown a brick through his window. She didn't know if he was ever going to let her forget that. Waiting for him to get out first, she grabbed her overnight bag from the back seat and slung it over her shoulder. Ben hurried towards her, reaching out to take it from her.

'Christ, that's heavy. What's in it?'

'My face masks. I thought we could have a pamper session.'

He looked at her in horror, and she laughed. 'And you thought *I* was gullible. I won't put you through that. Not unless you want to.' She winked at him. 'Where are we with the case now?'

'Hmm, just make sure you warn me first so I don't get the fright of my life. We've spoken to Isaac Cross on the off chance he could help us out with some kind of offender profile. But he didn't have anything specific he could tell us. It was an idea, probably a stupid one.'

'It's not. I think that's great that you asked him. It's a shame he isn't a forensic psychologist.'

'Yeah, we could do with Cracker on the case. There was one thing he said that was interesting though: he seems to share your opinion that this isn't some random, one-off killing.'

'Ah, I take it that wasn't what you wanted to hear, but it's a possibility we have to consider. Who's Cracker?'

They reached the front door and Ben unlocked it, pushing it open for her to step inside.

'I'm showing my age. You've never heard of the television show? It was big in the nineties; Robbie Coltrane played him. You know who he is, don't you?'

She shook her head.

'Christ I feel ancient. He played Hagrid in Harry Potter. Anyway, excuse the mess and the dust. I don't really do housework.'

Morgan thought it looked lovely, he'd painted and cleaned up; it was much nicer than the last time she was here. There was no mess that she could see from the entrance hall. She waited for him to follow her. He did, shutting and locking the door behind him.

'I only have a couple of house rules. You keep the windows and doors locked at all times, even when I'm here. At least until we have a better idea of who we're dealing with and why they're sending you messages. You don't let anyone in you don't know or you don't know very well.'

Morgan nodded. She knew he was thinking back to her letting a killer into her apartment not that long ago and what an almost deadly mistake that had been.

'I won't, I promise.'

'And you don't tell anyone that you're staying here. Amy knows, because it was her suggestion, but the fewer people we tell the better it is.'

She nodded, wondering if he was embarrassed to have her here and didn't want anyone from work knowing about it, or whether he was being overly cautious and concerned for both of their safety. He pointed to the door to the left.

'You can use that as a lounge; there's a sofa in there but no TV. It's a great place to read; in fact, that's all you can do in there really, or use your laptop. If you need to watch the TV then use this room.'

He pointed to another, identical, pine door opposite. 'That one has a sixty-inch TV, an Xbox and Netflix, but don't mess my games up if they're on. Apart from that you're good to go. Use the place as you want. I don't mind which bedroom you choose. I'm not fussy. I'll sleep anywhere, and if you get the urge to cook I won't hold it against you.'

Morgan began to laugh. 'Blimey, have you ever watched *Fawlty Towers*? You sounded just as welcoming as John Cleese when he played Basil Fawlty.'

Ben grinned. 'That good, eh? I love *Fawlty Towers*; it's a classic. I'd have thought you were a bit young to remember it. How come you know that but not *Cracker* then?'

'My mum, she loved it. Would watch reruns of it on Gold in an afternoon and giggle away to herself. I never really understood it, until one day after she'd died I was in the house alone and switched the TV on, to see Basil Fawlty striding around. I sat down and watched it. I wanted to know what was so funny and before long I was laughing so hard and crying at the same time. In a good way though, you know, happy memories mingled in with the sad. It felt as if she was there, sitting next to me on the sofa. I wish we'd done that more. It's the simple things you really miss when someone is gone; all the stuff you take for granted.'

Ben reached out both arms and pulled her towards him, hugging her in an awkward fashion for the briefest of moments before releasing her. He wished he could have hugged Cindy more. He missed her so much.

'Thanks, I needed that.'

'Have you eaten? I'm starving.'

'I did, sorry.' She didn't feel comfortable telling him she'd met Dan for a late lunch. She knew he disliked him with a passion and didn't want to cause any bad feeling between them. Especially not when she was stopping in his house.

'Don't worry, I don't expect you to make an announcement every time you eat. I can sort myself out. I'll grab a bag of crisps.'

Morgan felt awful. 'You can't survive off crisps.'

'Said who? I've been managing quite nicely, thank you very much. You get pretty much every flavour, mix a few bags together and you end up with the equivalent of a crisp roast dinner, without having to wash a single pot.'

'Urgh, that's disgusting and lazy.'

He shrugged. 'Works for me.'

'Thank you.'

'For what?'

'For this, for letting me stay and being so nice to me even when I've been a pain in the backside.'

He laughed. 'You might not thank me if my snoring keeps you awake all night. I'm going to make some sandwiches. I'll make extra and wrap them in foil. Help yourself if you get hungry.'

He headed towards the kitchen, and she went upstairs with her bag to choose one of the spare rooms. She opened doors. One was a home office/bedroom, another was a bedroom which was full of boxes. There was another, but it was too close to Ben's. She didn't want to hear every noise he made in the night. She also didn't want him to have to hear her thrashing around in her sleep. And when she woke up early, she didn't want to disturb him when she crept downstairs. The room with the desk was the furthest away, so she hauled her bag and threw it on the bed. She sat down next to it. Kicking off her shoes, she lifted her feet onto it. It was so comfortable she didn't want to move. As she lay there thinking through everything that had happened the last couple of days, she felt an overwhelming tiredness consume her entire body, even though it was a few hours yet till her usual bedtime. She didn't even realise what was happening as she allowed her eyelids to close for a couple of moments as her body gave in and let her sleep.

CHAPTER TWENTY-SIX

He followed her from a distance along the A591. She'd stopped off at a small country lane and the man had got out, waved and disappeared down it. He followed her all the way to Rydal Falls and watched her, not quite believing where she was heading. Parked along the quiet road, she drove through the gates of the large house which he knew had been turned into three apartments. She got out of her car and let herself in through the front door. He'd looked around one of the apartments himself when he'd been thinking about moving but had decided against it. On one hand he couldn't have asked for anything better because he knew the layout without having to do any research. On the downside, he also knew the copper he'd been texting off G's phone lived in the ground-floor apartment, which kind of threw him a little. She had been involved in a serious attack a few months ago and her apartment had been splashed all over the local paper. It made it very dangerous. He couldn't text her from anywhere in this area because no doubt they were now monitoring Gabby's phone. If they tracked it to this area, it would make it a no go for definite. They would be watching her for sure and waiting for him to turn up so they could catch him.

He turned around and drove off before anyone spotted him. He was going to have to think carefully about this one and revaluate whether the risk it posed to him was going to be worth the pay-off. He'd never expected E to live in this part of Rydal Falls. He thought she'd live in Kendal nearer to the college. But perhaps it was serendipity at its finest. His stomach a mass of churning knots, he didn't know if it was excitement at the risk following through with this would pose, or the fear of messing it all up and getting caught before he'd finished what he had to do.

He went home, needing some time to think things through. He had to be sure he wasn't letting his ego take over, because sometimes it did and he ended up in a bit of bother because of it.

His phone rang and he answered it.

'Have you finished work yet and are you coming to the pub?'

It was a simple enough question, one he should have been able to answer, but his brain felt as if it was in a different zone to the rest of his body.

'Hello, are you listening to me?'

'Yes, of course I am. I don't know, I'm a bit busy.'

'Suit yourself; we're here if you change your mind.'

The line went dead and he didn't know what to do. He knew he should go to the pub. It was the best thing to do; it was good to give the impression that you wanted to be with your mates. Even though it was the last place he wanted to be and they were only his mates because it suited him, not because he really liked them, he decided to get changed and go for a pint: a bit of conversation and then he'd come home to make his decision.

As he walked into the pub, he was surprised to see one of the regulars who hadn't been in a while, an older guy called Stan who had cleaned himself up, sitting at the bar. Sitting in front of him was a pint and a whisky chaser. That was the thing with living in such a small community: everyone knew your business whether you wanted them to or not. Sometimes they knew more about your life than you did. It could be frustrating and for him dangerous. He really liked his next potential target, but the fact that she lived in the same block of flats as the copper hunting him made things far more complicated than he liked. Maybe he could choose another victim.

He saw his friends by the pool table and lifted his hand, then pointed to the bar. They all shook their heads, so he was in for a cheap round. He stood next to Stan who was still staring at his drinks.

'Rough day?'

He nodded, then lifted his gaze and smiled. 'Oh hi, how are you?'

'Judging by the way you're staring at that pint, I'm probably a lot better than you.'

Stan laughed, but it was strained. 'Yep, probably. Can I ask you for a bit of advice? This is strictly between you and me, by the way.'

'Ask away. I don't know if I can give you the answer you're looking for though, and you're probably not going to find it in those glasses either.'

'Hypothetically, if you ever adopted a kid and you knew something bad had happened to them before they came to you, but you never brought it up or discussed it with them, would you tell them if they asked years later? Would you tell the truth or lie, even if it was for their own good?'

He blew out his cheeks. 'Wow, that's a big one, Stan. I suppose it depends on the severity of what happened and if it's having an impact on their life now.'

'It's a huge one. I've let my daughter down most of my life. We're just getting back on track, but we never told her that she was adopted, and this is going to tear such a huge hole in her heart. I don't think we'd ever recover from it, and I don't want to lose her again when I've only just found her.'

He looked at the pain in Stan's eyes. He could feel it radiating off his body in waves and it was quite intoxicating. He felt a spark of excitement as an idea began to form in his mind.

'You have to do what's best, what you can live with. If you can face your daughter, knowing what you know, then I wouldn't say anything if it's eating at you this much.' He pointed to the glasses of alcohol in front of him. 'Then for your own sake, you might have to come clean, tell her, and live with it. I'm pretty sure, even if she's mad at you, once she gets over the shock she'll come around and thank you.' He ordered a pint of lager and paid his money to the barmaid.

'I have to go see my friends. Good luck, Stan, with whatever you decide.'

'Thanks.'

He joined his friends at the pool table, but he couldn't take his eyes off Stan.

CHAPTER TWENTY-SEVEN

When Morgan's eyes opened she had no idea where she was and sat bolt upright in the bed, causing a wave of dizziness that took her breath away. It was still dark outside. She reached out for her phone, the backlight illuminating the desk and bookshelves opposite her. Her shoulders dropped and she sighed. Ben's. She was at his house, in his spare room. How had she got to bed? She didn't even remember saying good night to him. She sat there for a few moments, willing her breathing to slow down and waiting for the spinning inside her head to ease off. From somewhere down the hall, she could hear gentle snores and found it comforting. It was nice not to be alone, especially not with everything that was happening. Which reminded her: she checked her phone to see if there had been any further messages from Gabby's missing phone. There was one from Stan.

Night Morgan, love you. I think we need to talk, come see me when you can. I'd rather talk in person. You could come for tea if you like, I'm a dab hand at beans on toast. Xxx.

She didn't text him back, not at four thirty in the morning, but she would later. What was that about: they needed to talk in person? It was a bit cryptic for Stan. She wondered if he had something awful to tell her. Maybe he'd remembered something from her childhood that might explain the bad dreams and early mornings. Grabbing her clean clothes and toiletry bag, she crept along the hallway to the bathroom. Ben's door was closed and she could hear him snoring, so hopefully she wouldn't disturb him.

*

By the time Ben's alarm began to sound a couple of hours later, Morgan had cleaned the kitchen, put the recycling out and was in the process of making breakfast when she heard the shower turn on in the bathroom. When Ben came downstairs dressed in a shirt and tie, to a full English breakfast and a sparkling house, he looked at her and muttered: 'Wow. You've been busy.'

She shrugged. 'Had to do something to fill my time. I don't want you thinking I'm taking advantage of your good nature.'

Smiling, he shook his head. 'This was Amy's idea. You didn't ask to come here. But I'm glad you did, not that I expect you to clean up and make my breakfast every morning. This is a nice surprise though. It's been awhile since I've had company who cooked for me.'

Morgan detected a shadow of pain cross his face, only for a split second, and she realised he was meaning Cindy.

'Did I overstep?'

'No, you did not. Thank you, but honestly cereal is fine and I can fix it myself.'

'Yeah, after our conversation about a roast dinner flavoured crisp, I'm not so sure about that.'

'You're not going to let me forget that, are you?'

She shook her head. 'Never. So what's the plan for today?'

'We're going on a road trip?'

'We are, to where?'

'HMP Manchester, the prison formerly known as Strangeways.'

'Why?'

'I got a call last night. DNA from the crime scene came back as a match for a guy called Gary Marks.'

'That's fantastic. We have a hit and know who the killer is. Wow, amazing. Why didn't you tell me yesterday? Why haven't we arrested him yet and why do we need to go to the prison?'

'Woah, slow down. That's where we hit a bit of a snag. He's a prisoner and has been locked up since 1999.'

Her mouth fell open. 'I don't get it.'

'Me neither, but we need to go speak to him and find out why a match for his DNA has turned up.'

'What's he in prison for?'

'Have you heard of the Riverside Rapist?'

'Vaguely, I was a kid I think. I remember hearing things over the years, but never really took much notice because it was before my time.'

'He raped three women by the River Rothay. He used to tell his wife he was night fishing. Only he wasn't: he was out preying on women who were out walking, jogging or in the area. His wife figured out what he was doing and he killed her. She kept a record of what she'd found, though, which he didn't know about and they put him in the frame for the rapes. Not to mention they found his DNA on all three victims.'

'Jesus, that's horrific.'

'Yeah, it was awful. We need to go visit him and find out what's happening and if he has any connection to Gabby Stevens's murder.'

'It's a long shot. What are you expecting to find out?'

He shrugged. 'Who knows, but we can't ignore it.'

They ate in silence. Morgan had suddenly lost her appetite and had to force herself to eat. She didn't know what to think, this was so confusing and such a mess.

CHAPTER TWENTY-EIGHT

The journey to Manchester had taken a little longer than usual as the roadworks on the M6 slowed everything down to a crawl. As Ben finally turned the car into Southall Street, he looked for the nearest car park. For some reason Morgan felt uneasy. She'd never visited a prison before. The journey down had been a flurry of hands-free phone calls between Amy, Ben and the DCI discussing updates.

'We'll have to walk from here. There's no visitor car park.'

She nodded.

'Make sure you have your ID on you or they won't let you in, even though you're with me. They're strict about everything even the dress code. If visitors turn up wearing low-fitting tops or skirts that are too short, they don't let them in. I bet they must be gutted if they travelled a long distance to come see the love of their lives.'

'I suppose it makes sense. I can understand why.' She was glad she was wearing a trouser suit and shirt.

She let Ben do the talking once they reached the entrance. This was a chance for her to learn something new and fascinating. As they were let in through the doors to the security office, she wondered if she should have declined coming, if Amy with her harsh attitude would have been more suited to a prison visit with a convicted killer and rapist. Ben nudged her and she realised he wanted her ID. She lifted the lanyard over her head and placed it on the counter for the guard to study. Then they were being led through a maze of corridors and security gates to a room which didn't look much different to the interview rooms at the station, only it was bigger. The guard pointed to the chairs.

'Take a seat, they've gone to get him.'

Ben sat down. His feet in front of him, he crossed his legs. Morgan sat next to him, bolt upright, her feet flat on the floor and her hands crossed in her lap.

Ben whispered: 'It's okay, relax. There're cameras everywhere and he'll be handcuffed. He can't do anything.'

She looked at him. 'Oh, I'm not afraid of him. It's just, I feel like a fish out of water. I've never seen the inside of a prison, except for on the television.'

He smiled. 'It's a bit of an eye opener, but at least you're seeing it first-hand.'

The heavy, metal door scraped open and they both looked to see Gary Marks being led in. He was flanked either side by a prison guard. His hands were cuffed in front of him. He shuffled towards the chair. After what seemed like for ever he was finally seated. Ben nodded to the guards.

'Gary, I'm not going to mess around. I'm DS Ben Matthews and this is my colleague DC Morgan Brookes. I need to talk to you about an ongoing investigation that you might be able to help us with. Is that okay? Are you going to give us any trouble?'

Gary Marks looked at Ben, then turned his gaze to Morgan, letting it linger on her. He smiled.

'Nope, no trouble from me. I'm a model prisoner. Isn't that right, Jason?'

He turned to the guard nearest to him.

'You are.'

Ben nodded. 'Good, glad to hear it. Do you want to uncuff his hands?'

The guard shook his head, whilst looking at Morgan.

'I'm afraid I can't do that, sir, not with the present company.'

Gary was grinning at Morgan, who looked him directly in the eye, determined not to back down, but the fact that the guard thought he was still a danger to women after all this time didn't go amiss on her.

'Ah, apologies. I didn't think.'

'Don't you worry, boss. They think I'm going to jump right over the table and ravage your very pretty detective. It's been some time since I've had the pleasure of such lovely, attractive company. But despite what you may have heard about me, I'm not a complete animal. So let's cut to the chase. We could spin this out for some time so I get to appreciate my visitors, but I'm due my exercise session in thirty minutes, and my hour-long walk around the yard in the fresh air is the only thing that keeps me sane. I won't miss it no matter how much temptation you offer me.'

Morgan felt a spark of anger ignite inside her chest. Is that why she was here? Bait, to lure him to talk. She carried on watching Marks, too angry to even look Ben's way.

'I wouldn't expect you to, Gary, and Detective Brookes is not here as a bargaining chip. I'll be honest with you, I'm confused. I have a serious crime scene back in Rydal Falls and the forensics came back as a match for your DNA. Can you help me understand how that could have happened?'

Gary, who had been leaning forward, his elbows on the desk, smiled, pushed himself back and crossed his legs. 'You know, I honestly can't. I've been a bit incarcerated, in case you didn't notice. I'd love a chance to revisit my home town. It's been so long since I got to stroll along the riverbank. I'd like to have a wander around for old times' sake.'

His gaze fell back on Morgan. She stared back at him. He leant forward.

'You know, you remind me of someone. Have we met? Did you work here before you decided to become a copper?'

She shook her head.

'Where do you live? Maybe I knew your momma.' He was laughing at his own joke, and she found herself feeling more confused than ever. How could he recognise her?

Ben stepped in. 'Have you been out on day release at any time in the past week?'

'That's a definite no. I haven't been outside of these walls since my trial.'

'Do you have any family in Rydal Falls, a brother, cousin, son?'

'I don't believe so. I had an older sister; she's probably dead by now. I haven't heard from her in years. She doesn't do prison visits.'

'Have you ever given a sample of your DNA to an inmate which they could have planted at a crime scene intentionally?'

Morgan tore her gaze away from Gary to look at Ben; as horrible as his crimes were, she found Gary intriguing. He was charming in a strange way and still a good-looking man for his age.

'That's not my style, boss. I don't go giving away my most prized possession. I'm afraid there's nothing I can tell you. This has nothing to do with me. Have you considered that you might have come here on a bit of a wild-goose chase? That wherever you send your forensic samples could have fucked up?' He smiled at Morgan. 'Pardon my language.'

Ben shook his head. 'I have and I've been assured it's not possible.'

'Well then, boss, you have a bit of a problem and there's nothing I can do to help. It was nice to meet you, even nicer to meet you, Detective Brookes. Your hair is such a pretty colour. It matches your eyes and you really look good in that suit. It's a nice cut, very flattering.

'Guard, I'm done here.'

The guard looked at Ben, who nodded. Gary stood up. Despite his age, he was still an imposing figure. He must use the gym to keep fit because he didn't have the physique of someone who had given up like some lifers did. He shuffled out of the room and didn't look back.

They stood up as another guard came in to take them to the exit.
She asked: 'Did you get the answers you need?'

Ben shook his head.

'That's a shame. I'm surprised he talked to you. He doesn't talk
much; he rarely gets visitors. So to see him interacting like that
with you on the monitor was quite unexpected. I had a fiver bet
he'd clam up and not say a word. He must have really liked you.'

She laughed as she looked at Morgan, who couldn't speak. She
was furious with Ben and wasn't sure what to do about it. She had
the grace to know that this was not the time or the place to make
it known. They signed out and walked back to the car in silence.

*

Once they were inside where no one could hear, Ben asked: 'What's
wrong?'

She turned and stared at him. 'What's wrong?' She shook her
head in disbelief.

'Yes, what's wrong?'

'I was bait. You used me. You took me because you thought he
might open up more to a woman more his victims' age.'

She began to search on her phone, loading Google. Holding
the screen towards him, she showed images of the Riverside
Rapist's victims: one had shoulder-length dark hair; two of them
were redheads. 'I fit his profile, so you used me to get him to talk
and don't insult my intelligence by pretending you didn't. That's
probably why he thinks I look familiar. Until he walked into that
room twenty minutes ago, I'd never set eyes on him.'

'I didn't, not intentionally. I thought this would be good experience for you and that I'd know where you were and that you were
safe whilst I was here, and as for recognising you, that's easy. Your
face was all over the newspapers and news. He may be in prison,
but he's a lifer: they get access to the television and papers. I bet he
lapped it all up: the Potters' and O'Briens' murders, he was winding

you up. Trying to get under your skin. What else does he have to do? It doesn't mean anything.'

Determined not to turn this into a full-blown argument, she put her phone away, crossed her arms and turned to stare out of the window.

'Do you want to go get some lunch?'

'No.'

Ben shrugged. 'Suit yourself, you can wait in the car whilst I do. I'm starving.'

He drove until he found a McDonald's. Parking up he went inside, leaving Morgan sitting there. She had no idea what was going on with her, or why she was so angry with Ben, and she was frustrated that this trip hadn't got them any closer to catching Gabby's killer. Closing her eyes, she began to breathe deeply, calming herself down.

By the time he came back to the car with a huge grease-spotted bag and two coffees, she felt a little better. He got inside and passed her a burger. She wanted to tell him to shove it where the sun didn't shine, but it smelt so good that she took it from him.

'Thanks.'

'You're welcome. I've been thinking, it has to be a family match. I'm pretty sure he had a kid, although they would have only been a baby when it happened; but you know, it might be hereditary.'

'What?'

'Being a sick bastard. We need to be looking into his family and relations. I don't think the lab screwed up at all.'

He phoned Amy and asked her to begin the process of intelligence checking Gary Marks and his associates, relations. When they finished eating, he set off driving.

Morgan couldn't stop thinking about Gary Marks and the horrendous crimes he'd committed. Yet he hadn't come across as a monster; in fact, he'd been quite the opposite.

CHAPTER TWENTY-NINE

As they reached the A591, Morgan retrieved her police radio from her bag and turned it on. Ben was having a hands-free conversation with Darcy about Morgan's text messages.

'Good news is we've triangulated the area where the messages were sent from. Well, it's a three-kilometre area but still. Bad news is the location: it's basically in the middle of the A590, somewhere between Newby Bridge and High Newton.'

'Crap, the houses are spread out far and wide.'

'My best suggestion is that you do an intel check on anyone with a criminal record that might fit the parameters of the case who lives in that area.'

'Yes, that's mine too. Thanks, Darcy.'

'What we need is for him to get sloppy. The phone provider said they'd notify us when the phone connects to a mast. Unfortunately, he's kept it switched off, so he's either got spooked or is biding his time. I'll let you know the minute I get a notification. Good luck.'

Morgan heard the shout from the call handler for an available patrol to attend an immediate response to a suspicious death and turned the volume up on the radio so they could both listen. She waited for the address to be passed to the unit who had responded and felt a dagger of fear slice through her heart.

'Oh my God, that's the block of bedsits where Stan lives.' Grabbing her phone she rang his number; it rang out.

Ben put his foot down and began to drive as fast as he could to get to the scene.

'How many flats are there, Morgan?'

'Three. Stan said there's a drug dealer who lives in the ground-floor flat.'

'Well there's a good chance it's them. Don't panic.'

'I'm not.'

But she knew that she was, and she knew Ben could tell it too by the way the colour had drained from her face and her shaky voice.

The sky had been getting darker all the way back from Manchester, and as they approached the narrow street where Stan lived, large spots of rain began to hit the windscreen. The street outside the flats was full of police cars and an ambulance. All of them had their blue lights flashing, casting an eerie glow on the row of empty shop windows opposite.

Morgan's mouth felt dry and her heart was racing. She just needed to know Stan was okay. Ben slowed the car, and before he'd even parked she was out of the passenger door and racing to the front door. She saw Dan blocking the entrance to the flats. He held out his hands to stop her. She pushed past him; there was no activity outside the ground-floor flat, so she bounded up the stairs. Voices were filtering down from the top, echoing in the narrow space. The undigested burger she'd eaten lay heavy in her stomach. She reached the second floor, which was also empty. That left Stan's. Suddenly, the fight had gone from her and her knees felt weak. Ben was behind her. Reaching out for her, he shook his head.

'Morgan, you don't want to do this.'

She opened her mouth to speak but couldn't find her voice. She forced herself to walk up the remaining flight of stairs to where a paramedic was talking to an officer. They looked at her. She pointed to the front door which was ajar.

Ben's voice behind her addressed the officer.

'What have you got?'

'Elderly male, dead behind the door. He's been there a couple of hours. There's a rope around his neck.'

'Suicide?'

'No, I don't think so.'

Morgan didn't trust herself to speak. More footsteps ran up the staircase and this time it was Dan's voice.

'Morgan, do not go inside that flat, please.'

She turned, both Ben and Dan were watching her and she knew that she should turn around and let them deal with this, but she couldn't. She needed to see this for herself. On automatic pilot, she asked the paramedic and officer standing next to her on the small square of landing: 'Gloves?'

Both of them began to pull gloves from their pockets. The paramedic got his out first, and she took them from him. Tugging on the bright blue gloves, she took a step forward. Ben's voice was louder, behind her.

'Morgan, please. Let me, don't do this, you don't have to do this.'

She couldn't; she could not turn around now and walk away. She owed it to Stan to be the one to identify him. She owed it to Stan to be there for him now like he'd been there for her when her life depended on it. Shaking her head, she squeezed through the narrow gap and let out a sob.

Dan looked at Ben.

'Shit, why didn't you stop her?'

Ben had the authority to have ordered her to leave the scene immediately, but he hadn't. Instead, he shrugged.

'Why didn't you? Neither of us could have stopped her and you know that.'

He followed her inside and saw Stan's lifeless body on the floor, his glazed eyes, staring into the distance and a piece of rope wrapped several times around his neck. Morgan was staring at him. She hadn't touched him, which was good. Ben tenderly took hold of her arm. 'I'm sorry, Morgan, but you need to step outside now. I'll take it from here.'

A barrage of tears was building behind her eyes but she knew she wouldn't cry now, not in front of her colleagues. She shrugged her arm from Ben's grasp, gave one last look at the body of Stan, the man she should have called dad, then turned and went back down the stairs to wait outside in the car.

She was numb from head to toe and cold, so cold. She realised that for the first time in her life she was entirely alone.

CHAPTER THIRTY

Ben phoned Amy. 'Where are you?'

'Grabbing lunch, do you want some?'

'No, I need you at this scene, please. As soon as you can. Did you hear the log get passed over the radio?'

'No, sorry, boss. It's loud in here.'

'It's okay. I'm at Church Street, you can't miss all the police vans. There's been a murder.'

'Another? I'm on my way.'

'Thanks, I owe you. This one is difficult; it's Morgan's dad.'

He heard her gasp. 'Where is she?'

'In the car. She insisted on going in.'

'Christ.'

'Yeah, something like that.'

He walked out of the flats to see Dan bending down at the side of the car, talking to Morgan, and he felt a twinge of something in his chest. *Have a word with yourself, Ben. Stop letting him wind you up, what's the matter with you?* He nodded; the voice of reason was right. What was up with him? They were friends before he'd come along. He shouldn't be surprised to see him comforting her. He crossed to the car. Morgan looked as if she was in shock.

'Dan, can I have a word?'

Dan reached out and squeezed her hand then stood up and came towards him.

'Who was first on scene?'

'Me and Jack. I went in first had a quick look then waited for paramedics. It was pretty obvious he was dead, but you know.'

'Yeah, if Jack stays here, please can you take Morgan back to the station. Get her a cup of tea or something and try to keep her out of the way for a while.'

He nodded and Ben thought he actually looked miserable, which shouldn't have cheered him up but it did.

'It would be even better if you can get her to go back to my house. Tell her to take the rest of the day off.'

The look of surprise on Dan's face made Ben feel even better.

'Why your house?'

'She's stopping with me for a few days.' He didn't go into specifics and he knew he was being childish, but he couldn't help it.

'I'll see what I can do, but I'm not promising. You know what she's like.'

Ben did know.

She was fiery, stubborn, hard-working, motivated and he'd realised in the last ten minutes that he had feelings for her that ran a lot deeper than for most of his colleagues.

'Do what you can, thanks.'

He turned and walked back to the scene. He needed to forget this was Stan and push it to the back of his mind. He turned off the part of his mind that dealt with emotion because they were on limited time to discover as much evidence about this as possible. He didn't want Morgan hearing him talk about her dad as a body or a crime scene. There was no way he could focus if he was trying to make sure he didn't say anything to upset her. As harsh as it was that was the reality.

He watched as Dan got into the plain car and began to do a three-point turn. The car drove past and Morgan didn't give him a second glance. Her eyes were fixed on the road in front. As they left the street, the car which belonged to CID that Amy and Des were in took its place. Amy got out and waved him over as she went to the boot. He nodded in appreciation of the fully stocked box of supplies she'd brought with her. They needed to get dressed properly before going back into the crime scene. Amy ripped open the packet the paper suit was in and whispered: 'Poor Morgan, did you see her face?'

'I know, this whole thing is awful. But we need to focus. Morgan went inside but she didn't touch anything, so we're going to start fresh. CSI are on their way. We'll let them do their thing whilst we try and work out what the hell is going on and why Stan is dead. I don't understand why someone would want to kill him. It's not as if he had anything to steal. Morgan said he told her the bottom floor flat is lived in by a drug dealer. Des can you start knocking on doors? Find out who lives in there. Check if there's any CCTV in the area. Get all the enquiries underway.'

Des who had joined them nodded. 'Yes, boss.' He walked away, leaving them waiting. The CSI van pulled into the street and Wendy got out.

'Bit crowded here, what have we got?'

Ben explained to her. 'The pathologist is on the way; control have already requested they attend.'

'I'll get on then. Is it true that it's Morgan's dad?'

'How did you know?'

'News travels fast in that place, Ben, you should know that. The patrol sergeant was asking if Stan Brookes was related to her before I left.'

'She's on her way back with Dan. I've told him to take her home.'

'Poor kid, she's not having the best time since she joined up, is she? I'm surprised she's still here.'

He shook his head. Wendy disappeared through the front door and he looked at Amy.

'You can't protect her from everything.'

'No, I can't and what do you mean?'

She shrugged. 'People talk; at least if they know, they won't say something stupid when she's around. You know what they're like with their dark humour and inappropriate jokes.'

He sighed. He was itching to get into Stan's flat and take a proper look at the scene. He couldn't do much else for him or Morgan now, except to find out who had done this.

CHAPTER THIRTY-ONE

At Stan's apartment building, Wendy came outside and waved Ben towards her. He followed her up the stairs.

'You can take a look now: everything has been photographed and filmed.'

Ben bent down to take a close look at Stan. His skin had taken on the waxy appearance of the dead and had a yellow tinge to it. Even though he had seen death in many different stages over the span of his career in the police, he reached out his index finger and gently prodded his shoulder. It was hard to the touch, rigid, and he knew the basics, that rigor mortis typically set in around two to six hours after death depending upon the conditions. Stan's eyes were the worst; his eyelids were only partly closed as if he was looking down his nose. The rope around his neck had caused a red groove just below his Adam's apple and there were several scratch marks on the skin.

'Boss, are you okay?'

He glanced up at Amy. It was a simple enough question. He nodded, unable to speak his response.

Wendy came out of the small kitchen. 'Looks like he tried to loosen the rope as it was choking him. Poor bugger, you just can't imagine. I've bagged his hands. Hopefully, there's enough trace evidence underneath his nails to catch the bastard who did this. I mean who does this to a guy his age? It's just wrong.'

Ben stood up. 'Anything obvious in the rest of the flat?'

'No, this is the only way in or out. There's a window over there and a small one in the kitchen, but we're three floors up. There's no way whoever did this climbed in through one of them. They came to the front door.'

'And he opened it. He must have known them. I wouldn't have thought he'd do that unless he recognised them. This is a bit of a rough area and I just don't think given what happened not that long ago with Morgan, or the quality of his neighbours, that he'd open the door if he didn't know the person on the other side. We need a list of his family, friends, and acquaintances.'

'We need to speak to Morgan.'

'We do. I'm not so sure she's going to be able to help out on the friends' part, and I think there's just the two of them, no other family from what I gather.'

'Knock, knock.'

Declan's voice called through the gap in the door.

'Come in. Is it me or do you get here faster every time you're called out?'

'Ah, it's probably because it's you who's requesting my services. I wouldn't turn out this fast for any other DS. So what have we got here?' He squeezed through and looked down at the body.

'Oh, dear me. That's an awful thing to happen at his age. Who on earth would do this? Not a nice way to die at all.'

He placed the heavy case on the floor next to his feet.

Ben shrugged.

'You should know that this is Morgan Brookes's father.'

'Our Morgan Brookes?'

'Yes.'

Declan let out a whistle. 'Christ, what a shame. Does she know?'

'She ran in, but she didn't touch him.'

'Oh dear, bless her. What a terrible shock. Where is she now?'

'Hopefully, being driven home. I sent her away.'

'Wise decision, Ben. Well, there's nothing you can do for the poor guy now. You're going to have to pass him over to me, and

I'll take good care of him. I'll do everything I can for him. What's his name?'

'Stan Brookes.'

Declan crouched down and opened his case. He took his thermometer out.

'Well, Stan, I'm afraid you have me now; at least I'm better looking than Ben. I'll take good care of you, my friend.'

Ben stepped away from the body further back into the living area and loosened his tie. It was too hot in this small flat. Amy walked out onto the landing area, giving Declan room to work.

He spoke to Ben.

'You can wait outside too if you want. Wendy can help me.'

Wendy, who had been dusting the door frame for prints, nodded. 'Yes, no worries.'

Ben wanted to, he wanted to leave and go find Morgan, but couldn't. He had nothing to tell her as of yet and he owed it to her and Stan. 'I'm good, I'll watch. Wendy can still help you.'

Declan nodded and began to examine Stan's body. He was studying the rope around his neck when he said: 'Well, that's a nice little piece of evidence we have here.'

Ben stepped forward. 'What is it?'

Declan plucked something from the collar of Stan's T-shirt with a pair of tweezers. 'Ooh you little beauty. It's a lovely looking eyelash and it's not Stan's.'

'How do you know?'

Dropping the sample into a small evidence bag, he sealed it and wrote on it.

'Stan's eyelashes are grey; this one is black.'

'Bloody brilliant. Is it any good though?'

'Yes, of course it is. The lab can extract DNA from the follicle. Granted it's more difficult than head or pubic hair, but it can be done if there's little other evidence to go on.' Taking another sterile pair of tweezers, he whispered: 'Excuse me, Stan,' as he leant over and plucked one of his eyelashes out.

Ben grimaced as Declan carefully dropped it into an evidence bag. 'It's a control sample.'

'I know, it's just I don't like eyes much.'

Declan looked at him. 'You say the weirdest stuff at times.'

This made Ben smile for the first time since he'd arrived on scene.

When Declan had finished his initial examination he stood up.

'This rope around the neck, it's very similar to Gabrielle Stevens's as is the way he's been strangled with it. There are obvious differences to the scenes, but I don't think I'd be discounting the same killer. Rigor is in full swing. At a guess, he's been dead a minimum of eight hours, quite possibly longer. Which puts time of death early hours of this morning, sometime between four and six. Cause of death is asphyxiation due to ligature strangulation by another individual, and the manner of death is homicide. You can clearly see the marks in the skin made by the rope and the petechial haemorrhages in the inner eyelid. By the position of his body, it looks as if Stan opened the door and turned his back on his killer as he walked into the flat. He trusted this person to follow him in.'

Ben nodded. 'He definitely knew his killer then, but what connection could he have to Gabby Stevens?'

'I'd say so to the first part, but I can't help you with the second.'

'Who would he let into his flat in the early hours of the morning?' Ben felt the hairs on his neck prickle and his skin begin to tingle at the thought that entered his head and he quickly pushed it to the back of his mind, burying it. He was being ridiculous, completely stupid and he wasn't even going to give it another second of headspace.

'Not my job, Ben, that's for you to figure out and I'm pretty sure you will. I'm done here. Happy for Stan to be brought to the mortuary when you've finished.'

'Thanks, Declan.'

'Give my condolences to Morgan. Tell her I'll take good care of him.'

'I will.'

Declan left Ben staring at Stan's body, his head a swirling mess of jumbled thoughts all fighting to surface.

Amy popped her head around the door.

'What now?'

'Station, I need to see the DI. Where is he anyway? He should be here?'

'He's outside talking to the police and crime commissioner who is with him. They left some meeting to come here.'

Ben groaned. 'No way. Amy go tell him I need him and only him up here. This isn't a circus show, it's a crime scene.'

She left him there, alone with Stan and his thoughts.

CHAPTER THIRTY-TWO

Morgan let Dan drive her to Ben's house. She only spoke to give him the address and that had felt as if it was a huge effort. The words had sounded strange. Her voice was much quieter than usual. He stopped outside and opened the driver's door.

'No, it's okay. I'm okay. I don't need you to come in.'

'Let me make you a hot drink; at least let me get you inside and wait until they assign you a FLO.'

She shook her head. 'I need a bit of space, and you can tell Ben or whoever I don't need a family liaison officer, thank you.'

She slammed the door harder than she meant to but she didn't apologise. Instead, she tucked her shaking hands in her pockets to find the spare key Ben had given her. She didn't want to be here either. She wanted to be in her own apartment. Opening the door, she turned to wave at Dan who was staring at her as if she'd gone insane. Before she could change her mind and ask him to come in, she shut the front door; besides, she didn't think Ben would want Dan in his house. Bad enough he was having to babysit her, he'd be so angry if he came home to find Dan sitting in the kitchen drinking his tea.

She kicked off her shoes. Going upstairs, she changed out of her suit into a pair of black leggings and a black T-shirt, pulling her ponytail into a messy bun. She went into the bathroom and scrubbed her hands under the hot water tap, then rinsed her face under the cold. Her green eyes were filled with unshed tears waiting to fall. Today had to have been the most surreal day of her life. From listening to Ben interview the Riverside Rapist in a category A prison in Manchester to coming back home to discover… She closed her eyes and sucked in a huge, gulping breath as an image of Stan's dead body filled her mind. He was dead; she never got to say goodbye to him. Just like she never got to say goodbye to her mum. The past five years she'd had to live with the grief of losing her mum and then Stan as they'd drifted apart. He'd taken to the bottle and all but abandoned her and she'd blamed him for everything, hating him but not as much as he'd hated himself. She knew that now; they'd spoken about it and had just repaired their fractured relationship and now he was gone. She hadn't got to tell him she was proud of him for trying to sort out his life; she hadn't told him that she loved him flaws and all or that she forgave him, because she had.

Stan would be the first to admit to her that he'd messed up, but he'd tried. Since the night he saved her life, he'd done nothing but try, and where was she when he'd needed her? She hadn't been there to save him, too selfish hiding out here at Ben's house because she hadn't wanted to be alone. If she'd gone to stop with Stan instead this wouldn't have happened. The room began to spin and go fuzzy. She barely made it to the room that was her temporary bedroom before collapsing onto the bed.

Curling up into a ball, she hugged a pillow to her chest. All she'd ever wanted was a normal family life. It wasn't much to ask. Whilst her friends were dressing up trying to get into night clubs and pubs or get served at the corner shop for bottles of anything that would get them drunk, she had been mourning the loss of her mum. She did eventually try the cheap vodka and peach schnapps that seemed to be the drink of choice amongst her friends, if only to blot out the horror, but the hangovers weren't worth it. All she did was get ridiculously drunk and cry on a park bench about how shit her life was whilst everyone else was snogging. Then Stan would come home drunker than her and she couldn't stand it. Instead, she'd withdrawn from her friends and even more so from Stan.

That was when her teenage obsession with *Mean Girls* and Lindsay Lohan ended, and she'd come across a book called *The Silence of the Lambs* which had then sent her on an Internet search to find documentaries about serial killers on YouTube and been hooked. Fascinated yet horrified that people could actually do this to other people, she'd then begun to watch and read about the various killers that had been caught and made the headlines. One in particular caught her attention: Israel Keyes had been caught and charged with the abduction and murder of Samantha Koenig. It had struck a chord on a deep level with Morgan; eighteen-year-old Samantha had been abducted from the coffee kiosk where she worked. Morgan worked every weekend at a small coffee shop; sometimes she'd be left alone if it was quiet. The huge difference was she lived in the quiet Lakeland town of Rydal Falls; Samantha lived in Alaska and everyone knew the US was full of serial killers. The pictures of Samantha and their similar lives had been what propelled her to want to become a detective.

Now here she was, twenty-three and living the dream she'd spent so long thinking about. Only this dream was more like a nightmare. One she couldn't escape from. What did she do now and where did she go from here? Was the job worth the heartache it had brought to her so far? Lying on her back she thought about the Potter family and the O'Briens, murdered in the same house forty-five years apart. She had worked hard and helped to bring both families justice, and she realised that although the fire inside her chest had been dampened there was still a tiny spark there. She did want to carry on; she just wished she knew how to process the grief and guilt that was threatening to take her down into an abyss that she might never come back from.

CHAPTER THIRTY-THREE

Ben didn't leave the scene until Stan's body had been removed. He owed it to both Stan and Morgan to be here. As the private ambulance was driven away by the duty undertakers to take Stan to the mortuary, he sighed. There was a lot to do. He now had two investigations running and he needed someone to take over from Morgan. He was going to have to ask Dan. There was no way he could sideline him again; it would cause more trouble than it was worth. Maybe now he seemed to have reconciled his friendship with Morgan, he would be easier to work with, especially as he would need him to work Stan's investigation. Amy, Des and he would be helping, but he still had Gabby Stevens's killer to find and, if Declan was right, the link that connected both victims to their killer.

Back at the station, he was sitting at his desk when he heard a voice.

'You look like you need a stiff drink.'

'A bottle of whisky wouldn't be enough to drown my sorrows and blot out this mess, Amy.'

'I think I need one too. Where's Morgan?'

Before he could answer, Dan walked into the office.

Ben stood up.

'Dan, can I have a word?'

Amy grabbed the empty coffee mug off Ben's desk and left them to it.

'How is she?'

'Pretty shit. She wouldn't let me go in your house with her and said she does not need an FLO.'

'I didn't think she would. We can do that. Listen, I know things haven't been easy between us but I'm going to need someone to fill Morgan's place. I can't run two major murder investigations without her and I don't expect her to come to work. Is there any chance you can come up here and help out?'

Dan smiled. 'Yeah, it's pretty rubbish the circumstances but yes, I'd love to. I want to help.'

'Good, I'll clear it with your sergeant.'

*

An hour later, Ben had cleared Dan's relocation to his department and had requested everyone attend a briefing in the blue room. He watched them file in and take a seat. It felt strange not seeing Morgan rush in last like she usually did. He had photos of the crime scene up on the large screen.

'Thank you all for joining me. This is a difficult one. You are probably all aware by now that the body found at flat 13C, Church Street is that of one Stanley Brookes, who also happens to be Morgan's father.'

Heads were nodding and low murmurs went around the room.

'The pathologist confirmed it was homicide by ligature strangulation; whoever killed Stan knew him. Of this we are certain. He opened the door and turned his back on his killer to lead them into his flat. There is also a striking similarity between the rope and manner of death to Gabby Stevens's murder. At this moment, we can't rule out the same killer. The rope is being sent off for comparison to the rope used to bind Gabby. So top list of priorities is house-to-house and CCTV enquiries. I want every house, flat and shop knocked on. I don't care if the shops are empty, if you can see a camera then find out who owns the shop and go speak to them. There's a taxi rank further down the street. They have

CCTV. Ask them to check with any of their drivers if they have dashcam footage. See if they were parked up, picked up or dropped anyone off at the flats. Time of death is estimated between four and six a.m., so focus on those times. I want our resident drug dealer from flat A spoken to; bring her in if she's uncooperative. I want to know who called at her address last night, so we can speak to them. They may be potential witnesses and not know anything about it.'

Tom nodded in agreement with all of Ben's comments. 'What about Morgan? Someone needs to go speak to her and get a statement, list of his friends, associates et cetera.'

Ben replied. 'I will do that. Amy will take the statement.'

'Do you think that's a good idea?'

'What's wrong with it?'

'Well, she's a member of our team. We work with her. We're all probably a little bit too close to her for this to be done ethically. I think it might be better to bring someone in from Barrow or HQ to deal with Morgan.'

Ben had to stop his jaw from dropping to his chest. He felt completely floored and betrayed by what Tom had just suggested. Was he accusing him of not being professional? He didn't say this in front of a room full of his team and management.

'Whatever you think, sir.'

'It's the right thing to do. We don't want any accusations further down the line of not carrying out this investigation in a professional manner. The last thing we all want is for someone to involve PSD and have to suffer one of their nasty internal investigations.'

Ben had never felt so angry in his life. He knew Tom was right. This could be construed the wrong way, but Morgan was one of them. She hadn't done anything wrong. She needed to know her team had her back and gave a shit. What was she going to think when some stranger from another station turned up to start questioning her? And where did that leave Gabby Stevens's murder? They were hoping the killer was going to make contact with Morgan so they could trace his phone and locate him. He looked down at the large notebook in front of him. Picking it up, he stood up.

'Right, well. If you can get on with the tasks you've been given for now.'

Tom was watching him. 'What about a search team?'

'Erm, we have the murder weapon. It was still around Stan's neck when we found him. I don't think…'

'Send them in anyway. For all we know, Stan could have been a master criminal with a drug stash the county lines gangs would be proud of. We have no motive up to now. It ticks another box that we checked every investigative avenue.'

Tom's phone rang and he excused himself, leaving the room. Ben watched him go. He needed fresh air. He felt as if he was suffocating. He followed him, wondering if he should argue about bringing someone in to speak to Morgan and realised he couldn't because Tom was right. He also knew he needed to see Morgan and at least explain what was happening in person.

As he walked out of the station he heard Amy shouting to him.

'Ben, where are you going? Do you need me to come with you?'

'No, I'll be back soon. Hold the fort.'

He was going home.

CHAPTER THIRTY-FOUR

Morgan woke in a daze as the front door slammed downstairs.

'Morgan?' Ben's voice shouted in the hallway.

'Upstairs.' Her voice came out as a croak.

His footsteps as he ran up the steps echoed and she sat up on the bed. Even though she was fully dressed she felt awkward.

'Sorry, did I wake you?'

'I drifted off.'

'Where do I start?'

'What do you mean?'

Ben no longer had a tie around his neck, the top three buttons on his shirt were undone and he looked visibly upset. He came and sat down on the bed next to her.

'Start at the point where I was sent home.'

'I had to; you know that.'

She nodded.

'This is really difficult for me too.'

She studied his face and realised if she felt like a mess, Ben looked as if he'd aged five years since this morning. She smiled. 'Sorry, I know it is.'

'Well, I'm so sorry to say that Declan confirmed Stan was murdered; time of death between four and six this morning.'

Morgan bowed her head and whispered: 'I was awake, you know I'm always awake at that time. Why didn't I feel something or realise something was wrong?'

'Unless you're a psychic you're not supposed to. I never knew when Cindy died. I was at work; I didn't feel a wave of sadness or get a cold shiver. Her face didn't magically appear in front of me saying goodbye. That stuff happens in the movies or in books, not in real life.'

'I should have been there. If I'd gone to stop with Stan instead of coming here, I could have stopped this from happening.'

'How? How could you have stopped this, Morgan? For a start there's barely room for Stan in that tiny flat, never mind you. If you had been there then we might be dealing with two bodies, and I couldn't… I wouldn't know what to do if that had been the case.'

She sensed the frustration in his voice but pushed it away. 'I suppose you want a statement?'

He nodded. 'Yes, but I can't take it.'

'What do you mean?'

'Tom insisted someone from another station deals with you. He said it's too personal for us to be professional about.'

She felt hot tears prick at the corner of her eyes and lifted her finger to wipe them away. A burning sensation in her chest and stomach made her realise she was getting angry.

'What's that supposed to mean? Am I under suspicion? Does he think I killed Stan?'

Ben reached out for her hand and she shrugged him away. Standing up, she paced towards the window.

'Don't be ridiculous. No one thinks that. What motive would you have? It doesn't make any sense.'

Turning she looked at him. 'Well, for a start I'm always awake at that time in the morning. I've had a rocky relationship with him over the past five years.'

'But you were turning things around. I saw how proud you were of him. And how proud he was of you.'

Her head shook from side to side. 'Stan has no enemies that I'm aware of. He has no money, nothing of value to steal. He may have been an alcoholic but he never touched drugs. He has very few friends that I know of, probably a few old drinking buddies around his age. So where does that leave me?'

Ben stood up. 'A grieving daughter. Tom asked me to tell you that you have to take some time off; he's given you compassionate leave.'

'Fine, but I'd rather be in work doing something useful, and it stinks that you aren't allowed to discuss it with me or take my statement.' She began to grab what few belongings she had, stuffing them into her overnight bag.

'What are you doing?'

'I think it's pretty obvious. You might not think I have anything to do with this, but Tom does. If you can't take my statement then I can't be here. It looks odd and it puts you in a difficult situation.'

The rage was so hot inside her chest, she felt as if she was going to explode into a ball of flames.

'I don't want you to go, Morgan. What about the messages from Gabby Stevens's killer?'

'What about them? I don't care, Ben. I have to go home. I can't stay here; it's too difficult for the both of us. I like being on my own. I'll be fine. The mood I'm in, if he knocks on my door, I'll rip his bloody head off. Tell them to come to my apartment to interview me or take a statement, whatever it is. I'll be there; I have nowhere else to go and nothing to hide from anyone.'

The anguished look in his eyes shook her to the core, but she couldn't stay here. She needed to go home where she could think straight. He might not realise it but she wouldn't let Ben get himself into any trouble because of her.

Throwing the bag over her arm, she ran down the stairs and let herself out of the front door, turning around to place the spare key on the small hall table. She didn't slam the door. She was furious but not with Ben, just with everyone else.

*

She reached Singleton Park Road and the entrance to the large, converted house where her apartment was. Despite what had happened in the past, she did love it here. Grabbing her bag, she let herself in and threw it on the floor in the hall. It was good to be back in her own space; it was hers and she could walk around here naked if she wanted without worrying about Ben walking in on her. A wave of sadness so strong hit her that she felt a crushing sensation in her chest and collapsed on wobbly legs onto her armchair. As she stared out at the gardens, she took in deep breaths to calm her mind. She hadn't done anything wrong. What did it matter who came and took her statement? She hadn't murdered Stan. The only thing she was guilty of was being a rubbish daughter and as far as she knew that wasn't an arrestable offence.

CHAPTER THIRTY-FIVE

He felt euphoric, there was no other word for it. Everything was working out wonderfully. The police were chasing their tails whilst he was running rings around them in ways even he hadn't thought was possible. It was all coming together nicely, and it gave him a little breathing room. He was still torn: he liked the woman from the college but he was no fool and appreciated the danger this one posed. He asked himself two questions: was it worth it and did he want to risk it? As he lathered the foam all over his face, he stared at himself in the bathroom mirror. Yes, she was worth it, but no, he was unsure about the risk. It depended upon how the policewoman handled her father's sudden demise and what risks she herself would be willing to take to catch him. Would this throw her so far over the edge there would be no coming back from it? Another question, so many questions, his mind was super busy. He shaved carefully, then rinsed his face, running his hand over his chin and cheeks, making sure they were smooth. Appearances were everything: scruffy wasn't his style. He enjoyed wearing expensive clothes that fit well; looking good made him happy. Almost as happy as the last week when all his long thought-out plans had come to fruition; this was going to be hard to beat. Especially as the police had no idea what was going on. He'd given them a lot more credit than they deserved. He thought about G's phone in the lead-lined box under the seat in his car. It was tempting to message: maybe he could send his condolences, or was he being far too assertive for his own good?

He wasn't worried about the CCTV from the pub. All it showed was him having a friendly chat with a man he barely knew whilst ordering a pint. There was no crime against that. He'd joined his friends and spent a couple of hours playing pool. By the time he left, the man had been long gone, leaving his untouched drinks on the bar. That took some bottle. He had no idea how long Stan had been sitting staring at those glasses but he hadn't taken a sip from them.

He absent-mindedly picked up the coin he'd taken from Stan's bedside table. He knew a little about coin collecting. This was quite a rare one, and he wondered if Stan had known that. He tucked it into his trouser pocket – it was his now. A little good luck medallion. If he didn't get a move on he was going to be late. He didn't want to miss E coming out of class. He had to time this exactly right to get the most from it.

CHAPTER THIRTY-SIX

The doorbell rang and Morgan stood up. She'd waited hours for this and wanted it over and done with. Slipping her feet into the battered pink Converse she kept by the front door for going outside, she went to open the communal door. She didn't recognise the man and woman standing in front of her, but she did recognise the bright blue lanyards with Cumbria Constabulary printed across them.

'Morgan Brookes?'

She nodded.

'I'm DS Shannon Watts and this is DC Tim Burdon, can we come in?'

She opened the door and let them follow her into her apartment; there were three plastic wrapped bar stools at the breakfast bar and she had purposely moved one to the opposite side. She pointed to the blush pink and gold chairs she'd treated herself to from TK Maxx on payday.

'Take a seat. Would you like a drink?'

They shook their heads.

'No, thank you. Maybe you should make yourself a tea. I'm sure you'll be aware that we will be handling the investigation into your father's murder.'

She sat down. She drank coffee at work and when she needed a clear head. She didn't want a cup of tea. Ben or Amy would have known this. It was so unfair that she had to deal with two complete strangers. She wanted this to be over with and for her to be back at work, where she could keep busy and help to find who did this to Stan.

'I'm good, thanks and yes, I understand.'

'We're both terribly sorry for your loss. It must have been an awful shock for you.' Tim's voice was soft and soothing, and she liked him instantly.

'It is, it was.'

'We know how hard this is for you. Are you sure you don't want someone here with you? What about a friend or colleague, someone you trust? It can't be nice for you being alone with all this going on.'

Dare she tell them her friends were her colleagues? She didn't have a particular friend she could call upon in a time of need. She was well aware that she would be under suspicion for Stan's murder: how could she not be? They always looked to close family members and friends first. She didn't want them to think she was strange and a loner; it would only add more fuel to their fire. She could see their profile of the killer on the whiteboard in their office: single, mid-twenties, bit of a loner, no real friends, driven, selfish, killer, angry daughter.

'She's on her way but lives in Lancaster.' The little white lie left her lips without a second thought.

'Good, that's great. You should have some company. There's a lot to take in. Should we cut to the chase, ask our questions and then get your statement down?' Shannon asked, and Morgan liked that. She appreciated it.

'Yes, please.'

'There's a lot going on here. It's been a busy week for you. I'll tell you what we know and you can fill in the blanks.'

Morgan wondered if Ben had told them where she spent last night. She didn't want to bring him in to this on a personal level.

'Ben Matthews said that you spent the night at his house, in the spare room, because he was worried for your safety after you received a number of text messages from Gabby Stevens's phone, a recent murder victim.'

'I did; it was Amy's idea. DC Amy Smith. I didn't want to put him to any trouble, but they thought it was best.'

Tim was reading something off a notepad. 'I'm inclined to agree. Why have you come back here then on your own? Do you think this is the safest place for you to be at the moment, Morgan?'

'I didn't want to be a nuisance and, anyway, I wanted to be here. It was nice of him to offer but you know you get used to sleeping in your own bed, and I prefer to cry alone.'

'Basically, we need to know what your relationship with Stan was like, who his friends were, that kind of thing. You know the score. So do you want to talk us through your relationship and how things were with your father? We'll take notes.'

Shannon smiled at her. 'This must be so awful for you. I can't imagine how you're feeling.'

Morgan inhaled and closed her eyes. 'The last six weeks, Stan and I had been getting on great. He was really trying to clean himself up. He'd even been attending AA meetings at the community centre; he was like a different man.'

'What about before then?'

'We didn't have a good relationship, not since my mum died, five years ago. We drifted apart; Stan buried his grief in the bottle. I didn't like him much, or I should say I didn't like who he'd become, but we still spoke on the odd occasion we saw each other. I didn't hate him so much that I'd want to strangle him, if that's what you want to know.'

It was Tim who looked up from his notepad. 'We're not here to accuse you of killing him, Morgan, we just need the facts. Do you know who his friends were? Who his AA sponsor was, that kind of thing?'

She shook her head. 'No, I don't. Like I say, we've only been on proper speaking terms for six weeks. His mobile should have contact details of anyone he might be friends with. I don't think he used a computer; he didn't use social media. I know he used to drink in The Golden Ball; they might be able to help you with his friends. Apart from that, I don't think I can tell you much else about his life.'

'That's the pub Gabby Stevens worked in, right? Do you think that she and Stan could have had some connection? What about these messages that you received from Gabby Stevens's missing phone? Do you know why her killer would want to contact you?'

'No, I don't and I can't imagine how Stan could have a connection to Gabby. I mean he will have known who she was, if she served him regularly in the pub, but that's it. He's never mentioned her to me. Whoever it is sent four messages, and I told the team about them all. The high-tech unit have cloned my phone and downloaded all the evidence. I haven't had any further messages.'

'Why do you think that is?'

She shrugged. 'Maybe they realised how risky they were being and got spooked.'

Shannon was looking at Morgan. 'Or maybe they knew your phone had been cloned?'

'How would they know that? Unless they worked in the station, and I don't think so.'

'No, sorry. I'm thinking out loud. That's not very likely, is it?'

Morgan didn't like the way Shannon was looking at her, as if she were trying to capture an expression that might betray what she was really thinking.

'If they had even the slightest awareness of the workings of criminal investigations, they would know that the phone would be used as evidence to try and trace them. Are you going to take a statement about what happened at Stan's flat after we got called there? Or are you here just to ask about Gabby Stevens?'

Tim smiled. 'We have one from your supervisor, Ben, who was with you when the call came in, about what happened at the scene. Is there anything different you would have to add to it?'

'I don't know what he said so I couldn't say. This is my version of events: I heard the address being passed to officers over the radio and recognised it as the flats where Stan lived. Ben drove there; we were on our way back from interviewing a prisoner in Manchester. Officers were already on scene when we arrived; I ran into the flats hoping it was one of the other occupants. I didn't want it to be Stan, but I had this awful feeling in my stomach. As I ran upstairs, I knew it was. I squeezed through the gap in the door and saw him lying there.' She paused, gulping the air bubble away that was caught in the back of her throat. 'I looked at his body. I knew he was clearly dead and had been for some time. It was pretty obvious to even a non-medical person, and the paramedic at the scene had already called it anyway. Ben came in behind me and I left.

'I didn't touch anything, even though I wanted to cradle him in my arms. I was professional for what it's worth. Dan Hunt, one of the first officers on the scene, drove me to Ben's house. I stayed a couple of hours then decided to come here, and now you're here taking my statement. That is how my day went.'

Shannon stood up. 'Thank you, Morgan, that's very helpful. We'll let you get on and we'll be in touch if we have any further questions. The DCI asked us to tell you he doesn't expect you to come in to work. He's arranged for you to take some dependant's leave.'

She watched as Tim finished writing in his pocket notebook then closed it. Tucking the pen in his pocket, he stood up. 'We'll see ourselves out, take care. And we're so sorry for your loss.'

And then they were gone. Morgan knew they were only doing what they had to. How many times had she sat and asked people similar questions, not realising the devastating effect they had on someone until she was the one being questioned? Her hands were shaking. She waited until she heard the car doors slam and the engine start before she got off her stool. She walked to the front door, locked it, and put the safety chain on.

Taking a mug out of the kitchen cupboard, she made herself a coffee and booted up her laptop. Waiting for it to load, she sipped the warm drink and clasped the chain around her neck in her fingers. It was the last present she'd received from her mum and her most treasured possession. Something was going on; she couldn't decide what, but it had got Stan killed. Why had a killer chosen him? She thought about the last message she'd had from Stan. What had he been going to tell her and was it that information that got him killed?

Isaac had told her she needed answers to questions and now she had no one left to ask. The only thing which might help could be the Internet.

CHAPTER THIRTY-SEVEN

He couldn't have timed it better if he'd tried. She came running out of the building, her leather satchel held above her head to protect her pretty blonde hair from the rain. Her head bent low, she wasn't looking where she was going. He got out of his car, copying her, and put his head down then waited for her to bump straight into him. He held himself stiff, ready for the impact as she bounced off him, landing on the floor in a heap.

'Oh my goodness. I'm so sorry. I wasn't watching where I was going.' He stooped, holding out his hand to her, which she took as he tugged her to her feet. This could either go two ways: she'd be angry with him or laugh. She shook her head; her perfect pale cheeks tinged with circles of pink and she began to laugh.

'I'm so sorry. That was my fault. I wasn't looking at all. I didn't want to get my hair wet.'

He picked up her sodden satchel from the puddle it landed in, holding it out towards her. The flimsy skirt she was wearing now had a large damp patch on her bottom and he could see her pretty pink, flowery knickers.

'I'm afraid it's a bit late for that.'

He pointed to the back of her skirt, and she let out a squeal, her hands slapping against it to try and shield her modesty.

'Oh lord, sorry, I have to go.' She clicked the car key fob, and the Mini's lights turned on as she got into the car and started the engine. He gave her a moment then knocked on the window. She looked at him quizzically, and he waved her bag at her. Putting down the window, she laughed.

'Thank you, I'm such an airhead at times.'

He smiled. 'Anytime.'

She drove away, but as she reached the exit, she turned for one last look at him and waved. He waved back. He was a dripping mess and his suit was soaked but that had been worth it. She knew who he was, what he looked like and he didn't think she would forget him so soon. When it was time, she would open the door to him, a bit surprised that he was there, but without a doubt she'd open it, and he would take it from there.

He drove home happier than he'd been in a long time. He was on a roll and liked it. No one had a clue who he was or what the nature of this all was, but he did. It was as clear in his head now if not clearer than the day he'd conceived the idea. It was all coming together nicely. His father would be proud of him, of that he was one hundred per cent sure.

CHAPTER THIRTY-EIGHT

Morgan woke herself up thrashing around. Her eyes opened, and she thought she'd heard herself screaming in her dream. This time she remembered it; the woman with red hair had been covered in blood, so much blood. As she lay there shivering, she had been able to smell the acrid, earthy smell that blood carried in the air and she was terrified: it had been so real. Crawling out of bed, she'd made it to the shower, her heart racing and her body covered in a fine film of sweat. Standing under the spray, she let it wash away the bad dreams. She had fallen asleep last night before doing much research, so she went back to her computer now, wide awake and feeling as refreshed as was possible on the broken sleep she'd had.

She opened the page she was last on. The only thing about her family on the Internet were the recent articles about the Potters' deaths and also some short pieces about her mum's death and the inquest. More awake than last night, she took her time to read through the full articles instead of skimming through them. An article in the *Cumbrian News* stated that Sylvia Brookes left behind her husband and adoptive daughter. Morgan sucked in her breath. Adoptive daughter? She read the words again, even more slowly in case she'd read them wrong. But she hadn't. What did this mean? Surely it was an error. It had been written by a reporter she'd never heard of and that paper had a reputation for getting almost every story it printed wrong. She sat back, staring at the photo of her mum, an uneasy feeling making her empty stomach churn. All this time, if it was true, surely Stan would have told her or she'd have known about it.

She made herself some toast and poured a glass of orange juice. Her stomach felt like a mass of knots but she needed to eat something. Sitting back down at the breakfast bar, she nibbled her toast, staring at the black screen which had timed out.

Yet the more she thought about it, the heavier her heart felt. If she had been adopted, it would explain a lot, like the way Stan went off the rails after her mum's suicide. He'd admitted he never wanted her; he'd told her it was all Sylvia who was desperate for a baby and he'd gone along with it to make her happy. Christ, she was alone with no living family that she knew of and now she didn't even know who the hell she was. There was only one way to find out more.

She dried her hair then piled it into a ponytail and was dressed in minutes. She looked at the clock on the bedroom wall: it wasn't even five a.m. If she went to work now, she should be able to slip in and go upstairs to the office unnoticed. She could check the intelligence system for her family. Surely there would be something on there from her mum's suicide. There might not be much, but there could be something in a vulnerable child or adult report that mentioned her. She knew this was an absolute no: looking into the intelligence system for personal use was against the rules and she would probably end up suspended if they found out that she had, but what option did she have? She had to know what was going on and she'd been told to take time off because of Stan. She hadn't been ordered to leave or been suspended, at least not yet. Hopefully, the night shift wouldn't even notice her or think anything of it, as she often went in to work really early.

*

Parking on the main road, she got out of her car and walked the short distance to the police station, not wanting to drive through the secure gates and be captured on camera that way. Keeping her head down, she briskly walked to the side entrance and pressed her key fob against the security system. For a fleeting moment she wondered if it had been disabled, but the red light turned green and the gate clicked. She pushed it open and scurried through it to the back door the office staff favoured. Morgan felt like an intruder, as if she was about to commit the crime of the century, which was stupid. This was her place of work; she was doing this to find out if there was a connection between Stan and Gabby Stevens. There had to be one, somehow.

She made it up the stairs and into the CID office without passing another person. The automatic lights came on in the office and she looked around at the pale grey walls. They matched her mood. Her eyes momentarily landed on the whiteboard, Stan's dead face stared back at her and she looked away, pushing the grief that was threatening to surge out back down into the bottom of her chest. She went to her desk, sat down, and logged on to the computer. Deftly typing in her passwords, the screen she needed appeared as she accessed the intelligence system where all the records were kept. She typed 'Sylvia Brookes' into the search bar, her finger hovering over the enter button. Once she did this there was no going back; she could get in trouble.

You're already in trouble, Morgan, they think you had something to do with Stan's murder and if they connect him to Gabby, for whatever reason, they're going to come after you for that too.

She hit the enter key. A page loaded with her mum's name, but no photograph. There were various pieces of intelligence; police had attended a couple of arguments between her and Stan that she didn't recall. She clicked on one of the log numbers and saw it was a non-violent domestic. She read the comments and was horrified to see that the argument had been about her. She had only recently been placed with the family and it was causing problems between Sylvia and Stan. So it was true. She was adopted.

She felt stunned; not once had it even crossed her mind when she'd been growing up. There was the name and phone number of a social worker who was the point of contact between them and social services. Dazed, she scribbled the name and number down on a yellow Post-it note and tucked it into her pocket. She clicked off the computer. She had to get out of here and she had to find that social worker. She doubted she was still working but she had a name: Angela Hardy.

Opening the desk drawer, she saw the gift bag from Dan. Picking it up, she undid the bow and removed the small white box. Taking the earrings out of the box, she put them into her ears and whispered – *I need a guardian angel more than ever. Mum, what happened? Why couldn't you tell me who I was and why my adoption was a big secret? I need to know who I am. It would never have stopped me loving you.*

Dropping the bag and box into the wastepaper bin by the side of her desk, she stood up, grabbed a tissue off Amy's desk and wiped her eyes. She had to get out of here. As soon as it was a reasonable hour, she'd try and contact the social worker.

*

She left the station as she found it: empty. Once she was back in her car, she drove home. There was nothing else she could do now except try and track down Angela Hardy. She prayed there would be some mention of her somewhere on Facebook. Older people enjoyed keeping up with their family and friends on there: she was bound to be retired or near retirement age. Her heart raced the entire time until she reached the gates to her apartment. She didn't think about Ben's face if he found out what she'd done. She didn't want to betray him or his loyalty, but there was no way she was sitting around whilst everyone did their best to betray her. She wondered what Isaac would make of this. He'd told her to write down everything she could remember about her dreams as soon as she woke up, and today's had been an eye opener. Snatches of the past were now coming together. She had been adopted, why?

The woman with the red hair and same colour eyes as her – she was sure that was her birth mum. And the blood? She could only guess she must have died horrifically or been killed. Everything was interlinked somehow. If only she could sort it out into order.

Slamming her front door behind her, she kicked off her shoes. Thank goodness for Google. How did the police or the rest of the world get by before? It didn't bear thinking about. Everything must have taken for ever to find out. She typed the name 'Angela Hardy' into Facebook and a list of them came up; she was looking for any who lived in this area. The top two were both local: Windermere and Barrow. She clicked on the Windermere one first. She imagined that's the kind of place a retired social worker would want to live. The image of an older woman with cropped grey hair and a happy smiling face peered back at her. Her profile was private, so there was limited information she could read about her, but Morgan would have bet that it was her. It was almost nine. She already had the phone number for the social care officers in her phone so she rang it, praying someone else was an early bird like her and already at work.

'Good morning, Child Services.'

'Good morning, I wonder if you can help me? I'm Detective Constable Morgan Brookes and I'm trying to get in touch with an Angela Hardy. It's possible she's retired.'

'She is the lucky thing, retired six months ago. Thea Dexter has taken over all of Angela's ongoing cases. I can give you her number. I don't think she's in work today though, is it urgent?'

'I'm afraid I need to speak to Angela. It's about an old case she dealt with in 1999.'

'Blimey, that's old. Knowing Angela, she probably won't remember much herself.'

'Do you have a contact number for her? It's really important.'

'Can I ask what it's about?'

Morgan bit her lip. She wanted to scream down the phone *just give me the bloody number*. Instead, she forced herself to smile. 'It's regarding a very serious incident. I'm afraid I'm not at liberty to say just yet or I would.'

'Oh, yes. Sorry, I'm being nosey. I suppose I can give you her phone number.'

'Thank you, that's great and such a big help.'

She scribbled the mobile number down. 'Thank you, I really appreciate this. You wouldn't have an address for her? I need to speak to her as soon as possible and she may not answer the phone to an unknown number.' Morgan lowered her voice as if trying to be discreet in a busy police station. She knew she had to give her something more in exchange for the information she needed. 'I can tell you it's to do with a murder investigation.'

She could tell by the gasp the woman was impressed. She whispered back: 'Oh no, not that lovely girl. That's awful. It turned my blood cold when I heard about it. I don't know what number, but she lives in a cottage on Brantfell Road. You can tell which one it is: she's recently had a new front door on it.'

Morgan rolled her eyes; it was better than nothing but not particularly helpful. How was she supposed to know which was a new front door?

The woman laughed. 'Sorry, I meant to say it's the only one with a pink door. It's very quirky and very Angela.'

'Thank you so much. You have no idea how helpful you've been.'

She ended the call. If she was knee-deep in trouble at work, this wasn't going to make much difference when they hauled her in.

CHAPTER THIRTY-NINE

Ben burnt his toast and managed to spill the mug of tea he'd made all over the kitchen worktop. He hadn't slept properly; his reflection in the mirror this morning confirmed it. Tired didn't cut it, neither did stressed or frustrated beyond belief. Mopping up the tea with the only clean tea towel he had, he couldn't stop thinking about Morgan. He'd texted her late last night when he got home to see if she needed anything. She'd read his message but hadn't replied, which had hurt more than he wanted to admit to himself. He wanted her to know he was there for her and that she didn't have to face all of this on her own. He was worried about her; she had a reckless streak and he didn't want her to put herself in any danger because she was too stubborn to accept his help or friendship. The two detectives sent through from Barrow had seemed efficient, if not the friendliest of people. They'd said very little to him about it though; instead, they'd reported back to Tom, which had made him angry. His phone rang and he saw Declan's name.

'Morning, what's up?'

'It's almost eight, some of us have been up since the crack of dawn working. Are you in the station?'

'No. I'm not at work yet. I was going to speak to Gabby Stevens's college tutor. I'm at home making a mess of my breakfast.'

'Good, we need to talk.'

'We are talking.'

'No, I need to see you in person. Can you come here? I'd come to you, but I have a post-mortem in ninety minutes.'

'I'm on my way.'

'Good, text me when you're here. I'll come meet you.'

The line went dead, and he wondered what was so sensitive that he couldn't tell him over the phone. The heaviness in his stomach that had seemed to become a permanent fixture felt worse than ever.

Ben arrived at the hospital in record time. Parking his car took longer, but he managed to squeeze into a tight spot and hoped whoever was parked either side of him could manoeuvre. He called Declan.

'That was quick, I'll meet you at the WRVS tea station in the outpatients' department.'

Ben walked along the street, feeling as if he'd stepped into some Jack Reacher novel. Why was everything so cloak and dagger? The churning in his stomach hadn't subsided and he didn't think that whatever Declan was about to tell him was going to make it disappear. He found the outpatients' building and walked through the sliding doors. Following his nose, he could smell the coffee before he saw the small café area. Declan was already at the counter; he nodded at Ben. Paid for the two coffees, then said: 'Let's go outside.'

'It's pretty cold out there.'

'I know, but I don't want to talk about it here.'

He followed Declan out and they walked a short distance to where there was a low wall. Declan looked around and, satisfied there wasn't anyone in hearing distance, he sat down. Ben sat next to him.

Declan held out the paper coffee cup. 'Just a bog-standard cappuccino.'

Ben took it and pursed his lips, sipping from the small hole in the lid. 'Thanks. So what's all this top-secret stuff about? It's a bit unnerving. I gather this is something to do with work?'

'Look, we've been friends a long time and I have the utmost respect for you as a highly qualified detective. You're excellent at your job; the results you achieve speak for themselves.'

'And?'

'I fast-tracked the eyelash from the crime scene yesterday. I have a friend who works in the lab at Chorley. We sometimes go out for a drink, see each other, you know; he's a great guy and I really like him.'

'That's brilliant, I'm pleased for you, but it's no secret to me that you're gay, Declan. I don't care who you date as long as you're happy.'

Declan had taken a sip of his coffee and he snorted, spraying coffee all over himself.

'Christ, Ben, you idiot. I haven't dragged you here to tell you that. I'm getting to it.' He laughed and Ben joined in and it felt good. It also took a while for Declan to compose himself. Finally, he did.

'This is where it gets serious. He extracted the DNA from the eyelash follicle then ran it through NDNAD, the national DNA database. As you well know, all serving officers have their DNA taken and it's put onto a separate database so we can eliminate them from enquiries. You said yourself that Morgan entered the scene, yes?'

Ben could taste the coffee in the back of his throat; the bitterness was nothing compared to the coldness in the pit of his stomach.

'It was run through both and came back as a close match for Morgan. He also ran the sample again from the Gabrielle Stevens's scene and that came back identical with the sample from Stan.'

'What does this mean? She entered both scenes. Surely, she could have left it somehow. She touched a picture frame at the first scene. It must be from that.'

Declan was shaking his head. 'Did you let her go into the scene not wearing protective clothing, no gloves?'

'Of course not, but she did go in unprotected to Stan's flat.'

'Yes, but you said yourself, you were behind her and she never touched him and wasn't in there very long.'

'What about the DNA that matched the Riverside Rapist? How did that get there? It's all been screwed up somehow. It has to have been a major cock-up, because he's in prison and has been for years.'

'I had that rechecked; that DNA is remarkably similar to Morgan's. In fact, it's almost a match.'

'I don't understand.'

'I'm not one hundred per cent sure myself, but my best guess is that Morgan is somehow related to him. There must be a family connection somewhere along the line. I'm sorry, Ben, but from where I'm standing, Morgan could be the killer. I don't know why or how or what it's about, but you have to take the evidence seriously. I'm as devastated as you are. I like her a lot. She's clever, fiery, ambitious and driven… but so are a lot of killers.'

Ben stared at an empty cola can that was rolling around on the floor, the strong breeze sending it spiralling in circles. His head was a mess; he couldn't believe it, nor did he want to.

'Can you give me twenty-four hours before you tell anyone else?'

'Why?'

'To prove her innocence. I don't know. To find out what the fuck is going on. Do you really believe she's murdered two people? Please, Declan, I've never asked you for anything like this since we've known each other. I need you to sit on this just for twenty-four hours until I've looked into it. If I don't come up with any evidence to prove otherwise, I'll bring her in myself.'

Declan ran his hand through his hair. He looked as stressed as Ben felt, and he knew he was putting him in a difficult position.

'No, I don't believe it, but that's my heart talking and it's led me to make some terrible choices over the years. I'll give you twenty-four hours and not a minute more. I like her a lot, but I will not jeopardise my career and my life for her. If you want some advice from an old friend, neither should you. Take care, Ben, you could be dealing with someone who is inherently evil and very clever at disguising it. I don't want to lose you either.'

He stood up, reached out and squeezed Ben's shoulder then he walked back towards the outpatients' entrance, discarding his paper cup into the bin on the way in. He never looked back, and Ben had never felt so scared or alone in his life.

CHAPTER FORTY

Dan strolled into the office with a grease-spotted brown paper McDonald's bag and a tray full of coffees. Amy jumped up to high-five him.

'Thank God, I'm starving.' She took the bag from him, rummaging around inside it until she found her double sausage and egg muffin.

'You're welcome, hungry eh?'

She nodded, passing the bag back to him. He went to sit at the desk he was using. Morgan's desk. It didn't feel right and, as bad as he felt about her dad, he sort of felt relieved he was finally getting his chance to work in CID. He would show them how capable he was. His elbow knocked the mouse and the computer monitor came to life. Staring back at him was a picture of a fresh-faced Morgan in her black polo shirt and body armour. He pulled his bacon roll and the hash browns from the bag. Placing them on some serviettes on the desk, he turned to drop the bag into the bin and saw the gift bag. Picking it up, the box was still inside. He pulled it out and opened it. The earrings were gone. Looking back at the picture of Morgan, he realised that she'd been in here at some point since he'd left after ten last night. He felt sick to the pit of his stomach: she shouldn't have been here; the DCI had told her to take some time off. Why had she come in, sneaking around to use the computer when there was no one here? He didn't know what to do. He didn't want to get her into trouble, but he didn't want to drop himself in any either. He hadn't even managed twenty-four hours, and he was already having a major crisis.

Damn you, Morgan, and your selfish bloody tactics.

Now he was angry with her because, if he didn't tell Ben, he could get kicked out before he'd even started, but if he did tell he'd feel like a grass.

Amy came to take one of the hash browns and looked at him. 'What's up? You haven't touched your breakfast?'

He shook his head. 'Nothing, I like to take my time to eat.'

'What are you saying? I eat like a pig?' This made her laugh, and he wondered if she was nuts.

Ben, who had just walked in, shook his head. 'You'll get used to her weird sense of humour, eventually. Have we got any major breaking news since we clocked off last night? Has anyone come to the front desk to hand themselves in for being a sick and twisted killer?'

They both stared at him.

'That's a nope then. I thought as much. I need to sort some stuff out. Amy give me a few minutes then I need a word.'

He walked into his office and closed the door.

Amy whispered: 'Wonder what's got to him this early in the day?'

Dan looked back at the screen; he was afraid to touch it. Before he could change his mind, he went and knocked on Ben's office door.

'Yeah?'

He opened it a crack. 'Sorry, can I have a word?'

'Come in.'

He did, closing the door behind him. 'I don't know what to say; I don't really want to say but I think you should probably know.'

'What?'

'Morgan has been in and used my computer, well her computer.'

The look of disbelief on Ben's face made him feel better for telling him.

'When? This morning whilst I've been out?'

'I don't know. No, I think probably earlier like really early.'

'Right.'

'What should I do? Use another computer so you have it as evidence?'

'Evidence of what? That she's been in when she was told to take some compassionate leave? It's not really evidence, is it? She hasn't done anything wrong. Well except for being an idiot. No, you can use it. This is between me and you for the time being. Can you tell Amy to come see me on your way out?'

Dan nodded and left him with his head in his hands, closing the door behind him.

'He wants you to go see him now.'

She shoved the last of her hash brown in her mouth and stuck her thumb up.

He sat back down at the desk. Maybe he should phone Morgan to see if she was okay because she was acting strange.

CHAPTER FORTY-ONE

Morgan stared at the blush pink door and found herself falling in love with it. She was a goth at heart; on her days off, she nearly always wore black, loved her tattoos, winged eyeliner, and fishnets with Dr Martens. But she also loved the colour pink, just not on her. She'd been watching the house for almost ten minutes; she didn't know if Angela Hardy was home or if she'd talk to her, and the very thought of it made her feel sick. She had no choice really; Angela was the only person who could tell her who she was and where she'd come from. She'd dressed in one of her work suits, and her lanyard was around her neck. Inhaling deeply to calm the churning inside her stomach, she got out of the car and approached the front door. Before she'd even got through the matching pink gate, the door opened and Angela Hardy smiled at her.

'I was wondering how long it would take you to knock on my door. Not that I'm nosey, but Alice from work rang to tell me I was getting an official visitor, so I've been watching out for you.'

Morgan felt the heat as her cheeks turned red. 'I'm sorry, I've been trying to figure out what I need to ask so I don't waste too much of your time.'

'I'm retired, I don't have any plans today. You chose a good time to catch me. Please come inside.'

They went into a lounge with bay windows. Lake Windermere was just visible over the tops of the trees in the distance.

'Nice view, I love the lake.'

'It's even better from my bedroom. I spend hours up there reading and looking out at the water.'

'That sounds like heaven.'

'It is, well to me. Alice said you're investigating a murder but needed to talk to me about an adoption case from 1999.'

Morgan couldn't help thinking that if all this went to court, Alice and her foolproof memory would be an excellent prosecution witness on the stand against her.

'Yes, I am.'

'There was only one adoption I worked on that year. It was connected to the murder of Janet Marks in front of her children, by the man who would later be further arrested for being the Riverside Rapist.'

It was hard to breathe. Morgan felt as if the air had been sucked out of her lungs. The dreams, the woman covered in blood, what if that was all to do with her? She nodded. Trying to keep calm. She couldn't betray who she was; Angela would clam up and she wouldn't find out what she needed to know.

'There's not an awful lot I can tell you really. I had been on maternity leave and was thrust back in at the deep end on my first week back, but it's all in the papers. What do you specifically need to know about the adoption?'

Morgan was reeling: she had said 'in front of her children'.

'How many children did Janet Marks have?'

'A girl and a boy; the girl was three when it happened; the boy was slightly older. He was almost five.'

'What happened to them?'

'Well the girl was adopted almost immediately by a couple who had been desperate to have children. The boy stayed in care longer. It was like that back then. Girls always seemed to get snapped up first. The boy eventually got adopted, but I didn't deal with that. He had been passed on to someone else by then.'

'Do you have details of the families they went to?'

'I don't, sorry. Are you trying to trace them?'

'Yes.'

'It was a long time ago; I do remember there was an aunt. She was Gary Marks's sister, but I couldn't tell you her name it was so long ago. She wanted to take both children, but it was never allowed; a crying shame if you ask me. I recommended she should be considered, but they wanted them completely removed from the family. I bet if you Google it you'll find all sorts of information and a lot faster than going through the official channels. You never know, the aunt might have been able to trace them. She seemed like a lovely lady.'

Morgan stood up. She held out her hand and Angela shook it. 'Thank you.'

Walking back to the car, she felt as if she were living in some bad dream that she couldn't wake up from. Her mother had been murdered by her father, who just happened to be the Riverside Rapist, who she had visited in prison only yesterday, completely unaware they were related. She also had a brother out there somewhere. She wondered if he knew about her. And then the thought struck that perhaps he knew a lot more about her than she did herself. Could he be the killer? Was he responsible for Stan's murder? For Gabby's? Did he know she'd visited their father?

CHAPTER FORTY-TWO

'Amy, sit down, this is between us. Do not tell anyone else what I'm about to tell you.'

Amy sat opposite Ben. 'What's going on, boss?'

'I don't know exactly.' He needed her on his side, but he didn't want to involve her on such a level that if everything went wrong she'd get dragged down with him. He wouldn't do that to her. He was willing to risk everything to prove Morgan's innocence, but not at the expense of people he admired and respected.

'There are some discrepancies with the DNA results from both crime scenes. You know that there was a match to the Riverside Rapist, which is ridiculous because he's in prison. What isn't so ridiculous, and an explanation for, is that he must have a close family member who shares an almost identical profile to him. Stan's murder threw us off track yesterday, but I need you to get me everything you can on Gary Marks. Pull everything, case files, intelligence reports, newspaper articles. Then I want you to do an in-depth intelligence check on Morgan, but not on our system, and I don't want you to talk about it in front of anyone. Not Dan or those two detectives from Barrow.'

She was staring at him. 'Why Morgan? What's she got to do with any of this?'

Ben knew she was clever, and it wouldn't take her long to figure it out, but he was trying to protect her.

'So the official investigation into Marks, the RR. Then an unofficial investigation into Morgan, right?'

He nodded.

'You think this family member could be…?'

He held out his hand. 'Please don't say it out loud. I don't know what I'm thinking, this is so screwed up. It's blowing my mind, but I need to know. I need to figure out what the hell is going on before anything else happens. Did you get that statement from the landlord at the pub? I need to know if he's a potential suspect for Gabby Stevens.'

'I need to go back there. His partner has been away for a few days and back this morning. But there's so much to look into: what do you want me to do first?'

'I know, I'm sorry to put this all on you. Please just do what you can. Find out what you can. I suggest you start with Gary Marks and work your way forward from there. You can always ask Des to go to back to The Golden Ball.'

'What are you going to do?'

'Go back to speak to Marks, find out what he knows and why he gave us the runaround yesterday. The smug bastard knew something; he had a smile on his face the whole time. I've already arranged a visit.'

'You can't go on your own, take Dan?'

'I'd rather shit in my hands and clap, thank you. He's a sneaky little telltale. I'm trying but looking at him irritates me.'

'That might be, but you need someone there to have your back, witness anything that comes to light, just in case it turns into a disaster.'

'I'll take my chances and, besides, I don't want him to know anything that we've just discussed. This is between you and me. If this all goes horribly wrong and PSD get drawn into it, you deny all knowledge of me asking you to do background checks on Morgan. You understand, Amy, you need to use a computer that isn't linked to you.'

'How?'

'I don't know, go to the library or an Internet café.'

'Boss, this is Rydal Falls not London, we're a bit short on Internet cafés and such. I'll have to go down the library.'

She walked to the door. 'Amy.' Turning to look at him, he smiled. 'Thank you. No matter what happens, don't get involved on a professional level with anything to do with her. I'll take the flak should it come to that.'

She shook her head. 'You're scaring me, Ben.'

'Oh, and do not take Dan with you or tell him what you're up to. He'll be straight down the corridor to Tom's office to drop us all in it before I've had time to drink the coffee you're going to make for me, take my word for it.'

Smiling, she walked out and headed straight to the brew station to make him a drink. If Ben were a real drinker, he'd be pulling a bottle of whisky out of his bottom drawer and taking a nip.

As it was, he preferred coffee and needed to get himself together, ready to speak to Gary Marks again.

As he stared at the monstrous red brick building in front of him, it occurred that he'd been here only once before in the fifteen years he'd been a detective, and now he was walking into the visitor's entrance to HMP Manchester for the second day on the run. His phone rang and he looked down to see Amy's name.

'Boss, the guy from the pub checked out; his partner, Saffie, said she vividly remembers having to watch two episodes of *Mindhunter* with him, even though she doesn't really like it, and then they went to bed.'

'I'm sure he said he watched it because his girlfriend likes it.'

'Maybe he was embarrassed to admit it to you, especially when you were asking him about a murder. I've checked into Gary Marks's background, and he had two children at the time he killed his wife in 1999. A boy and a girl. According to the intel reports made at the time, the younger of the two, his daughter, witnessed her mum's murder; the boy was asleep. They were split up and placed into care.'

He let out a whistle. 'Morgan?'

That would explain the nightmares and insomnia; if she was repressing the memories from back then, her adoptive mum's suicide could have been the catalyst that brought them back to the surface. But did this make her a killer? He still found it hard to believe she could have anything to do with this.

'Not according to this. They were called Skye and Taylor, but that doesn't mean whoever adopted them didn't change their names to protect them. It would make sense; if they were still known as Skye and Taylor Marks they would always be hounded by the press. Every time he was up for appeal, or his crimes were talked about, it would remind the public about his kids. That's a terrible thing to have hanging around your neck for the rest of your life.'

'Where's her brother now?'

'That's the thing, no one knows. There's nothing on the system about them after they were taken into care, except for a couple of non-violent domestics between Stan and Sylvia Brookes who adopted Skye and changed her name to Morgan. Taylor dropped off the face of the earth.'

'Please can you go visit Child Services? Tell them this is urgent, a matter of life and death. We need to know where Gary Marks's children were sent. Names, addresses.'

'Do you think she knows?'

'I couldn't say, but this is going to devastate her if she doesn't.'

The line went dead, and he wondered if she had learned about her past, if that was the catalyst that could have set her off on a murderous spree.

Stop it, Ben, you need to believe she's innocent and prove it. If you give up on her, then you might as well give up on your entire life.

He checked in and went through the same routine as yesterday. Amy was right: he should have had someone here with him, but there was no one apart from her he trusted with this and he needed her back at home, holding the fort. The corridors smelt like school dinners and his stomach let out a silent groan, a reminder to feed it at some point. So consumed with disbelief since he'd spoken to Declan, he hadn't even thought about food. The guard pointed to the chair and ran through the rules again. It was a different one today, so he listened and thanked them when they had finished; as impatient as he felt, they were only doing their job and he respected that.

The room was silent. The only noise was the ticking of a large clock, placed so high on the wall that it couldn't be pulled down and used as a weapon. He could feel the pulse of his heart as it beat in synchronicity to the tick tock. Ben felt as if it were counting down the minutes to some huge, impending disaster. Bending his head, he clasped his hands together. Was it too late to pray for a bit of divine intervention, for him to be totally wrong about all of this?

The door scraped open and Marks was led in, again a guard either side. He waited until he was sitting opposite, studying him. He didn't see any resemblance to Morgan, but that didn't mean anything.

'Thank you for agreeing to speak to me again so soon, Gary.'

He shrugged. 'Yeah, I wasn't particularly busy, my diary is a little empty these days. Where's your pretty sidekick? I was kind of hoping to see her again.'

A ripple of disgust made Ben shudder. Did he know that could be his own daughter he was talking about? God he hoped not.

'She's on her day off. I'm not going to lie; things have taken a turn for the worse since I was here and I need your help. Yesterday I asked you how your DNA could have been left behind at a crime scene.'

'You did and the answer is still the same, it wasn't me. They don't let me out for day trips to the lakes no matter how well I behave.'

'I appreciate that, but realistically, the only way that could happen was if someone who was a close relation to you and shared many of the same DNA characteristics you do, left it there. I've been doing some digging and discovered you—'

The laughter that filled the room threw Ben off guard. He looked at Gary Marks, who had tipped his head back and was laughing so loud even the guards were staring at each other in surprise.

'What's so funny?'

He clapped his hands on his thighs and shook his head, composing himself. He still had a ridiculous grin across his face.

'This, all of this. I get it now. One of my kids has taken a leaf out of my book and turned to a life of crime. That's why you're so interested. I never saw this coming not in a million years. It's a bit of a revelation to be honest. You discovered what? That I fathered two bloody children I never wanted in the first place, that I went back home after each attack and played happy families. Don't get me wrong, it wasn't the kids' fault they were born. It was that bitch Janet's. I told her I didn't want any, so what did she do? A couple of months after we met, she went and got pregnant; told me it was an accident, but I didn't believe her. I found myself stuck with her; I was having a bit of a bad time. You see I had these urges, these fantasies, and they were getting harder to control. I realised that Janet with her neat three-bedroom council house might be able to help me. I tried, I did, and then Taylor was born, and I realised I quite liked the ugly ball of screaming baby. That threw me for six; I hadn't expected that to happen.'

'You were a good dad, you stayed around?'

'I was a fucking brilliant dad. I couldn't up and leave Janet. She had started acting all weird and didn't want to look at the kid despite her demanding she was keeping him in the first place. The doctors called it baby blues and gave her some pills.'

'Then what happened?'

'We did play at happy families for a year or so. I was too tired working then coming home to take over looking after Taylor, that those feelings I'd been having kind of went away a little, making it easier to live a normal life.

'Then she did it again; she told me she was pregnant again. I looked at her like she was the stupidest woman on the planet. I told her she was an idiot, that she didn't bother with Taylor, so how the hell was she going to manage another, and she cried for hours. Said that she felt better and maybe this time it would be different. There was no way she could have an abortion.

'I tell you I was raging that night. I left the house and went out looking for trouble, for a fight, for anyone to even look at me the wrong way. I wanted to strangle her with my bare hands.'

Ben was absorbing all this information. He stared at Marks.

'Janet had the baby?'

Marks tutted loudly. 'Yeah, the stupid cow.'

'How did you feel about this one?'

Marks was no longer smiling. He was staring at Ben with those cold, calculating eyes.

'I think you can guess. It didn't help matters, not for me anyway. Janet seemed to get her shit together though, said she'd always wanted a baby girl and loved her more than Taylor. How do you work that out, eh?'

Ben realised that Morgan's arrival had been the catalyst which had sent Marks from having sick fantasies to carrying them out.

'So which one is it?'

Ben didn't answer straight away. He was still trying to process what he knew.

'I'd hedge my bets on it being Taylor. I don't think Skye deserves the credit; I mean this is clever, right? What's going on is a credit to whoever is doing it. They left DNA at a crime scene they knew would link back to me? That's genius; I'd like to meet them, shake their hand and tell them their old man is proud of them.'

It struck Ben that if Morgan was the killer, she would have had to have known Gary Marks was her father and he didn't think she had the slightest idea. When they were here yesterday, she hadn't given the impression she knew about him. It had to be Taylor. He needed it to be Taylor because he didn't think he'd be able to get over this if it was Morgan. The betrayal would be worse than anything.

A voice in his mind asked, *even worse than losing Cindy?*

'Tell me, Gary, do you think your children know about you? Have they ever been to visit you and ask why you killed their mother and raped three innocent women?'

'Fuck you, she deserved what she got. They all deserved it; they had it coming to them.'

Gary Marks jumped up so fast the chair overturned with a loud clatter. Both guards rushed to grab him. He fought with them, his face an angry shade of red.

Ben could see a vein throbbing in his temple, pulsating with explosive energy. He jumped up and looked around for the emergency button, dashing across the room and slapping his hand against it. He stood watching as Gary Marks fought with the guards. He could hear the thundering of Magnum boots against the tiled floor in the corridor as they rushed towards the room. Marks realised he was greatly outnumbered and stopped fighting. He let his body go loose. Ben watched as he was dragged from the room, his shoulders hunched over and head hung low.

One of the guards led Ben back to collect his stuff.

'You sure managed to get under his skin. I've never seen him like that; he's usually a model prisoner.'

'Sometimes the truth hurts a lot more than you expect it to.'

CHAPTER FORTY-THREE

Morgan went home. She was drained and needed to figure out how to find Gary Marks's sister. She may be able to tell her more about her early years and where Taylor was now. It all came back to Taylor, the brother she never knew existed. Did he kill Gabby? And Stan? There was no way she could go back into work to check on the address system; she'd already pushed that to the limit. Technically, she wasn't doing anything wrong; she was still trying to figure out who killed Gabby Stevens. That she'd stepped straight into the middle of some horror story that just happened to be her life wasn't her fault. This whole thing was so unfair. It hit her then, the weight of the revelation from the social worker, and she had to sit down. All those bad dreams, the woman with the red hair... they weren't dreams, they were repressed memories. Isaac had told her to write them down: was he in for the surprise of his life when she went back for her first appointment. It would probably take years to sort out this train wreck.

She decided to phone him, because she needed to speak to someone about it and wasn't sure she should be spilling this much information to anyone at work. She dialled his number and he answered on the first ring.

'Hello, Morgan.'

'Hi, how did you know it was me?'

He laughed. 'I'm psychic; actually, I asked Amy for your number because it came up as private the last time you rang. It's not that exciting.'

'Oh, yes, I suppose it makes sense. I found out some stuff, quite a lot of stuff actually, and my head is a complete mess.'

There was a pause and she could tell he was walking around. 'Hang on, let me shut the door.'

'Sorry, is this a bad time? I can ring back.'

'No, it's fine. So what kind of stuff?'

She wondered if she should be telling him this, then realised what was the point of having a therapist if she couldn't talk to him? It kind of defeated the whole purpose.

'I'm adopted; I found out that I have a biological brother I know nothing about. My birth mum was murdered in the nineties and Stan, my adoptive dad who I had no idea wasn't my real dad, was murdered yesterday. It's all such a complete mess and I don't know what to do about any of it.'

'Morgan, I'm so sorry. I don't know what to say about any of this, well not on the spur of the moment. Where are you? Are you on your own?'

'I'm supposed to be stopping at Ben's, but I've nipped home.' She realised she didn't feel comfortable telling him every little detail, because where she was had nothing to do with any of this.

'Good, I don't think you should be on your own. Let me see, I can see you tomorrow if you want? We can bring your appointment forward.'

'Thanks, that's kind of you. I'm not sure. I don't know what to do about any of it. Sorry to have bothered you; I needed to get it off my chest.'

'Well I'm here to talk, if you need to. Let me know and I'll see you after my last client even if it's just coffee and a chat.'

'Thanks, Isaac, that's very nice of you. I better let you get on, bye.'

'Bye, Morgan, and take care.'

She ended the call. Stripping off her work suit, she changed into her staple of black leggings and a black sweatshirt that said 'Tired and Needy'. Never was there more appropriate attire. She was exhausted, mentally and physically, not to mention she felt sick at the revelation that her father was both a murderer and rapist who had killed her mother in front of her. How was she supposed to get over that? It didn't matter now: she had to compartmentalise it and get on with her investigation. When all this was over and she'd proved to Ben she had nothing to do with it, there would be time to grieve for Stan, her real mum and the life she lost.

It struck her that when she'd met her biological father yesterday, he'd come across as okay and not at all what she'd expected. Once more, she scoured the Internet looking for a mention of Gary Marks's family; the tabloids were her best bet. They thrived off stories like this and would have covered the trial in depth. Scanning the articles there was no mention of a sister, so she began to look for photographs of the court case. No idea who she was looking for, but it was worth trying.

As the screen filled with images from outside the court, she enlarged them, looking for anyone or anything that might stand out. About to give up, she spotted something in the left-hand corner of a photograph of Marks being led into the court; he'd turned to look at someone. Twisting her head, she saw an older woman standing there, her gaze fixed on Marks, and realised she looked vaguely familiar. Enlarging it even more, she stared and then she realised: it was the woman from the quirky cottage in the woods. Ettie.

It struck Morgan, as she was driving to the outskirts of Grasmere, that she only knew how to find Ettie Jackson's cottage by cutting across the Potters' garden. There must be an entrance to the woods where she wouldn't have to trespass. Pulling over, she began searching for directions on her phone and it struck her that she didn't even know the name of the woods. Typing 'Easdale Road' into Google Maps, she waited for the area to load and then zoomed in until the woods appeared on the screen. Covel Wood, that was it; but even if she found the entrance, she could walk for hours and not find the cottage. She was going to have to go through the Potters' garden.

She began driving again and before long she reached the entrance to their drive. Pulling onto the grass verge, she wondered if anyone was home. Instead of walking up the long drive, Morgan cut straight through the trees. Head down, she was almost jogging as she followed the sound of the rushing water. Glancing up at the house, it looked empty. She said a silent prayer for Olivia Potter as her gaze fell on the tree where she'd first found her body. She didn't think she would mind her using her garden as a shortcut while trying to unravel her crazy life and catch another killer.

Hopping over a mossy, drystone wall which bordered the woods, Morgan landed on a pile of twigs that cracked underneath her feet. It sounded as if a gun had been fired and the birds nearby took flight squawking in fright. Morgan had to steady her own breathing. She picked her way through the trees, hoping she was heading in the right direction to Ettie's cottage. It occurred to her that once again no one knew where she was; if she got lost, she could end up wandering around for hours and a lot of good that would do her. She stood still, closed her eyes and waited until she had her bearings. All she had to do was walk uphill following the wall. If she could find the part where it had collapsed, she was heading in the right direction. As she walked uphill, the drystone wall got higher. She remembered the part of the wall where there was a pile of loose stones on the floor. Turning to face the woods, she saw the narrow path leading to the cottage. It was almost overgrown, but it was there. These woods made her feel as if she was in a different time and place and she wished she was. It was soothing and peaceful; maybe she needed a house in the woods away from people. It struck her then, who would she need to hide from? The only family she had left didn't know her. She would never spend time with her real father, and the brother she never knew existed was highly likely the killer she was hunting. Rounding a corner, she saw the cottage with its lilac door and beautifully planted front garden.

The door opened and Ettie smiled at her. Arms across her chest she nodded. She heard a loud swooping noise as the biggest black bird Morgan had ever seen swooped down and landed on the picket fence a few feet away. Startled, she stepped away from it.

'Don't mind him, he's nosey. Aren't you, Max?'

The bird flapped its wings.

Fascinated, Morgan watched him. 'Is he answering you?'

'God knows, I like to think so. I think birds are a lot cleverer than we give them credit for; well, he certainly is.'

'Hello, Morgan, I've been waiting for you.'

A feeling of déjà vu washed over her. Hadn't Angela Hardy said almost exactly the same thing? Morgan opened the gate and walked along the path.

'How did you know?'

'I had a feeling yesterday. I knew something was wrong and, whilst I'm happy to see you again, I fear you're not here for a social visit. Or maybe I'm completely wrong and you've come for some more of my sleep-better tea.' Ettie turned and walked inside. She followed her.

'Please, take a seat. I insist I make a pot of tea before we start.'

'I think brandy or something stronger might be better. Unless you have coffee; I'd love a cup of that.'

'I have both, although I'm more of a gin drinker. Which one will it be?'

'Coffee, please.'

Ettie busied herself making drinks and Morgan took her time looking around. The shelves full of jars of herbs and whatever else were mesmerising. There was a shelf with baskets of different crystals and she wanted so much to reach out and touch them all. There was also a bookshelf stuffed with old books on plants, herbs, gardening and healing. She let out a huge sigh. This little cottage was like something out of a fairy tale and it had the most comforting feeling inside it.

Ettie carried over two mugs and placed one on the battered pine chest in front of Morgan. Going back to the kitchen, she carried over a plate of cake, stuffed with buttercream and jam.

'You made this? It looks amazing.'

Ettie shook her head. 'Gosh no. M&S make better cakes than I do. But that's our little secret.'

'So, Morgan, what brings you back here?'

From out of nowhere came a loud sob, so violent it racked her entire body. Ettie rushed over to her. Gently holding her hand, she sat next to her on the soft, grey leather sofa.

'Oh dear, are you okay, flower?'

She shook her head, gulped and whispered: 'I'm sorry, I don't know where that came from.'

'It's okay, your job must be difficult. You must see some tragic, awful things at work and then you're supposed to go home and carry on as if nothing has happened, when all the time you can't switch off because the awful images are there, in your head, and you can't get rid of them.'

'Ettie, you seem so lovely. I need to tell you this isn't strictly linked to the murder I'm investigating; I want you to know that. I don't want to lie to you. I want to be honest with you.'

Ettie nodded. 'I know, I also think I know why you're here.'

'You do?'

'You look so much like her; I only met her a handful of times but she was a beautiful woman.'

'Sylvia?'

'No, I imagine she was a lovely lady but I'm talking about your birth mother.'

'How?'

'I knew this day would come; I knew from the day it happened and you were taken away that you'd be back. I'll tell you everything

I can. I don't see what harm it can do. I'm sorry too for your loss. When I read about Stan Brookes's murder, I knew you would come looking. I had decided a very long time ago as long as you were old and mature enough to handle the details that I would tell you everything when the time came.'

Ettie passed Morgan a handful of tissues and she took them, dabbing her eyes then blowing her nose.

'Do you know about your birth father?'

She nodded.

'Gary was my younger brother; there were just the two of us. Growing up, he had some issues that my mother and aunt tried to brush away. They idolised him and didn't see the way he would switch off and turn into someone completely different. They'd make him drink cup after cup of camomile tea, which he hated, and instead of getting him professional help they let him get worse and worse. I'm not saying it's their fault. I loved them dearly; they were wonderful. But there are some things that can't be ignored or brushed under the carpet. I think they thought it was a passing phase, that getting caught peeping in girls' windows was what teenage boys did.'

'When he met Janet, he seemed to settle down: as far as we knew, he had. Then she got pregnant with your brother, Taylor; a couple of years later you came along. Did you know you were called Skye? I don't blame Sylvia for changing your name. If I'd have got custody of you both, I would have done exactly the same. I tried; I really did. I wanted to take you both on and bring you up. The courts wouldn't let me because of how serious Gary's crimes were. They wanted you removed from the family for your protection. It was heartbreaking. Even though I only saw you both a few times, I still loved you.'

Morgan was trying to absorb what Ettie was telling her.

Ettie continued. 'Thankfully, my mother and aunt had both died by the time Gary murdered Janet. The shock would have probably killed them anyway. How did you find out about me?'

'I spent ages scouring the Internet and the reports of the murder, then I tried the court case and was clutching at straws really. I was hoping I might see someone I recognised that I could ask about it, and there was one picture of you. Gary was on his way into court and he turned to look at you.'

'It was hard; despite everything he's my brother. We got on okay, nothing more than the usual sibling arguments. I felt like I had to let him know I was still there for him, even though it broke my heart what he did to Janet and those other women.'

'I need to find Taylor. Do you know anything at all about him? How did you know that Stan and Sylvia had adopted me? Did you know who I was the last time I visited? I'm sorry, there are so many questions and I only have you to ask.'

'I knew you were adopted by a family called Brookes who lived in Kendal, because there are things you find out around here without a lot of effort. I had no idea when you visited last time to investigate the Potters' murders that you were Skye. Why would I? Although you did look a little familiar. You're called Morgan now and I didn't connect the two together. But looking at you today, I realised who you were.'

'What about Taylor?'

She shook her head. 'He was taken into care out of the county. I think it's despicable they split you both up. You should have stayed together. If you'd come to me, you would have. He probably wondered why he wasn't good enough to go with you. I imagine he's carried that around with him his whole life.'

Morgan felt a surge of sadness for the brother she didn't remember. It was unfair but it didn't mean that Gabby Stevens or Stan should have died because of it. And where did that leave her? Did he want to kill her too? An icy cold shiver ran down the full length of her spine.

'I don't know what to do about any of it. My whole life has been thrown upside down. I've lost everyone I ever cared about only to find I have a monster for a father.'

Ettie squeezed Morgan's hand. 'You have me. Now you've found me I'm here for you. You're welcome here anytime; it would be lovely to get to know you. I've waited so long for this.'

Morgan smiled at her.

'Now, eat that cake and drink your coffee because you look as if you haven't eaten a good meal in days. You need to keep your strength up to do the job you do.' She picked up the side plate and passed it to her. Morgan realised she was pretty hungry and ate every bit of it, then washed it down with the coffee, which tasted heavenly.

Ettie stood up and went to her wall of glass jars. Returning with a couple, she handed them over along with a scrap of paper: a phone number written neatly across it. 'I think you might still have those bad dreams, especially with all this new information, but hopefully as time goes on and you begin to heal they'll get fewer. This is soothe-yourself tea, same instructions as last time. Steep a couple of teaspoons in hot water before bed with a drop of honey to sweeten it. I also want you to have my phone number, so you can ring me whenever you need to.'

Morgan took it. 'Thank you.'

'I'm here for you, Morgan, whenever you need me. I always have been, you just didn't know it.'

She stood up. 'I know. I'm sorry, I have to go but I'll come back when I can.' Reaching out, she pulled Ettie towards her and hugged her tight. She smelt of lavender and lemon, and something else she couldn't quite put her finger on. Family, she smelt of family.

As she left and walked back down the garden path, the raven was still sitting watching her. It was a bit of a trek to get back to her car but it had been worth it. A thought crossed her mind: had she unwittingly put Ettie in danger by coming here? If the killer was Taylor and he'd killed Stan because of her, what was to stop him doing the same to Ettie? Then where did Gabby come into this? Was this some grudge harboured since childhood against her because he got sent away and she didn't and, if so, did it mean he was going to kill everyone she cared about? If it did, it meant he knew a whole lot more about her than she knew about him. She prayed not: the thought of finding a brother she never knew she had, only to have to lock him up and send him to prison for life, unnerved her.

She realised she was scared for the few people she did care about. Would he go after Ben and Amy? What did this mean for her? Was it hereditary? After all, she was a killer's daughter. Was it like a disease growing and spreading inside of her until one day it couldn't be contained? Pain shot through her chest so intense it made her double over to catch her breath. No, she would never hurt anyone unless she had to in a life-or-death situation. She couldn't kill someone for fun.

There was only one person who she trusted; she needed to tell Ben all of this.

CHAPTER FORTY-FOUR

He couldn't wait any longer; the feeling when it came was undeniable. It wouldn't be soothed away with reading a book or drinking alcohol: he'd tried both plenty of times. As he drove to the large house his next girl lived in, he knew that he was putting himself at risk of being caught, but he couldn't help it. This thought made what he was about to do even more delicious; imagine how Morgan was going to feel, knowing he'd been that close to her. That whilst she was moping around feeling sorry for herself about Stan, he'd been strangling the woman in the flat above her. He stopped the car. If he was feeling this risky, why stop now?

Pulling out the heavy box from underneath the seat, he opened it and took out the phone. He looked around to see where he was, because he'd been on autopilot and hadn't taken any notice of his surroundings. He was so consumed with the desire to kill again. He'd stopped in the middle of Kendal: a small side street off the main road through town. He was far enough away from Rydal Falls that it wouldn't make the slightest bit of difference if he sent one message and turned it back off. He pressed the side button, waiting for the phone to come to life and realised that it may well have died; it hadn't been charged for days. Then it came to life and he smiled: it was meant to be. The low battery alert beeped as soon as the home screen came on. It was on three per cent battery. He typed quickly:

Do you know? On my way to see my next girl, maybe see you soon.

It sent and the screen went black as the phone powered itself off. Even though it had no charge, he put it back into the box. There was taking risks for the good of his plans and there was being stupid. He wasn't stupid.

He wasn't sure how he was going to play this. How good his sister, Morgan Brookes, was at being a detective. He knew enough that she was on the right path, but he didn't know exactly how much she'd discovered about him and their past life. Maybe she was oblivious, too overwhelmed with her grief for Stan that she was at home feeling sorry for herself. Somehow, he didn't think she would be. From what he knew about her she was driven. He thought about being completely brazen and parking outside for everyone to see, and then decided against it. His mother would be mortified at his actions and the path he'd chosen, after all those years of trying to banish all the bad thoughts from his head by making him repeat Bible verses and attend church with her. How he'd hated her dragging him to every church function, Bible classes and Sunday School. He supposed she'd done her best. She had known all about his father and been terrified he would turn out like him. Well, he had, because everything she had put him through had the opposite effect on him. He hadn't turned to God to be his saviour; he'd ended up hating everything that He stood for. The day he'd come home drunk after being to his friend's fifteenth birthday party, she'd been enraged by his behaviour. This had set her off on one of her biblical rants and, despite the room spinning from the large amount of cheap vodka he'd drunk, the name she'd let slip had stayed with him. He heard her high-pitched voice in the back of his head and lifted his hands to his ears to block it out. *Years of looking after you, nurturing you and hoping you'd turn to God and be a good boy have been a complete waste. You're going to be just like him, just like that monster Marks and you'll burn in hell together.*

He'd stumbled upstairs to bed, but it had somehow stuck in his mind. Who was that monster, Marks? He didn't know what she was talking about. He'd vomited twice in the toilet then collapsed into bed with the room spinning so bad he'd ended up retching into the waste bin by his desk. When he woke up, he didn't remember the party, but he did remember what she had said, and when he could see straight enough to focus on the screen of his knackered phone, he'd googled 'Monster Marks'. What had come up had shocked even him. Underneath several links to an art museum in Memphis and an advert for some Monster socks and energy drinks, he'd seen a headline that had caught his eye: 'Cold-hearted monster Gary Marks nicknamed the Riverside Rapist was in court today for the final verdict on the lengthy trial.'

He'd read the article, wondering if this was what she meant. He didn't think she was referring to an art museum. It had played on his mind and eventually he'd gone around asking his friends who had much younger, normal mothers if they remembered the Riverside Rapist. They had and would then tell him tales about what it was like following the news at the time of the attacks, the horror and fear. This should have scared him; at the very least repulsed him. It hadn't; it had excited him beyond anything he'd ever known and given him hope that he had a life outside of his mother's strict regime.

He decided to leave his car in a busy street near to where E lived. He hadn't spent years being discreet to go and blow it when he was so close. He would walk the rest of the way. There was a field separating the house from the street where he'd left his car and he decided to cut across it. Less chance of anyone seeing him approach, and it would take him straight to the rear garden, where he could watch and wait until it was time. He enjoyed this part; the watching was almost as much fun as the killing.

CHAPTER FORTY-FIVE

Ben drove straight to Morgan's. He needed to speak to her. Where the hell was she and why hadn't she answered his calls? She needed to know about her family. He thought he knew her well enough that he'd know if she was genuinely taken aback by it all or whether she had been lying to him all along. He tried phoning her several times, but it went straight to voicemail, and he couldn't help wondering what she was doing. His mind was in turmoil. He couldn't bear the thought of her not being the person he had got to know and trust. He also needed to go to the college. There was a chance that Gabby Stevens had met her killer there, and that brought him back to the connection with Amy's cousin, Isaac, who had told Morgan he lectured at the college. He had never felt so alone in his entire life. He was running two murder investigations practically on his own. He had a bad feeling about Isaac Cross; they still hadn't confirmed his alibi for the night Gabby was killed. He would follow up on that and speak to him first. Could he possibly be Morgan's brother? How did he broach the subject with him of being adopted? If he was totally innocent, it wouldn't matter in the least, but if he was Taylor Marks then that would be like telling him that he knew who he was. The only links they had were that Gabby and Stan both frequented The Golden Ball, but John's alibi had checked out. The connection both Gabby and Isaac had to the college also needed clarifying. Gabby's friends had said she had a crush on her teacher, but he had no tangible evidence to bring him in for questioning and, if he did without firm proof, it would send

Amy over the edge. None of it explained Stan's death though: he had no links to the college.

Ben could feel the pressure behind his eyes mounting. It felt as if his brain was overheating and about to explode. He needed to speak to Morgan. He was putting everything at risk by asking Declan to sit on the information he'd told him. Where the hell was she? He drove through the gates and parked next to a blue Mini which wasn't Morgan's. As he reached the front door, a woman came rushing out with a stack of books under one arm.

'Sorry, I'm late. Can I help you?'

'I've come to visit Morgan; she lives in the ground-floor flat.'

'Ah, right. I don't think she's here; at least her car isn't.' She kept the door open for him and stepped to one side. 'But you'd better knock. Sometimes she turns up in all sorts of different cars. I think she must work at a garage.'

Ben laughed. 'Actually she's a detective, but you better not tell her I told you that.'

'Really, wow. I need to speak to her then. I've been thinking about joining the police; I always fancied being a police sketch artist.'

He realised that Morgan was probably going to kill him for this and he should have kept quiet.

'Anyway, I better get going. I don't want to miss the start of class again.'

'Do you go to college?'

'Yes, the sixth form. Well, I teach an art class there. It's not as enjoyable as I hoped; I need a different career: something a little more exciting.'

'This is a long shot, but did you know Gabrielle Stevens?'

She was in the process of putting the stack of books in the car and turned to him. 'Not on a personal level, but I recognised her photograph in the paper, and I do remember seeing her around. She was a little older than the other kids, so I noticed her. It's so awful what happened to her.'

'How about Isaac Cross?'

She shook her head. 'I don't think so. Is he a student? I'm pretty new.'

'No, he teaches psychology, I think. Thank you, I'm sorry to have kept you.'

She grinned. 'That's okay, it's not every day I get interrogated by a nice policeman.'

'How did you know? I never said.'

'I might teach art, but that's a Cumbria Constabulary lanyard around your neck, peeking out of the collar of your shirt. You're wearing a suit and looking for Morgan, who you just told me is a detective. I'd say you're either her boss or a colleague, maybe her boyfriend, possibly all three.'

He laughed. 'We work together.'

'Oh, that's good then. Well, if you get lonely and want some company, you know where I live. I cook a mean spaghetti bolognese and always have plenty of wine in the fridge. See you around, hopefully. I'm Emily.'

She got into her car and drove off, leaving him a little speechless at what had just happened. Had she been flirting with him? Surely not. It had been that long he had no idea, and even though she was a little too forward and not his type, he felt flattered.

He let the front door slam shut behind him and crossed to Morgan's front door, avoiding looking at the staircase. He could understand Morgan being able to come back here because she had been unconscious when she'd been attacked. It was him who had the memory of her dangling from the banister, choking to death, ingrained in his mind. He rang the video doorbell she'd had installed and knocked on the door for good measure. He could hear nothing from inside. Leaning forward, he pressed his head against the door and whispered: 'Where are you, Morgan? Please don't let me down.'

He left the empty house with a sinking feeling inside of him. What did he do now? He had to speak to her but he couldn't sit around waiting for ever. He had leads to follow on two murder cases. He googled 'Isaac Cross Psychotherapist' on his phone and found a link to his website. He clicked on the image of the man with a thick head of hair and dark stubble. He looked to be in his late-twenties, so he was around the right age to be Taylor Marks. He didn't look anything like Morgan, but not all siblings looked alike, that didn't mean anything. He would go and speak to him in person. He liked to think that his copper's nose would tell him if he was on the right wavelength.

Isaac's home/office address was at the bottom of the page. Could it be this easy? Was he about to catch the killer? He hoped not for Amy's sake. He didn't think she'd forgive him for this and he wondered if he should ask her to come with him. Then he realised he couldn't because of the family connection, and if he was wrong then it might do irreparable damage to the relationship she had with Isaac.

CHAPTER FORTY-SIX

Amy found it hard to believe that Gary Marks was Morgan's dad. She either didn't know about him or she was very good at misleading people. Reading about his gruesome crimes on the computer in front of her in the small library, it was hard to contain her emotions and her language. At least at work she could talk and swear to herself loudly; next to her were three pensioners all trying to log on to the computers and it was painful listening to them asking each other how to do it. At least they were learning, that was good and she applauded them for it. If only they could do it a little quieter. She was thinking about Isaac and his connection to Gabby Stevens: it didn't mean anything; she was sure of it. But the knowledge sat heavy on her chest. She would rather ask him outright, face to face. She would know if he was lying, she was sure of it. She'd always been close to her cousin, Sophie, so had hung out a lot with her and Isaac since they'd started dating. She thought that he'd become a friend. She tried to remember if it had ever been mentioned about him being adopted though. She was sure Sophie had never said anything. She looked around the small library that was outdated by at least twenty years. It was a shame because this place was more of a community hub than the actual community hub on the main street. Sighing, she grabbed her bag and slipped out, unnoticed.

Isaac's house was on a newer estate. It was a good ten-minute drive, and she really should be on her way to Child Services, but she had to speak to him. She phoned him before she set off to make sure he was home. The phone rang and rang. When he answered it, he was breathless.

'Did I disturb you?'

His breathing was laboured, and then laughter filled her ears.

'No, I've been out walking. I left my phone behind and could hear it ringing from outside. I rushed to answer it because I knew it might be someone important. I shouldn't have bothered.'

'Charming.' He didn't mean it. He was joking; she knew that.

'Can I come see you? We need to talk.'

'Well you can, I've got a client later. What time are you thinking of?'

'Now, if it's okay.'

'Fine by me. Are you bringing coffee, or should I turn the coffee machine on?'

'You can make them; I can't be bothered going to a café and waiting ages to get served.'

'What's this about, Amy? You sound a little strained.'

She shook her head. Damn he was perceptive, which is probably why he made such a great therapist.

'Work stuff.'

'Okay, are you coming on your own?'

'Yes.' She ended the call, hating that she was in this situation and having to doubt her own friend's innocence. Who was the most likely out of Isaac or Morgan to be a killer? She knew she'd be devastated to find out it was either of them.

When she arrived, the house had all the curtains and blinds drawn, which wasn't like Isaac. He usually put her to shame in the domestic department. Parking across his drive she walked up the short path and knocked on the door. It was ajar and opened slightly.

'Isaac.' There was no reply, so she shouted a little louder as she stepped inside. 'Isaac.' As she wandered in and closed the door, she wrinkled her nose and wondered what that pungent smell was.

CHAPTER FORTY-SEVEN

Morgan stared at the message box on her screen, there was one new message. She opened it and a wave of bile rushed up her throat. He had another victim in his sights; a cold shiver ran through her body. She needed to tell Ben. She rang his phone again and again until the battery on her own was almost dead. Where the hell was he? The only time he'd given up his phone was at the mortuary and yesterday in the prison. She wondered if he'd gone back there to see Gary Marks, then realised that it was possible he was attending Stan's post-mortem. The drowning feeling as grief crushed down on her made it hard to breathe for a couple of minutes and she stopped, sitting down on a mound of fallen rocks. The river was so loud as it rushed past and she sat there staring at the frothy, bubbling water until it got a little easier to breathe. Across the riverbank, she was going to have to go back across the Potters' garden to get back to her car she'd abandoned outside the drive. Everything felt surreal, like it wasn't happening to her and she was an outsider observing. Taking the piece of paper Ettie had given her, she typed it into her phone before it died, in case she lost it. She had nowhere to put the jars of tea, though, and had balanced them on the drystone wall whilst she'd clambered over it. Mesmerised by the water, she wondered what would happen if she were to fall in and get carried downstream, maybe drown. Who was going to miss her? Ettie was lovely, but they hardly knew each other. Would Ben miss her? They had grown close and they led similar lives, both of them lonely. Dan might miss her for a little while, maybe Amy, but she had no one who would mourn her properly and that made her sad.

There was a loud flapping noise followed by a squawk as a raven flew by and landed on the wall next to her. Max, it had to be. She tilted her head to look at him, and he copied, tilting his to stare back at her with shiny, black eyes.

'Hello, Max.'

The bird began preening his feathers, watching her the whole time.

'Did Ettie send you to keep an eye on me?' She laughed, and the sound echoed through the woods. *Get a grip, Morgan, you're talking to a bird; you need to see Isaac Cross more than you realised.*

As she came through the gate, she saw Dan, not in uniform, leaning on the bonnet of her car. His own car was parked behind.

'What are you doing here?'

'I'm supposed to be asking you that question. One of the neighbours phoned in to say they saw a woman entering the grounds of the empty house where a family was killed. When they passed your car reg over the radio, I knew it was you, so I came.'

'Thanks, but why are you not in uniform?'

She was relieved to see a faint redness creep up his neck. 'Ben needed someone to help out whilst you're on compassionate leave.'

'Oh.' She was helpless to disguise the hurt that filled her entire body and was now etched across her face. 'He replaced me?' She didn't add, *with you.*

'Only for a couple of weeks until you come back, then I'm back on section. What are you doing here, Morgan?'

She didn't even know where to start. How did she explain it all to him without sounding like she was having a breakdown? It was Ben she wanted to tell everything to, not Dan. He wasn't the one who could help her.

'I don't know, I wanted to think and clear my head. There are some lovely woods across the river. I went for a walk.'

Dan laughed. 'Morgan you're nuts. You do know there's a public car park on Grasmere Road where there are actual footpaths and you don't have to trespass to get to it?'

She smiled and shrugged. 'Really? Well you learn something new every day. Sorry to have messed you around. I'll go there next time. Thanks for coming, Dan.'

'You're welcome. I have some more crappy news for you so don't thank me just yet.'

'What?'

'Your front tyre is completely flat. Did you run over a rock when you drove along the grass verge?'

'Bloody hell, no, I don't think so.' She rushed around to the passenger's side to see her very flat front tyre and wanted to scream at the top of her lungs.

'Have you got a spare?'

She shook her head.

'Come on, you look fed up. I'll take you home. Then come back with my stuff when I finish work and get your tyre off. I'll take it to the garage, if it's still open, then come back and put it on for you.'

'Thanks, Dan.'

She got into the front seat of his car, feeling deflated. Dan was the last person she wanted rescuing by; he would tell everyone about this and she was under enough scrutiny as it was. She closed her eyes and wondered when she was going to get a break and her life would get better, because it couldn't get much worse.

CHAPTER FORTY-EIGHT

At the station, Ben walked in to an office containing Des, who was sitting on the corner of the desk – a mug in one hand – chatting to the two detectives from Barrow: Shannon and Tim. He nodded at them. Crap, how had he forgotten they were working from here whilst investigating Stan's death? He was walking the finest of lines. He should tell them and also Tom about the DNA, Morgan and her brother, but where did he start with that one? He would come clean and explain it all once he'd got hold of Morgan. His phone had died on the way back from her flat and his car charger had decided not to work. He went into his office and heard Shannon call him.

'Ben, can we have a bit of a catch-up about the post-mortem and investigation?'

He turned and smiled. 'Of course, I just need to plug this in. Can you give me a couple of minutes?' He waved his phone at her and shut the door. Picking up his desk phone, he dialled Declan's office number and hoped he wasn't in the middle of dissecting someone.

'Good morn—, no, sorry, afternoon, pathology.'

This must be the lovely Susie with the green hair who was driving his friend mad.

'Hi, it's Ben Matthews, is Declan around?'

'He's in the mortuary, but I don't think he's doing much.'

This tickled Ben more than it should. She did need to work on her phone manners a touch.

'Should I go see?'

'Yes, please.'

She slammed the receiver on the desk and he heard her yell: 'Declan, phone,' in the background. He peered through his blinds, hoping that Shannon wouldn't decide to walk in before he'd had this conversation or he was screwed.

'Hello, did you hear that? It's like a foghorn.'

'She's trying.'

'Oh, she's trying me all right. Have you spoken to Morgan or done whatever it is you needed to do?'

'No, I can't find her or I should say I can't get hold of her, but I will. I'm looking at two detectives from Barrow through my office blinds. Is there anything I need to know before I speak to them?' He didn't want to directly ask Declan if he'd told them.

'Nope, you asked me to sit on it and I am, at least until nine a.m. tomorrow and then it will have to be disclosed.'

'Thank you, that's all I needed to hear.'

'I'm worried about you, about Morgan, about this whole damn mess. You need to think hard and carefully if you, my friend, are walking along the right path. There's a fine line between loyalty and doing the right thing.'

'I know, just a few more hours. Thank you.'

Declan hung up. Ben didn't blame him. He was annoyed and worried, but that made two of them. Where the hell was Morgan? A gentle knock on his door snapped him out of it.

'Come in.'

Shannon walked in; Tim was still chatting to Des. He craned his neck to look at them. Judging by the laughter they weren't discussing work.

'What's up? Take a seat.'

She sat down. 'This is a bit of a mess, isn't it? It must be difficult for you.'

A voice whispered in his head *you have no idea*.

'We have very little to go on at the moment apart from the fact that Stan Brookes knew his killer. We've collected CCTV from The Golden Ball the night before he was killed.'

Ben sighed. 'Had he lapsed? He'd been going to AA and doing so well. Morgan will be gutted.'

'Tim is going to view it, but according to the landlord he ordered a pint and a whisky chaser. He sat at the bar and stared at them for over an hour but didn't touch them. We'll check to see if he met anyone there. Apart from that, we have very little to go on.

'Morgan said his friend list was small and she wasn't joking. His phone literally has her number and his AA sponsor's along with his landlord and the community centre.

'The occupant of the middle-floor flat is a young lad who is agoraphobic and barely leaves, and when he does his mum has to take him out. He said he has never seen Stan. The woman, Julie Platt, from the ground-floor flat, said she saw Stan come and go but didn't know him and had never spoken to him. He's only been there six weeks.'

Ben's phone finally lit up and he picked it up, powering it back on. As he did so a barrage of missed call alerts began to beep.

'You're popular.' Shannon laughed.

'So what are you going to do?'

'I suppose we could speak to Morgan again and see if she can give us anything more, see if she can account for her movements between the hours of four and six the morning he was killed. I know she's a member of your team, but she said herself their relationship had been strained for years and they only began really speaking after he saved her life. There might have been some bad blood about the necklace he stole from her. I believe it was a treasured possession and she was devastated when he took it?'

Ben's mouth fell open. How did she know about that? Dan, slimy, two-faced Dan who pretended to be her friend whilst all the time he was stabbing her in the back. He was going to kill him.

'Is that all you have? It's not much, is it? I told you Morgan was at my house; she stayed over in the guest room.'

Shannon eyed him suspiciously. 'Does she stay over often?'

'No, absolutely not. It was Amy's idea; she was worried about her after receiving the text messages from Gabby Stevens's phone.'

'That's another thing I'm struggling with. Why would a killer send her a text message? It's a bit convenient, isn't it? Did Morgan know her before she was killed?'

Ben felt his entire body drain of what little fight he had left in him. Shannon was going after Morgan and she didn't even know about the DNA. If he came clean about everything now before he'd spoken to her, he was going to get Declan in trouble.

'What are you implying? That one of my most trusted team members killed Gabby Stevens, took her phone and sent herself text messages? Then snuck out of my house to go and murder her dad, who she didn't have any issues with?'

Shannon stared him straight in the eye. 'It seems that I am.'

CHAPTER FORTY-NINE

Amy sipped the coffee and stared at Isaac. 'You look rough. What's up?'

'Nothing much.'

She looked around at the sink full of dirty dishes and the bin that was overflowing with takeaway containers, causing the awful smell. 'Really, you look like shit and this place stinks; it's a mess. You haven't even opened your blinds.'

'Sophie left me. I decided to slob out for a bit and eat junk food. Isn't that what you're supposed to do when you're dumped?'

'Yeah, it is. I'm sorry, I thought you guys were going to be together for ever.'

He snorted. 'So did I.'

Amy, not known for her tact, decided to ask him outright: she didn't have time to be wasting here with him. Ben would probably kill her when she told him, but it had to be done and she was the right person. When this was over, she'd come back and clean up, bring him a chicken casserole or whatever it was you were supposed to do, but she had to get back to work.

'Hey, I'm sorry but I have to ask: did you kill Gabby Stevens?'

She stared at him, watching his expression. It changed from morose to one of disbelief.

'Are you for real, Amy? Are you seriously accusing me of killing someone?'

She shrugged. 'I don't believe it, but you know people are asking questions. I thought I'd come straight to you.'

'Jesus, talk about kick a guy when he's down. No, I did not. Why would I do that? I help people. I don't go round murdering them for fun. You're my friend, do you honestly think I would do something so horrible?'

'Where were you the night she was killed?'

'Here, with Sophie, and you can ask her. She's not exactly going to lie for me when it's obvious she doesn't love me anymore.'

She reached out for him, pulling him close. 'No, you dweeb, I just wanted to check. I have to go, but I'll come back when this is over. I'll bring you food and we'll watch *Die Hard* and eat pizza. You can sob into the pillow and tell me all about what happened, okay.' She headed towards the front door. 'Oh and empty your bin, it stinks.'

'Thanks, Amy, thanks for calling. I'm so glad you came. I feel so much better now.'

She waved and shut his front door behind her.

He was telling the truth; she knew that one hundred per cent.

CHAPTER FIFTY

Morgan didn't speak: what was there to say? Ben hadn't phoned her back and she desperately wanted to talk to him. He made her feel safe and would know what to do. Her phone rang, startling her from the daze she was in. She didn't know the number and thought about ignoring it but couldn't.

'Hello.'

'Hi, I'm sorry to bother you, is this Detective Brookes?' The voice was faint but Morgan thought she recognised it.

'It is, can I help?'

'It's probably nothing, but you said to ring. It's Charlotte Stevens.'

Morgan put the phone to her opposite ear furthest from Dan and turned to look out of the window.

'Hi, what can I do?'

'Well, I've been going through Gabby's things; you know, like you said to. It's the hardest thing I've ever had to do, but it was also nice as well. I found a stack of her diaries from when she was a teenager. I don't think I'll be looking at them for a very long time, but it's nice to know they're there when I feel up to it.'

'No, I can't imagine you will, but at least you have them for when you're ready. It will be like hearing her speak all over again, although teenage diaries can be a little bit brutal or at least mine are. I'm sorry to ask, but was anything missing?'

'Well I don't know for sure if they are – she could have lost them for all I know – but she had a pair of earrings that were very sentimental to her. Her gran bought them before she died. They were Pandora; the Pandora bag and receipt are still here, but the box and earrings aren't. I know she would never have given them away.'

A thousand images began to fill Morgan's head: the silver gift bag; the huge pink bow. She stared at her reflection in the car wing mirror and could just see the tip of the earring she was wearing. Her voice came out almost a whisper. 'Can you describe them for me?' Morgan knew exactly what she was going to say.

The air in the car was suffocating. She could feel the throbbing of a pulse in her head as her heart pumped the blood around her body much faster than normal.

'They weren't expensive, just sentimental. They are a small pair of angel wings, with the tiniest diamond stone in them.'

Morgan thought back to her conversation with Dan when she'd told him about the messages from Gabby. He'd mentioned text messages, but she hadn't told him that: she'd only said messages. How did he know she hadn't been referring to WhatsApp? It was weak, she knew, but next to the earrings, she knew with a gut-wrenching feeling that she was right. It was Dan. He was Taylor. Her tongue felt thick inside her mouth and her throat was dry. She couldn't look in his direction because she knew he was listening to her.

'Thank you, Charlotte, I'll add that to the list. Take care.' She hung up; her phone was on its last bit of charge. She needed it. Still staring out of the window, the car began to slow and she heard the steady tick of the indicators as he pulled into a lay-by overlooking Lake Thirlmere. The only other vehicle was a camper van, but it was empty.

She spoke as calmly as she could. 'What's up? Why have you stopped?'

Dan's voice was calm, steady and didn't waver. 'I don't know, you tell me?'

She glanced at him; he was smiling but it didn't reach his eyes. Those eyes: the more she stared at him, the more they looked familiar. They weren't like her green eyes; they were much darker. Like the eyes of the monster who had created them.

'Nothing, just a victim of a burglary who realised some jewellery was missing and wanted to add it to the list. Obviously, the stuff will be long gone, but you know how it is, you have to play the game.'

Dan nodded. 'Yes, we do. Are you okay though? You've gone a bit pale.'

'I'm exhausted and I feel really ill. Can you take me home, please? Don't worry about the car tonight, we can sort it out tomorrow.'

He reached over, his fingertips brushing the loose strands of hair to one side which had fallen out of her ponytail. 'Aw, you're wearing them. I'm glad you like them.'

His touch repulsed her and she wanted to rip the earrings out and scream at him. The thought that he'd given her jewellery from a girl he'd murdered made her stomach clench hard.

'Yes, they're lovely. Thank you.'

She looked out of the window; she could make a run for it if she followed the footpath then veered into the bushes. She may be able to hide until help arrived. It was her only option. She couldn't sit here and let him kill her. Without thinking, she drew her arm up and backhanded him in the face as hard as she could. She felt the warm spray of blood as she bust his nose.

He screamed. 'Ahh fuck.'

Opening the car door, she ran towards the footpath and the lake, hoping to God someone was around. In a matter of seconds, her legs were hurting and her lungs were on fire. She wished she'd actually attempted to finish the bloody Couch to 5K instead of messing around. Her fingers were curled around her phone. She would phone for help as soon as she put some distance between them. A car door slammed behind her and she knew he was coming for her. He wouldn't stop until he was choking the life out of her. He had no other option but to kill her now she knew who he was.

'Morgannn. Morgan, come back here. What's wrong with you? Why did you just hurt me like that?'

He was coming; she could hear his footsteps on the path. She saw a tiny gap between some hedging and pushed herself through it. Thousands of sharp thorns were tearing her skin and clothes, but she didn't stop and squeezed on through until she was on the other side. Then she began running again. She could see the edge of the lake where people were canoeing but it was some distance away. Running blindly through bushes and skirting around trees, she took out her phone and hit the call button. It rang and was answered immediately. Out of breath she could barely speak and managed to gasp 'Help', before the screen went black as the battery died.

CHAPTER FIFTY-ONE

Morgan crouched low, pressing against the trunk of a gnarly, ancient pine tree, trying to breathe silently, which was almost impossible her lungs were burning so much. She heard him in the distance, running down the narrow, stony path.

'Morgan, don't be stupid. What's wrong with you? Why are you freaking out like this?'

She shuddered at the thought of the earrings and him touching her hair, wanting to rip them away from her skin, but she had nowhere to put them, and if she made it out of here alive they were evidence. Looking around, she had two choices: she could either stay here and hope he gave up looking or carry on running towards the lake and the people out on canoes. But she had no idea if she was heading in the right direction and they could be across the other side by now. Would they even hear her if she was calling for help? By the time they turned around she could be dead. *That's a lot of what ifs, Morgan...* She looked around on the ground for something to protect herself with as she heard him thundering through the bushes. He was close. She spotted a fallen branch, large enough to do some damage, and crawled towards it.

A shadow fell across her back, blocking out the filtered sunlight coming through the trees.

She turned around to see Dan towering above her. His face was a bloody mess, and she took some pleasure knowing she'd managed to hurt him: that was for Stan and Gabby. Stalling for time, she asked him.

'How come your DNA didn't come up as a match?'

He grinned. 'Do you think I'd be so stupid as to hand in a sample of my own DNA, I got a friend to swab his cheek for me after a few pints of lager. All I had to do was swap it when I had to go to get mine done, in the blink of an eye they had his DNA under my name, so easy and until you came along, untraceable.'

'Why?'

'Why not, I was always going to come after you, Morgan. You got the happy ending I didn't, imagine my surprise when you turned up your first day as a student on area. I couldn't quite believe it, then I figured it was meant to be. I knew who you were and you had just saved me the hassle of coming looking for you.'

Her heart was racing as she backed away in the direction of the branch, shuffling along on her bottom, her hands behind her, and then her fingers brushed against it and she knew she had a fighting chance. All he had was his bare hands, which wasn't much comfort. He'd already managed to strangle two people with them, using rope. She was not going to be the third. She needed to keep his attention focused on her and not the fact that her arms were getting a tight grasp on the branch.

'Why are you doing this, Dan, or should I call you Taylor? You're my brother. We should stick together not be like this.'

'Dan is fine. I don't know Taylor. He's a snot-nosed kid who slept whilst his mum was murdered. But you, you were there for the whole show. What did you think when he stabbed the woman who loved us? Did you scream for her? Did you try and stop him?'

Morgan caught glimpses of the murder in front of her eyes: Gary arguing with the woman who was her mum. She was watching from the stairs, scared of the noise and too scared to do anything. She looked at Dan: she had been a three-year-old child, helpless, how was she supposed to stop it all? He'd have killed her. But that was then, she wasn't helpless now. Her other hand slowly wrapped itself around the branch. She hoped it wasn't too heavy to lift.

'I was a toddler, what could I have done, Dan? I didn't know what was happening until I saw the blood and it was too late. What's your excuse? Did you have your teddy close by whilst you slept? Do you still have it?'

The fear inside her had turned to a burning rage at him, at the injustice of her entire life, and she could tell he sensed a shift in her.

'No, I don't. You, you had a picture-perfect life, didn't you? You got a happy family and a happy ever after. What did I get? A Bible basher of a substitute mother who didn't do compassion and liked to remind me every single day that I was going to hell just like my daddy.'

'A happy family? Stan never wanted me. He was drunk for most of my childhood. And then Sylvia killed herself when I was fifteen. So why did you have to kill him? What's so happy about that, you stupid arsehole?'

'I killed him because he was going to tell you the truth about me, about our dysfunctional family. I didn't want you to know about me until I was ready, and he was about to ruin it whilst the pair of you played happy families.'

She was enraged. He took a step towards her, but she turned, grabbing the heavy branch and jumping up, her feet planted wide apart to keep her steady. She held the branch like a rounders bat, ready to use it if he came any nearer. There was laughter in the distance and she heard voices coming down the path. This was her chance. Dan lunged for her before she could scream, but she'd already swung the bat and it cracked against the side of his temple with a dull thud. He hit the floor, out cold, and she dropped it her hands were shaking so much. Glancing at him there was a trickle of blood running down the side of his cheek from the cut, and a part of her wanted to check he was okay, but she knew he could be faking it. Instead, she ran towards the voices, praying they had a phone she could use to ring Ben.

She burst through the bushes onto the path, towards the voices, and two women with the three kids all screamed together; the sound was ear-splitting. Morgan held up her hands, realising she must look a state. She was bleeding; her clothes were torn, and she was panting hard as she tried to catch a breath.

'Police, it's okay, I'm a police officer. Have you got a phone?'

The older woman pulled one from her pocket, handing it to her nervously. The slightly younger one had wrapped her arms around all three kids and was pulling them towards her protectively. Morgan rang 999 and asked for officers. The call handler asked her location, but she didn't know where the hell she was.

'Where are we?'

'The public footpath down to Thirlmere; tell them to park at the lay-by near the bus stop just before Swirls Car Park.'

This meant nothing to Morgan, but she relayed the information to the call handler, who told her to stay on the line. She turned to the family and smiled her best everything-is-going-to-be-okay smile.

One of the kids stepped away from his mum and asked: 'Are you hurt; you're bleeding? We have some Paw Patrol plasters in the car. I'm always falling over and hurting my knees.'

She smiled, touched by his thoughtfulness. 'I'm okay, thank you, it's just a few scratches and it looks worse than it is.' She had no idea what she looked like but was doing her best to keep them calm. Then she passed the phone back.

'Please can you stay on the line? I need you to go back to your car and lock yourselves inside it and wait for the police to arrive. This is deadly serious.' She glanced over her shoulder towards the densely wooded area she'd emerged from, trying to convey just how dire her situation was without terrifying the three cute kids in the process.

'Yes, we'll do that. Are you sure you're okay? You should come with us. We can all wait in the car.'

'I can't, I have to make sure he doesn't follow. Please go now and tell them where I am when they arrive.'

The women turned, grabbing their children's hands, and dragging them back along the footpath back to their car.

Morgan's heart was racing. Exhausted, she sat down on a rock, watching and listening to make sure Dan wasn't sneaking up on her.

CHAPTER FIFTY-TWO

Amy could hear her phone ringing on the front seat of the car where she'd left it and answered it.

'Hi, this is despatch. I have a bit of a weird one. I couldn't decide what to do and you're the only one who answered. I've tried Detective Brookes and your boss; sorry, you've caught the short straw. Should I put her through?'

'You better had.'

'Thank you.'

'Hello, Detective Amy Smith. Can I help you?'

'Yes, please. You have to help her. She's in trouble. I don't know what to do.'

Amy tilted her head back and rolled her eyes, thinking about the shitty day she'd had so far and how this call was about to send it into orbit.

'I'm sorry, can you slow down? Who do I need to help?'

'Morgan Brookes.'

Amy sat upright, a chill settling over her. 'What do you mean?'

'I'm her aunt. It's a long story, but she came to see me earlier and I gave her my phone number. I had a phone call ten minutes ago and it was her; I'm sure it was her voice.'

'What did she say?'

'"Help", she gasped for help and then that was it.'

Amy was already inputting Ben's collar number into the airwaves radio to call him direct. 'Can you stay on the phone, please? I need to get some details and speak to my boss.'

Ben's voice answered.

'*Yeah?*'

'You need to speak to this woman; she's phoned 101 because she got a phone call from someone gasping for help. She said it was Morgan.'

'*Oh Christ, where is she?*'

'I'll tell her to hang up and you can ring her.' She threw the radio onto the seat.

'Hello, can you give me your number so my boss can ring you back?'

She wrote the number on the back of her hand, ended the call and sent it to Ben. Then she began driving back towards the station because she didn't know what else to do.

Ben was in his car, the phone on hands-free and his radio on full blast as he listened to the woman.

'Ettie, thank you for ringing. We'll find her, I promise.'

'Good, she knows about her brother and father. This is all something to do with those two. Can you let me know when you find her that she's okay?'

'Yes, I will.'

He hung up; picking up his radio, he was about to call it in when a grade one emergency call was passed over the air.

'*All available patrols to the A591 and the public footpath down to Thirlmere near Swirls Car Park; officer in distress.*'

He put his foot down, listening to the different collar numbers tell the operator they were on their way. He knew where the footpath was, he'd walked it a few times over the years, but what the hell was she doing there? He rang Amy, who sounded as frantic as he felt.

'Jesus, she's never allowed out of the office after this, right? I can't take this. I'm almost thirty and if I haven't got grey hair by the end of today it will be a miracle. By the way, I spoke to Isaac and it isn't him, I'm sure.'

'I was going to speak to him, thank you that saves me a job. I know it isn't him. It isn't Morgan either; it has to be Taylor, and either she knows who he is and found him or he came looking for her.'

His voice cracked and he couldn't speak. The nearest patrols were in Keswick and Kendal. He was going to get there first. Driving way faster than the speed limit, he reached the part of the road that passed along Thirlmere. He stopped the car and got out. He had cuffs and his radio, nothing else.

A family were in the car. The driver had her phone to her ear; the other woman got out.

'Are you police?'

'Yes.'

'She's down the footpath, quite a way down. She wouldn't come back with us, said something about making sure he didn't follow.'

Ben nodded, opened the boot and grabbed the only thing he had that was any use, which was the tyre iron. Not even pausing to close the boot, he took off down the footpath. Christ he didn't run like he used to, but he pushed himself on.

'Morgan, Morgan, where are you?' His voice echoed down the path.

'Ben, down here.'

The relief made his knees want to buckle, but he kept pushing on until he rounded the bend and saw her standing there, brandishing a large rock in her hand. She was cut and bleeding, but nothing major. He ran to her and pulled her close, holding her tight.

'What happened?'

She squeezed him then let go. 'Dan, it's Dan, he did it. He's my brother. He killed Stan and Gabby. I hit him hard on the head. I think I hurt him.'

'Good. Did he hurt you?' He was looking at the tears in her clothes.

'No, I got these running through the bushes. Just scratches. Are you on your own?'

'No, patrols are on their way, so is Amy. Where is he?'

'Out cold through the bushes.'

She headed towards the space she'd emerged through and he followed, squeezing and breathing in to get through the gap. Morgan waited for him on the other side, then led the way back to where she had left Dan.

She let out a groan and whispered: 'He's gone.'

'Are you sure we are at the right place?'

She frantically searched the wooded area, looking for him, but couldn't see any sign he was still here.

'There's the branch I used to hit him with.'

'You should have hit the bastard into next week. Wait until I get my hands on him.'

She smiled, and Ben thought that despite the cuts, grazes and dried blood, she had never looked so tough.

The sound of shouts and boots pounding along the footpath was the most welcome sound he'd ever heard, not that he was afraid of Dan Hunt, but he was afraid for Morgan. He took hold of her hand and tugged her back towards the path. Her hair had pieces of twigs and leaves stuck to it, and her eyes were sparkling with tears he knew she was too stubborn to shed in front of him or anyone else. Her face was criss-crossed with fine scratches and grazes, all superficial though. He couldn't say that her clothes had fared so well; they were ripped and torn but they were going to need them for CSI anyway. He let go of her hand as they reached the path.

'Down here.'

Two officers appeared, red-faced and out of breath, which made him feel better.

'Our suspect is Dan Hunt; he is unarmed that I know about, but dangerous.'

Two more officers joined them, and one of them asked: 'Our Dan Hunt?'

'Yes, police officer Dan Hunt. He has a head injury so may be disorientated, but he's taken off on foot. Hopefully, he can't be too far. We need a dog handler. Is there one on shift?'

He didn't wait for an answer and asked on the radio. 'I need a dog handler at Thirlmere. I have Morgan with me; she's safe. She has superficial cuts and bruises; can you ask the DI to attend the scene? I want as many officers as we can spare to search for the suspect, Dan Hunt, who is unarmed but extremely dangerous.'

There was silence and he knew the control room operators were probably too shocked to take it in. Dan was one of them, one of their own.

The calm voice of the control room inspector came over the airwaves.

'Ben, what do you need? I'll call the dog handler in; she's due to start soon anyway. Task force are already on their way to you. Do we need air support to search? That's a huge area; he could be anywhere.'

'Yes, please, ma'am. I'll take everything you can give me.'

He turned to the officers. 'We'll wait for the dog to come search; this needs to be coordinated and I need armed officers. It's too dangerous to send you in blind, as there's no knowing how he's going to react. He's hurt and probably incredibly angry that he's been caught, plus a head injury. Two of you go back to the car. There's a family up there to get a statement from. I'm taking Morgan back.'

He let the two officers at the back go first, then gently took hold of Morgan's elbow, who looked shaken but alert, and led her back along the footpath to the safety of his car.

CHAPTER FIFTY-THREE

Dan had waited for her to come closer, but she hadn't, and he had to admit he was grudgingly impressed with Morgan. The moment she'd run towards the voices, he'd sat up, surprised at how blurry the trees were. She'd caught him a good one. Instead of following her, which was foolish, he'd gone the opposite way. If he could make it back up to the road, he might be able to thumb a lift with someone. Tell them he was hurt and needed a ride back to town. He lifted his hand to his head where she'd cracked him with the branch. He wasn't lying; he was bleeding, panting and out of breath. He heard the sound of passing cars on the busy A591 above him. He had minutes to get up there and try to get a lift before the police sirens began. There was a stile which led to a tiny footpath. Clambering over it, he followed the winding path and it led him out near a bend in the road that couldn't be seen from where he'd left his car. A small van from the local wholesalers came into view, and he stumbled into the road holding out his arms. It stopped and the driver jumped out.

'Mate, what are you doing? Trying to get killed?'

'Can you help me?' Dan turned so he could see the blood that had trickled down his face, staining his collar.

'Oh God, I'm sorry. You're hurt. Do you want an ambulance?'

'No, I just need a lift back to Rydal Falls; if you can drop me off that would be great.'

'Yeah, of course, get in.'

Dan tilted his head. The sound of sirens in the distance, faintly, filled the air and he rushed to get into the passenger side before

the police arrived. The driver was already in and buckled up. Dan
thanked him and shut his door. There were seconds in it; if he didn't
drive away now, the police would come flying past and wonder
why he was stopped in the middle of the lane. The engine started
and he began to drive. Seconds later, they were passing the lay-by
where his car was. He saw a car full of kids and two women; one
of them was on the phone. He turned his head away from them
so they couldn't see the blood.

'So what happened to you then?'

'I was out for a hike around the tarn and missed my footing. I
took a tumble and hit my head on a tree.'

'Ouch, that looks pretty deep, you might need stitches.'

He smiled. 'I'll live, my wife is a nurse. She can patch me up.'

If he'd noticed that he wasn't dressed appropriately for hiking,
he never said; in fact, Dan realised he looked like he'd come out of
a bad business meeting. He had shirt and trousers on, not a hiking
boot or backpack in sight. The lad driving didn't seem remotely
bothered about it though. He probably hadn't seen past the blood,
so he didn't worry too much.

As they reached the outskirts of Rydal Falls, he asked: 'Can
you drop me off near Singleton Park Road, please?'

'I can. Are you sure that's where you want to go though, not
the hospital?'

'Positive, thank you so much for stopping. Not many people
would have.'

The driver slowed down. 'Whereabouts?'

'Here is fine. I'll walk the rest of the way to clear my head.
Thanks again.'

Dan jumped down, shut the door and waved. Then hurried
towards the house where both Morgan and Emily, the girl from
the college, lived. He had two choices: he could wait for Morgan,
but it was very likely she would have Ben with her, or he could pay
Emily a visit. No woman could resist an injured man. She'd let him

in and then he'd have his fun with her before it was over. The net was closing but he still had time. He needed three to make it to the ranks of serial killer. He would prove to them all that he wasn't like his dad. He was far better. As he walked through the entrance to the house, he realised he was already on number three: she would be number four. How had he forgotten about his dear old mum? Had she been psychic and predicted this, or had she turned him into it with all the bullshit she'd fed down his throat about good and evil? He didn't know, didn't really care if he was honest. He knew it was over, but there was still a little time to make a really good last impression.

As if by magic, parked outside the address was the blue Mini belonging to the pretty woman he was about to murder.

CHAPTER FIFTY-FOUR

Morgan groaned as they reached Ben's car. 'I'm hurting in places I didn't know existed.'

'Yep, you're going to be bruised to hell. Seriously, Morgan, you're going to have to choose a gentler form of exercise. Extreme sports are one thing, but you take it to the next level. Hunting killers is far too dangerous.'

She smiled at him; he was right, although on both occasions they had hunted her. She saw Amy get out of an unmarked car.

'Where is he, Ben? It creeps me out. He could be watching us now.'

'I don't think so. He's either crawled off and died, which would be my preferred ending to this story, or he's out there wandering around. We've found his car already, where he and Morgan left it, so he should be on foot. The search team will find him though. Blackpool were scrambling a helicopter with thermal imaging; it will pick him up. We'll get him, and until we do, you are coming to my house, no ifs or buts.'

'I'd rather stay until he's in cuffs. I want to see him get arrested; I want to be the one to arrest him. I promised Charlotte Stevens I would.'

'Morgan, you have done more than enough. You've found the killer and solved two murders: I'm giving you a direct order.'

Amy peered over Ben's shoulder. 'Damn right, no ifs or buts. Jesus, you're a liability, Morgan, and look at the state of you.'

Ben nodded. 'Morgan we'll stop by your place to get some clothes and then I'm taking you home. A DI can take over here,

Amy; although I think task force will tell him to do one, it's theirs now. I don't care whose it is, I just want him caught.'

'You better let Wendy sort her out first though, boss.' She pointed to the CSI van which had parked behind them on the grass verge.

Morgan saw Wendy walking towards the car and got out.

'Flipping heck, what happened to you? Don't move, I need to photograph and swab you, or do you want to go back to the station and wait for me? I've been asked to photograph the scene and remove the evidence. Is it true you whacked Dan with a branch?'

She nodded.

'Good effort. What do you want to do?'

'I don't want to go and sit around the station. Can you do it now?'

'I can, but I need your clothes. Are you going to the hospital? I can do it there.'

'No, no hospital. It's just scratches. Do it now, please.'

Wendy shrugged, but began to snap the lens cap from her camera.

'Can you stand over by the bushes?'

Morgan did as she was asked whilst she photographed her. Then she walked back to the van with her so she could take some samples. Once that was done, she climbed into the back of it. Wendy passed her a large brown paper sack and a packet containing a white paper suit.

'I'll do you a swap.'

She took them and waited for her to slam the sliding door shut. It took Morgan a while to peel off her torn clothing; everything was hurting and stinging, but she did it and dropped them into the bag. Then tugged on the white suit.

Sliding the door back, Ben held out his hand for her and she stepped down.

'Wendy, I almost forgot.' She began to remove the earrings and wondered if her guardian angel had been around today, because this could have turned out a lot worse than it had.

'What are those for?'

'I'm pretty sure they belong to Gabby Stevens. Her mum phoned to say she was missing a pair of Pandora angel wing earrings. Dan gave these to me as an apology for being an idiot to me when I came to work up in CID.'

Wendy was staring at her in horror.

Amy looked at the tiny wings in the palms of Morgan's hand and whispered: 'Sick.'

Scooping them into an evidence bag, Morgan felt relieved to be rid of them.

Ben turned to Wendy. 'Are you all done?'

'Yes, for now. I'm going to need to photograph your injuries properly back at the station, Morgan. You can tell me if you have any I've missed or any bruising that develops over the next few hours, but for now you're good to go.'

She got inside Ben's car as he went to talk to the DCI who had just arrived. She felt exhausted and closed her eyes, lying back against the headrest, wishing Ben would let her stay and hunt Dan down.

CHAPTER FIFTY-FIVE

He rang the bell for Emily's apartment, and her voice crackled through the intercom.

'Hello?'

'Hi, sorry to disturb you. I've had a car accident and hurt my head; I was wondering if you could lend me a phone. My friend, Morgan, lives in the flat below you, but she's not in.'

'Oh gosh, hang on I'll be right down.'

He smiled to himself as he waited for her to answer the door. He heard her run down the stairs. There was a slight pause and he knew she was looking through the spyhole at him. Then the door flew open.

'It's you. Oh look at your poor head. Are you okay or should I call an ambulance?'

He looked at her with a confused expression.

'I'm Emily; we met at the college once in the car park.'

'Yes, we did. Sorry, Emily, my head is a little battered at the moment. No, thank you, I don't need an ambulance. I just need a phone to ring for someone to get my car out of the ditch.'

'Come in, you can clean yourself up or I can do it for you.'

'Dan, my name's Dan by the way. Are you sure you don't mind? I work with Morgan. I was hoping she'd be able to give me a hand, but she's not here.'

'Course I'm sure. You can come in and wait for her.'

He followed her in. He had no idea how much time he had to enjoy her, but he was grateful for the chance to have a little more fun. Maybe he could hide out here for a few days. They would never suspect him to be hiding in plain sight.

As she opened the door to her apartment, the sausage dog that featured heavily in most of her Instagram photos came flying down the hall at him, barking furiously.

'Frankie, stop that. It's okay, he's a visitor.'

The dog ignored her and ran straight towards him, didn't want him to go any further. He'd forgotten about the dog. As soon as he could, he'd snap its neck.

'Hey boy, what's up?' He bent down to stroke it, and it nearly took the end of his fingertips off.

'Ouch.'

Emily looked mortified. 'Frankie.' She grabbed his collar. Dragging him towards the bedroom, she pushed him inside and shut the door.

'I'm so sorry. I don't know what's got into him; he's usually a sweetheart.'

'It's okay, maybe it's the smell of the blood on my head.'

'It probably is, bless you. Come on, let's get you cleaned up.'

She led him to the open-plan kitchen area; the layout was identical to Morgan's. Just thinking her name sent a spark of anger coursing through his veins. The fact that she'd got one over on him infuriated him. Emily pointed to a chair tucked under the breakfast counter. He pulled it out and sat down, watching her as she pulled out a first aid kit and filled a bowl with warm water. He could spare a few minutes and let her clean him up. It might make him feel better to get the dried blood off his chin and head. His nose had doubled in size and there was a dull ache in the side of his head where that bitch had hit him. Emily had a pair of latex gloves on. She soaked some gauze pads in the warm water and gently held them to his head, then began to clean him up. He closed his eyes; it felt so nice having someone take care of him. It had been such a long time; the gentle movement was soothing, and he let her continue.

'Am I hurting you?'

'No, not at all. It feels great to get this blood off, thanks.'

She carried on until he sensed she was almost finished.

'One last wipe and you should be good.'

As her hand came up to blot his wounds dry, he opened his eyes and reached up for it, gripping it tight.

'What are you—?'

He was on his feet. Both of his hands wrapped around her delicate neck, he noticed the small gold E that dangled from a chain. That would make a lovely gift for someone. She tried to scream, but his fingers gripped her neck so tight she couldn't. Dan towered over her and smiled.

'You're a lovely woman, so beautiful. I'm so glad we met.'

The fear in her eyes was delightful and he drank it up. Squeezing harder, her hands reached out for something, but he didn't notice. He was staring into the beautiful blue eyes. Water exploded all over his face, blinding him. He released his grip and she pulled away from him. Screaming at the top of her voice, she fell to the floor, scrabbled to her knees and then ran for the bathroom: the only room with a lock on the door.

CHAPTER FIFTY-SIX

'Ben, I just want to go home, please, get myself cleaned up and, if I'm honest with you, have a really good cry in the bath. You have too much to do. You don't need to babysit me. How about you come back when you're done? You can tell me you found him, that you have him in cuffs in person and we can share a bottle of wine to celebrate.'

He laughed. 'Sorry, Morgan, no go. Dan knows where you live and I don't want to leave you on your own.'

'I'll be okay. He's probably hiding up a tree out by the lake. It's hard to believe it; I can't believe he is my brother and that Gary Marks is my birth father. It's so much to take in.' Her entire body juddered with repulsion.

'I know. I went back to see him today. Declan had phoned to tell me there was evidence taken from Stan that he sent off and the results were back.'

'That fast?'

'The guy in the lab has a bit of a thing for him, so he rushed it through extra fast. Declan wanted to help us find Stan's killer. Only, it came back as a close match for you. I couldn't believe it. He agreed to sit on the evidence for a day while I tried to figure out the connection.'

Morgan was swirling with emotion, surprise, anger, but the predominant one of all was a deep respect and a warm fuzzy feeling of love for Declan and Ben. They had both put themselves at risk of losing everything for her and she wouldn't forget that ever.

'It also was a family match to Marks, and I realised that you were his daughter and that there was another child too. So I went to speak to him.'

She looked at Ben, so thankful that she had his friendship. It made her feel better knowing she had him, Declan, Amy and Ettie in her life and on her team. 'What did he say?'

'Not much, just that he thought his daughter wouldn't be clever enough to do this or strong enough. Then he lost his shit and got dragged out. He obviously has no idea how clever or strong you are, or how stubborn. I'm glad you're on my side, Morgan. You fight for the good guys.'

She laughed. 'Good, I'm glad he has no idea about me. He can go rot in hell and take Dan with him.'

The car turned into the drive of Morgan's apartment. There was a blue Mini parked there.

'I met your new neighbour, by the way; she seems very nice and a little forward.'

'What do you mean?'

'She asked me round for a meal. I didn't know what to say. Obviously, I was flattered; you know, at my age I'm not going to say I'm not. I don't get many, if any, offers.' He started laughing, and she elbowed him in the ribs.

'Ouch, anyway, I said no.'

'Why? She's lovely. You can say yes to whoever you want.'

'Oh, she is lovely, there's no denying that, but…'

'But what?'

He stopped the car and turned to look at her. 'She doesn't strike me as a warrior-type woman, and I've realised how much I like those.'

'What does that even mean?'

A deep red blush crept along his neck, rising up his cheeks. He turned away. Ben's radio beeped and his name was called over the airwaves at the same time as his phone began to ring, and he shook his head. 'Ah, sorry, Morgan.'

'Don't apologise for doing your job, Ben. Now answer them. I'm going in for a bath because I look and smell terrible. When you're done, I'll be here waiting for you to come and tell me you caught the bad guy so I can sleep tonight.'

She got out of the car and left him there, open-mouthed. She didn't turn around but shouted: 'Answer your damn phone.'

Grinning, she let herself into her apartment and closed the door. Upstairs, the cute sausage dog was barking frantically. She ignored it and went to the bathroom to survey the damage and run herself a bath.

Stripping off the white paper suit, she went into the bedroom where the full-length mirror was. Dressed in her underwear, she stared at the multiple scratches and grazes. There were dark circles of bluish bruises forming on her arms and knees. Leaning forward, she began to pick the dried leaves and twigs out of her hair, a smile on her face the whole time. The dog was still barking; it must be locked in the bedroom above her, because it was scratching at the door and polished wooden floorboards like crazy. She'd never heard it make this much noise before and wondered if Emily was okay. She might be diabetic or have epilepsy and the dog might be trying to get help for her. Morgan's foot was hovering over the tub full of lavender-scented bath salts, but she didn't put it in. Cursing her overactive imagination, she grabbed her dressing gown off the back of the bathroom door, pulled the door to and ran upstairs to knock on Emily's door.

The dog went into overdrive, but she couldn't hear any other movement from inside the flat. Pressing her ear to the door to listen, she then tried the door handle. It was locked. She opened the letterbox and shouted: 'Emily, is everything okay?'

The dog's yipping was constant now, and she had the sinking feeling that everything was not okay. Crap, what did she do now?

It was probably innocent; she might have gone out and the stupid dog got itself inadvertently shut in the bedroom. She turned to go and phone the police. She was on the stairs when the door opened a little. That was weird. She went back and pushed it open slightly.

'Emily, what's going on?'

Heaviness settled across her shoulders, pressing down on her. She wished Ben was still here for moral support. She didn't want to go inside, but what if Emily needed first aid? She'd sworn an oath to save life and limb when she joined the police. A voice inside her head whispered: *yes, but that is when you are at work, dressed in your uniform with handcuffs and a taser to defend yourself. It didn't mean when you're knackered and only wearing a dressing gown.* The dog was still barking, yipping, and if nothing else, she could let it out of the bedroom and throw it a bone or something to shut it up, so she could have a bath in peace.

Pushing the door open, she stepped inside. The dog was whimpering now.

'Hey, dog, I'm coming, give it a rest.'

A scream so loud it made her physically jump off the floor came from the bathroom.

'Help, he's going to kill me. Help, help.'

She knew then that, somehow, he was here. He'd come here; the fear inside her was crippling. She had nothing to defend herself with, no phone and she was tired of this bullshit. She didn't answer Emily, trying to listen and figure out where he was. If he'd opened the door to let her in, he was close. He wasn't in the bedroom or the bathroom because both doors were shut, with Emily in one and the dog in the other. Every beat of her heart intensified as it pumped the blood around her body. Her eyes fell on the closet a few feet behind her. She would have to run past it to get out of the front door. It was just big enough for a man to hide in. She could see the open-plan kitchen and lounge and wondered if she could make it to the knife drawer in time, but then realised she didn't even know which was the knife drawer because this wasn't her home. Time seemed to have slowed down as she saw the closet handle begin to turn.

She pushed herself forwards, towards the kitchen, as the door slammed open. Sunlight through the large picture window in the lounge glinted off the huge knife he was holding. Still she ran, looking for something, anything, to use to protect herself. There was a bottle of Dettol disinfectant on the kitchen counter with its lid off. She reached out for it; grabbing it, she turned as he ran at her and prayed it would hit him in the eyes as she shook the contents in the direction of his face. It splashed in his face and he shouted, but he didn't let go of the knife. She was cornered. Still he kept coming closer, the knife wavering in the air as he rubbed at his eyes with the sleeve of his shirt.

'Did you think I was going to let you get away so easy, Morgan? I like to finish what I started.'

Morgan grabbed the nearest thing to her, which was the kettle, as he lunged towards her. Memories burst through the black fog in her mind and she was there, standing on the stairs, a small child still rubbing sleep from her eyes as she wondered what the shouting had been and come down the stairs. She'd watched as her father had plunged a knife into her mother and saw the bright red blood as it sprayed everywhere, helpless to do anything and so scared. But she wasn't three now and she would not let him kill her.

Dan lifted the knife, about to sink it into her neck, and there was a loud thud as he dropped it to the floor. Morgan watched it as it clattered on the tiles. She kicked it away from him with her foot, and realised Emily was standing behind him with the remains of a broken glass vase. Dan was sinking to his knees and, determined not to let him get away a second time, she lifted the kettle high and smacked him across the side of the head where she'd hit him earlier with the branch. His eyes fluttered and he dropped to the floor. She bent to pick up the knife; this time she'd check he was out cold before she left him.

Emily was screaming at the top of her voice, but at least she was alive to do that.

'Morgan.' She heard Ben's voice and footsteps running up the stairs. He ran into the apartment to see Emily screaming with tears running down her face and Morgan standing over Dan's crumpled body, a knife in one hand, a copper kettle in the other. She heard him asking for backup on the radio, then watched as he pulled a pair of cuffs from his pocket and knelt down. He cuffed Dan's limp arms.

He looked up at Morgan. 'Are you hurt?'

She shook her head. Standing, he took hold of her hand and pulled the knife from it.

'Let go, Morgan. It's okay, you're safe, he's not going anywhere.'

She released the grip on the handle of the knife and let him take it from her.

'Is he dead? Is the fucker dead?' Emily sobbed.

'No, he's unconscious but breathing. You're both safe now, patrols will be here soon and take him away.'

Emily ran to let her dog out of the bedroom. Scooping him up into her arms, she squeezed him tight. Then she walked across to Morgan whose feet were rooted in the same place. Emily kicked Dan in the ribs, then stepped over him and hugged Morgan in the strangest hug ever. The poor dog was squashed against the pair of them, but it didn't seem to mind. Morgan hugged her back and whispered: 'Thank you.'

Emily let her go. 'No, thank you. Jesus, he seemed so nice, and then he tried to strangle me. That's the thanks I got for trying to sort his face out. I didn't think I was doing that bad of a job. I mean, I'm no nurse, but I was gentle.'

Ben laughed somewhere behind them, and Morgan felt a smile begin to spread across her face, thawing the frozen expression she'd been wearing.

She turned to Ben. 'How did you know?'

'I didn't. You left your phone in the car. I brought it back and your flat was empty. I heard the commotion up here and came up to find this.'

CHAPTER FIFTY-SEVEN

In minutes, Emily's flat was filled with officers. Realising she was only wearing her dressing gown spurred Morgan into life. She whispered to Ben: 'I'm going back downstairs; you know where to find me. I'm not giving any statements until I've had my bath.'

'Did he hurt you?'

'Not this time.'

She stepped over Dan's body and walked out of the front door. Passing two paramedics on the way up the stairs, she recognised Luke, who seemed to come to all the jobs she needed medical help with. He looked at her scratched face and asked: 'Are you okay, Morgan? Do you want me to check you over?'

'I'm fine, Luke, thanks. These are just scratches.'

He nodded. 'This place is like a disaster magnet; I'd consider moving somewhere a little less exciting if I were you.'

She laughed. 'Yes, it's seen some crazy stuff, but I still like it here.'

'Take care, Morgan.'

And then he was walking through the door to Emily's, and she ran down the stairs.

She felt numb inside, but also free. Locking the door behind her, she checked her closet, just to be sure there was no one hiding inside it. Then she grabbed her iPad, poured herself a gin-sized glass of wine and took herself into the bathroom, which smelt divine. The expensive bubble bath disguised the awful smell which was emanating from her of soil, dried blood and sweat. At least she had something to tell Isaac when she went for her appointment. She wondered whether the nightmares and insomnia would go away now she knew who she was, but there was still a lot to process. It might take some time to come to terms with the life she'd never known and the consequences of that awful day. She couldn't help feeling sad for Dan; she had got lucky with Stan and Sylvia, and she wondered if he would have still turned out the same if they'd stayed together and never been split up. She didn't know, that would be for someone a lot more qualified than her to determine. At least things could only get better from now though. She wanted to get to know Ettie better. She realised she'd left her jars of Ettie's special tea in Dan's car, which would probably have been seized as evidence. Hopefully, she wouldn't need it now, but it gave her the perfect excuse to go back and see her. She was the only person in her new family that she wanted anything to do with.

Putting her playlist on, she blasted Aretha Franklin, took a huge mouthful of wine and stepped into the bath. Her aching body melted into the water, and she lay back amongst the bubbles, sipping her wine and singing, 'R.E.S.P.E.C.T.'

Closing her eyes, she let Aretha take over the singing and smiled to herself. She'd stick with being a detective; singing wasn't one of her better traits, but finding killers certainly was.

EPILOGUE

Gary Marks lay on top of his bunk, fully dressed, his feet crossed and his hands behind his head. A lot of information had come his way the last forty-eight hours and he was still trying to process it all. He hadn't thought about his kids since the early days of his arrest, when he'd realised he'd lost them and the life he could have had, if only he had walked out of the door that day like Janet had asked him to. He hadn't ever felt particularly guilty for killing her, but he had wondered if he'd screwed little Skye up for the rest of her life. Although if he had, she had put it to good use. To think she'd been the detective sent to interview him and hadn't known the bad guy in front of her was the same one who probably haunted her dreams. It hadn't been hard to see the resemblance to Janet, even her mannerisms and the way she stared at him with the same feisty expression Janet had that fateful day. They were looking for a killer who shared the same DNA as him, which meant it could only be Taylor or Skye. Was she that bold to kill people and pretend to be the one hunting them? If she was he'd be surprised and more than a little bit proud.

His cell door was opened, the metal grinding against the concrete floor as it was pushed inwards. The guard set his tray on the small table. Gary nodded but didn't get up. He wasn't too excited about a bowl of porridge with solid lumps in and some burnt toast. He was confined to his room after his little outburst with the copper who had come back to see him, desperate for some snippet of information that would help him catch his killer. There was a folded newspaper on the tray; at least they'd forgotten to take that privilege away. He got up slowly, there was no need to rush, nothing to rush for, and took the few steps to grab the paper. The headlines screamed at him and he felt the wind knocked from him as he sat heavily back onto the hard mattress.

COP ARRESTED FOR BRUTAL KILLINGS

His eyes fixed on the headline; he was speechless. Little Skye was more screwed up than he'd given her credit for. Looking down at the photograph, he realised that this wasn't the woman who'd been to see him, though, it was a man, with a large gash on his head as he was led in handcuffs from the entrance to a very nice Georgian house. Taylor, this was Taylor then. He studied the photograph for any sign of Skye. She wasn't on it, but the guy leading Taylor out to the waiting cop van was the same one who had been here. Was that the reason he was cooped up in this metal box unable to go for his hour's exercise in the yard? He nodded his head; this was a mess. Both his kids had joined the police and both of them were connected to that copper and not in a good way. He read the article, amazed and a little in shock. He wasn't sure what to think or do, not that there was much he could do about it. Then he stared at the guy walking his son out to the van: Ben Matthews. 'You, my friend, are screwing with the wrong family,' he whispered to his picture. He wondered if Taylor would get sent here, or if they'd decide he needed a secure mental facility. It would be pretty cool if he did come here; he could finally get to know him.

Removing the front page of the newspaper, he folded it into a small square then tucked it inside the *Speak Spanish in Four Weeks* book on his shelf. It had been there for four years and the most he'd learnt was *buenos días*. He nibbled some of the burnt toast, folded the paper back in half and left it all on the tray. He had some serious thinking to do. He'd neglected his family for far too long. It was time he stood up to the mark and showed them what he was made of; he'd start with that smarmy bastard Matthews first. All he had to do was to plot how, and that shouldn't be too hard. He was a model prisoner until that little blip the other day. If he behaved well, all he had to do was to bide his time and when the chance came along, take it.

A LETTER FROM HELEN

Dear reader,

I want to say a huge thank you for choosing to read *The Killer's Girl*. If you did enjoy it, and want to keep up to date with all my latest releases, just sign up at the following link. Your email address will never be shared and you can unsubscribe at any time.

www.bookouture.com/helen-phifer

I hope you loved *The Killer's Girl* and if you did I would be very grateful if you could write a review. I'd love to hear what you think, and it makes such a difference helping new readers to discover one of my books for the first time.

I love hearing from my readers – you can get in touch on my Facebook page, through Twitter, Goodreads or my website.

Thanks,
Helen Phifer xx

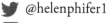 Helenphifer1

@helenphifer1

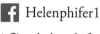 helenphifer

 www.helenphifer.com

ACKNOWLEDGEMENTS

The hugest amount of praise and thank you goes to my fabulous editor Emily Gowers, I've loved working with you. Thank you for polishing these ideas into stories worth reading, that takes some doing and for that I'm very grateful.

Another huge thank you goes to the whole team at Bookouture, every single one of you are amazing. I can't tell you how proud and thankful I am to work with such a talented group of people and be published by the best there is.

As always thank you to my fabulous readers who keep coming back for more, no matter what I put them through. You are the real stars, your loyalty and love of my stories gives me the warmest, fuzziest feeling inside a writer could ever wish to have. Your love for Morgan Brookes and support for this new series was simply amazing.

I also have to thank the people of my home town, who are quite happy to stop and chat to ask about my books even on the days when I look like I've been dragged through a hedge backwards and scare myself when I look in the mirror ☺ you support and praise me so much I'm surprised my head fits out of the door at times. That you root for a local author as much as you do is the most wonderful thing ever and it means the world to me.

I can never thank my husband and kids enough for not reading anything I've written, it saves lots of embarrassment and I don't love you any less for it – honestly. I'm eternally grateful that you all support me the way you do and encourage me whilst asking for McDonald's deliveries and Primark shopping trips in between my writing sessions. I love you all very much and I'm so lucky to have such a fabulous, crazy, loving family with the most amazing grandchildren I could wish for.

A special thank you goes to my amazing friends and coffee club members Sam and Tina, thank you keeping me sane and making me laugh, lots.

Helen xx

Made in the USA
Las Vegas, NV
29 August 2021